MW00529676

MIDDLEMAN

JAYNE RYLON

HAPPY ENDINGS PUBLISHING

Cover Art by Jayne Rylon

Editing by Mackenzie Walton

eBook & Print Formatting by Jayne Rylon

Version 6

Ebook ISBN: 978-1-941785-76-8

Print ISBN: 978-1-941785-77-5

A standalone novel from NYT and USA Today bestselling author Jayne Rylon.

I don't kneel for any man. Not anymore.

I had the perfect dominant boyfriend. Then Cortez left me to save the world.

After two and a half years lost drowning my misery in bad decisions, one man changed everything.

Rogan is the perfect submissive, who puts me back in control of both him and my life.

Until Cortez comes home.

Who am I? Cortez's bottom or Rogan's top?

Maybe I'm both.

Maybe I was made to be their middleman.

ADDITIONAL INFORMATION

1

CORTEZ

Have you ever known you were about to wreck the person you loved most?

I scan the letter clutched in my shaking hands for about the millionth time before crumpling it and stuffing it into my pocket. The shit-ton of sexercise I've been getting lately has burned calories like the end-of-summer bonfire I won't be taking my boyfriend to after all. Dread killed my appetite. It's tough to eat when you're constantly worried about an inevitable summons cutting short the steamiest affair of your life.

So when I jam that confirmation of our relationship's expiration date into my pocket, my fury nearly leaves me bare assed. With a twitch of my fingers, I tug my belt loops and hitch up my too-loose cargo pants until they're precariously perched on my hipbones again.

My boyfriend doesn't seem to mind my fashion faux-pas. He knows better than to offer me a belt, which I would find plenty of other wicked uses for. Besides, then he couldn't stare at the spot where my defined muscles disappear beneath that waistband.

You see, Kaden's an artist. One hell of a painter, who rationalizes his inappropriate gawking at sexy men as a study of the human form for his work.

If the circumstances were different, I might get off on the appreciative scan he'll no doubt give me once he finishes tinkering in his studio downstairs and comes to bed.

Tonight I'll be too guilty to enjoy his lusty appreciation.

What once would have been my dream come true is about to become his—no, *our*—worst nightmare.

I'm going to leave him.

Not because I want to. Because I have to. I doubt he'll give a shit about semantics, though. My dick doesn't either. It's mad as hell that this will be the last night it gets to sink into Kaden Finch's tight ass while I ride his smoking hot, compact-yet-powerful body.

Everything I've trained for has led me to this next level in my career. The idea of this opportunity used to excite me as if it's a promotion or some shit. No, it's an obligation. A duty to our country that I've sworn to undertake. I can't back out now. No matter how badly I'm starting to wish I could. It sucks donkey dick that to continue to call myself a man of honor, I have to do something that feels so wrong.

I never made Kaden any promises or accepted the ones I could see swimming in his adoring gaze. Fuck, how I wish I could. What the hell did I do to myself?

Falling for a guy I had no chance of keeping... Stupid. With a capital fucking S.

Worse, what will I do to *him* when I let go?

Maybe it's my pride talking, but I think I'm about to cause some carnage. The best I can hope for is that Kaden will hate me for my betrayal. That he forgets me quickly and moves on with his life. He has so much to offer a partner, it would be a waste otherwise.

My fingers curl into a fist at the thought of some other lucky bastard topping Kaden, who's my idea of the perfect submissive. Until I sigh and force myself to relax. I should be grateful to his future lovers for picking up the pieces I'm about to leave scattered on the ground behind me.

God knows there will be a line from here to our favorite club, Romeo & Julian, once guys realize he's back on the market. I've enjoyed watching men drool over him, knowing that for a little while he was mine.

Selfish fucker that I am, I don't bother putting on a shirt when I hear his springy footsteps echoing off the metal slats of the spiral staircase that leads to this loft above his studio and gallery. There's no use in pretending. It's only going to get peeled off again momentarily.

It's impossible for me to leave without saying a proper goodbye. Besides, if anything will turn him from friend to enemy, it will be this. Using him, then walking away as if his surrender means nothing to me. As if it isn't the best gift I've ever been given. Like every birthday, Christmas, and my personal favorite holiday—BJ and steak day—all rolled into one.

Committed to my lame-ass plan, I don't dissuade him from automatically sinking to his knees before me after he strolls into the bedroom we've shared during the past couple months of sultry nights.

I never meant to stay this long. To get attached.

Kaden has destroyed every last bit of my better sense. His onslaught began with a volley of coy yet naughty grins. He shot them at me one-by-one like flaming arrows for weeks whenever our paths would cross at the bar.

Once I caved and bought him a beer or three, I became addicted to the wicked smile and dimples that appeared as he shared one of his wild stories.

They told me how committed he was to enjoying every moment of life. That ability to make each day the best day ever and find something to smile about—even when life tried to feed you a shit sandwich—was a skill that had been snuffed out in me by immense responsibility before I'd met him.

After years of existing in a quasi-military environment, I envied his creativity, freedom, and spontaneity. It appealed to the parts of me that felt stifled by my intelligence career. He had flown beneath my radar and taken my libido hostage. From there he'd seized my heart before I could formulate a strategy to keep him safely relegated to the friends-with-benefits zone.

Not especially savvy for a guy who was supposed to be impervious to espionage.

But how could I resist someone like Kaden?

Sure, he's toned and so damn fuckable it twists my balls up to look at him. He's also fierce, determined, and relentless when he has his eyes on the prize.

And by *prize* I mean my cock.

Except now we're both going to pay the price for indulging in ecstasy so often and so thoroughly. I'll never come so hard again in my lifetime. No one will ever satisfy me as well as he has. Only now I'll know what I'm missing.

This.

A gorgeous boy dropping to his knees between my feet, sharing my desires and fulfilling them because they're his as much as they're my own.

Kaden nuzzles my inner thigh with his cheek as he

breathes deep, inhaling my scent. I wonder how long it will linger on his sheets before that last trace of me evaporates from his world.

He brings my passion alive as easily as he transforms a random assortment of colorful brush strokes into hyper-realistic depictions of objects or people I swear I could reach out and touch. The man is incredibly gifted. He sees the world in a way I never imagined before I met him.

"I missed you," he whispers.

He couldn't make me feel more like a champion and a steaming pile of dog shit simultaneously if he tried. Maybe I can show him, one last time, how vibrant our attraction is. If I fuck him well enough, there's a possibility he'll eventually remember me with something other than hate in his heart. After the initial wounds scar over and the sting of my desertion has faded, maybe he'll understand that this was real. As stunning as one of his masterpieces.

"Same goes." I fist my hand in his unruly chestnut hair, which is speckled with a rainbow of oil paints, and tilt his face toward mine so he can read the truth in my eyes. *Deny this, I dare you.* "Always does when you're not around. Always will when I'm away."

Shit, shit, shit. I don't mean to give him false hope. Or telegraph my exit.

It's harder than I thought to do this to him. To us.

His clever fingers distract me from my downward-spiraling emotions. They meander from my knee up my thigh toward my growing hard-on. Even the sickness roiling in my gut can't keep my cock from responding to him.

I don't dare take my eyes off him, not even long enough to blink, when he licks his lips then unfastens the button of my jeans. At times like this it's hard for me to consider myself the one holding the power here. It's obvious to me that he has it all.

He slides the zipper down carefully enough to avoid an injury that would put a premature end to our fun yet fast enough to prove he's as desperate as I am for what's about to come.

Greedy, he plunges his hand inside my pants.

I can't tell who moans louder when his fingers curl around my length and pump me a few times, as though I need any help stiffening up for him.

My jeans hit the floor, giving him better access to my crotch. He doesn't waste any time before his mouth is on me. His parted lips connect with my balls, allowing his humid breath to wash over them. His eyes are wide and so damn persuasive as they peer up at me, silently requesting permission.

"Go ahead." I put my finger below his chin and lift slightly. "Suck me."

He does. So well that I nearly forget my mission. That's become a habit around Kaden. It's probably for the best I'm being ordered to leave before I lose myself to him completely.

An entire season of owning him and I'm nearly ready to rip the damn paper in my pocket to shreds. What would I do with myself if I didn't go through with my assignment? Could I live with shattering my promises to the organization that saved me, taking me in when I had nowhere to go? How could I ignore the debt I have to pay? How could I support my boyfriend without a job? Despite his rising success in the art world, freeloading isn't my style.

The fact that I'm even considering those options

proved how far I've drifted from the man I was proud to be. The one who would never shirk his responsibilities, or fail to repay a debt. Especially an obligation this monumental.

How will I stand myself knowing I've turned my back on Kaden and the faith he's placed in me by being so open and giving? Don't I owe him too?

Either way, I'm screwed. And so is he.

Except he doesn't have a choice in the matter and he's oblivious to the dead end we're rushing toward.

My cock wavers the slightest bit at that thought. Kaden's right there, sucking harder, deeper. Flicking his tongue in precisely the right place along the underside of my shaft to keep me racing toward our invisible finish line. He distracts me from the confusing shit that has me riled up, channeling my energy into the best outlet I've found since my organization trained me to be one of its deadliest weapons.

My voice is coarse when I bark, "Get me good and wet. I'm not going to take it easy on that ass tonight. You're getting all of me."

If he only knew how much of me he already had.

He grunts and applies himself. Or the thought of the fucking he's about to get turns him on enough to have him swallowing me down as if I'm a slice of blueberry pie—his favorite dessert. No matter the reason for Kaden's fervor, I'm not about to complain.

When he sinks all the way onto my shaft, I grip the back of his head and hold him in place, reveling in the flex of his throat around my shaft. Only when he chokes do I haul him off my length, grinning at the twitch of his hips that proves he's enjoyed my display of control as much as I have.

"You ready for me?" I ask.

"Have been the whole damn day," he grumbles with an endearing pout. "If I didn't have a deadline for that portrait, I'd have hunted you down at lunch. And again for an afternoon quickie. Or three. Fuck, I've never been this horny. My dick is sore from being hard so much. At least you're here now to take care of me."

Ouch. Direct hit.

"I doubt I have anything to do with that. You're sexy as fuck and you know it. You were made to be tied to a bed and fucked endlessly."

"Yes, please." He kills me when he bites his lower lip and peeks up at me through his heavy-lidded eyes and a veil of thick lashes.

"Clothes off. Now." My commands are short because I can barely talk when I need him this intensely. He hurries, swiping his tattered jeans and paint-stained tank top from his luscious body, revealing the ink embedded in his skin. Everything about him is colorful and unable to be constrained by lines.

Before he's entirely free of the fabric, I grab him, wrapping my arms around his middle. Then I fling him toward the bed. I don't have to be delicate with Kaden. He's tough. He can handle my hunger. In fact, he's confessed how much he loves to be treated roughly. It's another way I acknowledge his strength. I hope he gets that.

Kaden groans as the edge of the mattress hits him in the gut. He braces his hands on the bed and automatically shifts his feet until he assumes a wide stance. He drops his head onto his folded wrists, leaving himself exposed to accept my advances. He's perfect.

I'm not afraid to show him I think so either.

I grab his ass cheeks, one in each of my palms, then spread him open. His cock and balls hang heavy and thick with arousal even as his hole clenches in anticipation. Rather than plunging inside him immediately, I do something I've never tried before. Something he's confided that he fantasizes about.

At least I can give him this before I break his heart.

Without hesitation, I bend forward and bury my face between his cheeks, lapping at him and swirling my tongue around his puckered hole. Probing it and grunting in chorus with each of his wild moans.

"Oh, shit. Oh, fuck. Cortez!" he shouts over and over as I treat him to a tongue-bath. From his ass to his balls and back, I pause only to suck and nip that really sensitive spot in between. I channel him and recreate the fantastic sessions we've had where he treats me to the same blinding pleasure.

I eat him until his thighs are quivering in my hands, which brace and steady him. Then I do it even more. Eventually he breaks. "Fuck me. I need your cock."

I pull back far enough to slap his ass, which is no punishment at all for Kaden, who enjoys being over my knee on occasion. "That doesn't sound like begging to me, boy."

"Please. Please, Cortez. I need it. Fucking *need* you. Please."

"That's better." And pretty much guarantees he'll despise me for making him admit it when I go. I reach over to the nightstand to snag a condom and the mostly empty bottle of lube stashed there. With a few quick jerks, I've sheathed myself and slathered my shaft in the gel. I'm thankful for the resulting coolness and the control it helps me regain.

I want to go out with the bang of a lifetime.

Seconds later, my hard-on is poised at the entrance to his body, nudging his ass and pressing against his clenched muscles. I consider using my fingers to ease him open. No. I want him to feel every inch of me acutely. Besides, I don't think he's up for waiting a moment longer judging by his escalating pleas.

I bend over him so that my chest rests on his back. Then I wrap my fingers carefully around the front of his neck and sink my teeth into his shoulder, pinning him in place as I breach his opening and tunnel inside.

I may not be able to keep him, but for right now—this moment and a few more—he's mine.

Only mine.

All mine.

And I give him every bit of me in return. For keeps.

"Ugh!" He doesn't waste breath on real words as he struggles to accommodate my thickness. It's his own damn fault he's hot enough to make me this hard.

I drive forward bit by bit until I'm seated fully within him. He holds me tight, clamping around me as if he doesn't plan to ever let me go. Maybe he doesn't.

I'm sorry, Kaden.

I run my hand down his back, along his spine, helping him relax so I can begin to move. I retreat until only the tip of my cock stays embedded before working my entire length into him once more. By the time I've gotten a dozen or so strokes in, he's rocking against me, making his cock swing in heavy arcs below us.

When I reach beneath him and grasp it in my fist, it coats my palm with slickness. He shudders.

"Close already?" I rasp in his ear, glad I'm not the only one about to burst.

"Yeah. Better take your hand off me or I'll come." He tries to shift out of my grip.

No way. In fact...

"Turn over." I take my cock out of his ass, then nudge him onto his back so that he's looking up at me. There's nowhere to hide the raw emotion that consumes me when I'm with him like this. Good. Let him see it. Let him know how I feel since I won't be able to reassure him that his memories are true after tonight.

Before I realize it I'm leaning down, balancing on one forearm that I place beside his head. I capture his mouth with mine. When he opens to me, as he always does so sweetly, I plunder.

We kiss franticly for a while. When we're both mindless, drunk on ecstasy, I slip back inside him. I enjoy the searing pleasure of introducing myself to his ass one last time.

Kaden's cock is trapped between our abs. I stroke it with my rippling muscles every time I plow into him. He throws his head back, breaking our lip lock while exposing his neck to me. I take full advantage, peppering it with open-mouthed kisses, licks, bites, and sucks.

It's one of his most erogenous zones.

He wraps an arm around me, crushing me. Probably would have hugged me to him with both arms if I hadn't pinned the other to the mattress above his head at some point during our tussle. His legs cross in the small of my back, helping me penetrate him deeper even as my lunges become shorter and sharper.

"Yeah. Fuck. Right there." He meets me thrust for thrust. If I hadn't topped him every night for months I might doubt his submissive tendencies at times like these, when lust overrides logic.

Too far gone myself to chastise him for the demand, I give him what we both crave.

I drill him over and over, exactly where we both like it so much.

The pitch of his moans changes as he clings to the sizzling live wire of pleasure we generate together. Hell, I'm pretty sure my grunts are at least as loud as his. It's hard to tell over the racket the metal frame of his bed makes as it slams into the exposed brick wall. Good thing there are no neighbors in this charming old building.

"You gonna come for me, Kaden?" I stare into his eyes as he nods. "Shoot all over me. Show me how much you've loved having my cock to yourself."

Shut. Up.

Fuck more, talk less.

I try to block out the encroaching pain and concentrate only on our rapture.

Again, Kaden helps me by calling my name before he freezes. I know this moment well, though I've never seen it affect him so profoundly before. I'm right there with him. We teeter on the pinnacle of blazing desire for a moment, which seems to last forever, before it's too much for either of us to handle.

Kaden thumps the mattress with his fists as he shoots. His come sprays across my torso, blasting me with sticky heat. Proof that he feels this too.

With a roar, I unload in him. My orgasm seems endless as my balls pump and pump some more, filling the condom I wish I hadn't worn. Just this once.

Empty, I sag forward, smothering him beneath me. My panting buffets the beads of sweat dotting his temple. And when I can move again, I reluctantly withdraw, sliding from his body as surely as I'm about to slink out of his life.

Fuck.

Flopping to my back, I fling my arm over my eyes so I don't have to meet the accusation in his or see the light of his love for me extinguish when I break the news to him.

My heart stops galloping in my chest when he beats me to it.

"You *have* to go." He kisses my jaw with a tenderness he's never shown before, startling me enough with his quiet confidence to make me jerk. "Your handler called the gallery today. Told me you have to report no later than tomorrow morning or get fired. And that's before he started dropping phrases like court-martial and treason."

"Shit!" I yell, struggling to find some way to explain. There isn't one.

"Hey, don't freak out. It's fine. I'll be here when you come home."

Is *he* actually trying to comfort *me*? What kind of fucked up shit is that?

And...hang on. "What?"

"The guy said it's a three-year assignment." Kaden blinks up at me with those wide eyes of his, innocent despite everything we've done. He's never seen war. He doesn't understand the true depravity human beings are capable of or what I'll be facing. "It'll be a bitch not having you again for so long, but what we have is worth the wait."

"That's *if* I come home. Big if. A regular tour of duty in the military is bad enough. This is something I can't even tell you about. Could never call you, send an email, nothing. Besides, you're not going on ice. No way could you last that long without a cock up your ass." A man as sexual as Kaden would never make it through thirty-six months of abstinence in his prime without either coming to despise me for the extended dry spell or finding some action on the side. Hell, neither would I. "Going without isn't possible for either of us, is it? So I'm saving us the trouble of cheating, feeling guilty, falling apart, and ending up bitter and hateful after wasting years of our lives."

Besides, that's the best-case scenario. Some guys I know came back damaged goods. It was hard not to after living a double life, always watching your back, never knowing who was friend and who was actually foe-pretending-to-be-friend so they could stab you in the back. PTSD, ingrained paranoia, the inability to resume a normal life—these are real risks I face. I knew that when I accepted a counterterrorism post with an agency too secret for a public name.

I've trained for this since I was seventeen. I've prepared to make sacrifices.

I just never understood how much I'd be giving up until now. When I've been activated. Called to duty at the worst possible moment. When I have to abandon the love of my life. The man of my dreams. Someone I never thought I'd find because I couldn't imagine a man as flawless as him could be real.

It's the highest price they could have demanded. The problem is that when I counted the cost of my decisions, I didn't figure in a partner. Never imagined I'd find one like Kaden. I hadn't meant for him to pay so dearly for loving me. I refuse to make that burden any heavier.

"That's awfully big of you." Kaden rolls from the bed. I try to focus on things more important than the flex of his abs or the glistening trails of his seed decorating them. "Don't do me any favors, fuck face. If you can't man up and tell me it's already over, and would have been anyway without such a convenient excuse, then I'll do it for you. Get the hell out of my bed. And my life. I already packed your bag. Take it and go."

The authoritative tone of Kaden's marching order rings through the tiny loft apartment. It has my cock twitching despite our recent fuck. To know that a man as strong-willed and defiant as him willfully surrendered to me boosts the buzz of my post-climax high.

Because I also know I don't deserve his devotion, I obey his command.

A solider at heart, it's easier for me this way.

Maybe Kaden realizes that and gave me one final parting present.

"Take care of yourself, okay?" I reach out but let my hand drop when Kaden rears back, out of my reach forever.

In silence, I put on my pants and the T-shirt that got "ruined" when Kaden and I fucked on the floor of his studio last week. It will always be my favorite. A reminder that maybe some of his true colors have rubbed off on me.

After lacing up my boots, I collect my duffle. It easily holds the sparse belongings I'd temporarily housed in the dresser we picked up at an estate auction one lazy Saturday. With him, even shopping could be fun. I put my arm through the canvas straps and toss the bag over my shoulder. Then I grab my phone, erasing my presence from his life all too easily.

Completely.

"I love you, Kaden." Probably should have told him so before now.

He flashes me the finger in response.

Somehow that makes me grin instead of pissing me off. He's a fighter. He'll survive just fine without me.

Satisfied with that at least, I put one boot on the top stair and then the next, the heavy clanking of my soles ringing ominously in my ears as I descend from the highest point of my life. My footsteps are the opposite of his lighthearted ones on the way up a half hour ago. When I open the front door and pause to memorize the tone of the chiming bells that hang there, I think I hear him say softly, "Try not to get yourself killed, asshole."

Why not? It couldn't hurt worse than this.

Without Kaden, there's not much to live for.

2

KADEN

TWO YEARS LATER

The bells above my gallery's front door emit a cheery jingle, letting me know someone's come in. Hopefully they intend to browse my work instead of merely soaking up some free, admittedly shitty, air conditioning. Since I like to eat, and pay my bills, and share my creative genius with the world and stuff like that, the sound of an incoming customer usually inspires me to grin and hold back giggles like a dude getting his first BJ. Today it irks me. The tinkling breaks the spell I'd been casting while wielding my brushes as if they're wands and I'm the fucking Harry Potter of the erotic art scene.

The noise reminds me that I'm not actually witnessing my creation come to life like some indecent Geppetto. It's not me, the painter, the image of the model is staring at adoringly. No, his loyal affection is aimed at his lover, who hired me to capture his syrupy sweet gaze in a portrait that will last forever. Far longer than the emotion itself, as we both know.

I'm not an idiot. Fear of loss drives the majority of my commissions. Having experienced a nasty breakup myself,

I understand the desire to preserve memories while the fickle flame of affection is burning its brightest. Nothing wrong with banking on peoples' need to freeze time to make my living, is there?

Would it be torture or a treasure if I had a reminder of Cortez to stare at day in and day out? I pointedly ignore the haphazard pile of unfinished and abandoned canvases in the corner of my studio. So what if most of them feature a muse who bears an uncanny resemblance to the sexy bastard, huh? At least I haven't added anymore to the stack in over a year. A couple more months and I might even work up the nerve to start painting over them. Then I can pretend our connection was duller than I remember. Let it fade into a black and white version of those vivid, saturated recollections of bliss...

After a few more blinks and a shake of my head, my errant thoughts and the grand vision I had been teasing into being are reduced to a bunch of meaningless oil streaks. I drop my brush halfway through the swirl I was applying to the canvas to investigate what's going on in the front room.

Now that I think about it, it's probably just the delivery guy trying to tempt me with his admittedly stellar package. Too bad for him. I don't fuck the same guy more than once.

Not anymore. Not A.C.—After Cortez.

Though the courier is sizzlier than the fajita plates from the restaurant across the street on Taco Tuesday, he's already had his turn. Claimed his tiny sliver of me. Or was it me that had a piece of him? It had felt that way when I fucked him long and hard enough against the counter that my ancient cash register had crashed to the floor.

Neither of us had bothered to stop to right it either.

The guy certainly hadn't complained about the rough ride I'd taken him for. In fact, he's hounded me nearly every day since for a do-over. As tempting as that sounds, it makes me twice as sure I can't indulge in a second serving without risking a bout of unwanted heartburn. We have a hint of chemistry. Not atomic-bomb level explosions of attraction like I'd had with Cortez. But there's something there. A spark.

So no, we definitely will never hook up again.

It took me forever to remember how to get off on casual sex A.C. It was only in the past six months or so I mustered some interest in hooking up with more than my palm in the shower. It's like smoking a cigarette after mainlining heroin. Hardly gives me a buzz at all.

Still, I'm not about to risk another year and a half stretch of total celibacy. Bad enough I'd gotten fucking depressed, like actually clinically depressed, for the first time in my life.

Cortez lifted me to the highest of highs before dropping me. After what had seemed like an endless free fall, it took a few face-first bounces and skids across the pavement before I could dust off my broken wings. I came dangerously close to splattering into total road kill, even picking up a few bad habits. You know, like drinking alone until I blacked out and smoking pot more than recreationally to help forget.

I became one of those real hardcore, moody, mentally unstable artists.

Eventually, I evolved. I don't have to get high on chemicals or the rush of endorphins that come from submitting in order to soar. Never again will I be the naïve dreamer bending my knees and flashing my ass for any dominant man who catches my fancy.

These days, it's *me* who decides when, where, with whom, and how often.

I have a couple strict rules—no sleepovers, no repeats, and absolutely no tops allowed.

Nope, those luxuries aren't for me.

So the delivery guy is out of luck. Hoping to avoid any awkwardness, I pause and call, "Leave it on the counter."

"Excuse me? Leave what exactly?" The clear, formal tone of the newcomer's voice is nothing like the husky smoker's rasp of my delivery dude. This guy sounds like aged whiskey tastes. Smooth. Tempting. Unwise to overindulge in. Great.

"Sorry, thought you were someone else. Hang on a second." I wipe my hands on my jeans as I retreat from my creative nook. I don't bother to grab a shirt since I'll only wreck it like most of my limited wardrobe. Splatters of paint dot my skin, blending with the tattoos inked across my chest and arms. New guy will have to deal with me as is. If he's in the right place, he won't mind since I specialize in nude portraits of the male variety.

Hey, I can't help it if my job is awesome. I'm into my work. You'd be obsessed too if you spent all day bringing gorgeous hunks to life so people can admire and ogle them for eternity, pretending they're flawless sex-bomb gods instead of mere humans.

It's a voyeur's dream gig and I've never minded watching. Especially since I can transform my models into anything that pleases me.

And double especially since paintings don't talk back.

Or break your fucking heart.

I emerge from behind the shoji screens that separate my studio from the retail side of my shop. My customer's sculpted ass—he's bent over, scrutinizing the fine details of my work on display—is the first thing that catches my artistic eye. Next is the expensive material and impeccable tailoring of his navy suit. Then his traditional haircut, which does a decent job of taming his onyx locks. A few errant strands inspire my imagination. They break free from the confines of his light and stylish gel job to curl over his brow, softening his rigid features the slightest bit. I'd love to see his hair mussed on his pillow following a mind-blowing fuck.

Except I don't do these kinds of powerful men anymore, remember?

Or I should say, they don't do me. And I'm guessing he's a hell of a lot less flexible in his role. A dude like this isn't built for kneeling.

With a huff of regret, I notice the fancy watch he checks as I keep him waiting for the briefest moment. I know his type, though I can't say I've had the chance to play with many of them up close and personal. Patrons of the arts. Serious collectors. Men who have risen high enough that only a handcrafted, one-of-a-kind collectable can give them an advantage in the spending races they compete in against their peers.

Maybe he can afford to give one of my spare hotties a home on his wall. Hell, he can own a whole harem of them for the right price.

Though I've become notorious in my specialty, it's not every day someone like him strolls through my door. Most of my wealthy clients commission a single special painting of their boy toy via a discreet online inquiry form that keeps their salacious intentions under wraps.

I don't mind helping people indulge their dirty little secrets. In fact, it adds something to the final piece. A knowing smile or a glint in the eye of a sensual nude model, preserved forever in a picture that captures him at his peak seductiveness. I consider it a public service for future generations to document so much studliness.

A man like this—executive, commanding, somebody who has their shit together—they'd be sure to keep a tight rein on their boyfriends. By coming here in person in broad daylight, he's also proving he doesn't give a damn who knows it.

If I say that doesn't turn me on, I'll be lying.

Even better, it means I'll be able to boost my bank account. At the end of the day, as long as I can survive doing what I love, that's what matters most to me. That's all I have left that brings me true joy, to be honest.

"Is there something I can help you with?" I ask, surprised when he flinches at the nearness of my inquiry. He doesn't strike me as the jumpy type.

He spins and smiles tightly at me. Even that pinched expression can't hide how handsome he is. Damn. "Yes. I'd like to arrange a portrait for my partner. I heard you're the right person for the job. After checking out your gallery, I'd say the recommendation was understated."

Though I don't advertise myself as a LGBT artist, I'd somehow fallen into this line of work. I'd like to think that's because, as a gay man myself, I'm capable of delivering an honest and unbiased representation of my subjects. I understand the intricacies of their bond, even if I no longer have—or want—that in my life. Or maybe I'm getting a reputation that drives other business away. I don't do this sort of work exclusively, but it seems like every week I get more and more requests like this. Let's be honest, they're my favorite.

Regardless, I'm thanking the universe that the newcomer is on our team. I might have shed a tear for all my fellow gay guys if not. I'm assaulted by a flash of regret that I don't kneel for men like him anymore. The first time I've had that thought in years. What the fuck?

Maybe I should turn him down. Tell him I'm too busy. Name a price he'll never pay.

It could be dangerous to expose myself to that kind of charisma. Even if he's taken. It's better not to be tempted, even by something I can never have. Reminded of what I've lost.

"We can probably work something out..." Why don't I jump at the chance? Say yes and lock down a date like I normally would? He makes me nervous.

"What would it take exactly to get you to take the job?" His steely gray eyes narrow and I can see him engaging negotiation mode. He must be one beast of a businessman. I wish I didn't find his metamorphosis so intriguing. Or arousing.

Here's the point where I should make up some shit to get him the hell out of my gallery. Pronto. I open my mouth, but instead of fabricating an ironclad excuse, I hear myself say, "You'll need to be willing to spring for the best. I don't come cheap."

Why does that make me sound like a hooker bargaining for a couple extra bucks before blowing their mark? I lick my lips. Probably because sucking him off sounds delicious. Too bad he's in a relationship. If not, I might offer him the fuck buddy discount.

Shit.

"My boyfriend is worth it." He shrugs one shoulder. Though he's tall and broad, he isn't bulky. I wish I could paint him instead of his beau. I have a feeling that when I return to my easel, my subject might take on some of this stranger's lanky qualities.

"In that case, I charge ten grand for nude portraits. Five-thousand due at the sitting and the balance upon delivery of the final approved artwork."

He doesn't even blink at my highest tier quote. "Is the frame included?"

"Yeah." I nod. "I hand-make them out of a wood that complements the palette we end up going with. Museum quality."

"How far in advance are you scheduling out?" The guy looks at his fancy watch again. I'm sure it's got a date function for this planet and likely a few others somewhere in those ornate dials. I hate what his frown does to his mouth, pinching his lips tight. "I've been busy. Probably haven't left enough time to have it finished by our anniversary."

"I have a rush fee option, but I warn you, it's steep."

He doesn't hesitate or flinch. "I'll pay you double."

"For twenty grand I'll make time whenever you need me."

Why does his hot cocoa gaze seem to snap to mine at that? I'm not trying to be dirty or even flirty for that matter. If nothing else, I respect committed guys. You know, the ones that don't bail on their partners. I'd never interfere with someone's relationship.

Instead of pouncing on my poorly worded response or taking the opportunity to make an innuendo-filled crack, he turns humble. Somehow that's even sexier on him, that hint of gentleness.

Help me.

"Thank you." The corner of his mouth tips up slightly. Even that's enough to make his already handsome face come alive. Oh yeah, I'll be doing some unpaid sketches later. He doesn't have to know he's my new muse. "I've got just under a month until the big day. It'll be five years."

"Congratulations." I mean that sincerely. "That's a long time."

The milestone where things start to become a forever sort of relationship, I'd guess. Although, hell, I thought that after only a couple months with Cortez. Thank God he ditched me before we got any closer. I wouldn't have survived.

He chuckles. "Yeah, it's funny. Sometimes I can't believe it's been so long and other times it seems like forever."

The creases in his forehead and chiseled cheeks make me sure he's faced ups and some pretty serious downs with his lover. Who doesn't? Kudos to them for sticking it out and working through their issues instead of bailing when things got rocky. Maybe the road will be easy for them from here on out. I hope so, for this guy's sake. He seems pretty decent for such a smoking hot rich guy. Not dickish in the least.

"I'm sure time flies when you're with the right person." His boyfriend is one hell of a lucky bastard. Probably young, fit, and gorgeous to land someone of this caliber. At least my job would be easy. "If your boyfriend is available to pose Saturday, I'm free."

"Wait." He swallows hard. "I think you misunderstood."

"How so?"

"I want you to paint a portrait of *me* to give *him* as a gift." He rubs the back of his neck. "Christ, is that pretentious? No one does it that way, do they?"

"Uh..." It would be a first. Usually the dominant partner commissions a portrait of their lover as a

25

keepsake. Sort of a visual representation of their possession. A way to show them how prized they are.

Ho-ly fuck. I suddenly want this job more than my next breath. I haven't been this excited about a project since I was hired to paint a foursome and they got frisky during their modeling session.

That had been hot. This corporate raider stripping down for me, baring himself wholly, and allowing himself to be vulnerable, giving all of himself to his lover against his natural instincts to dominate...whoa. Surface-of-the-sun level scorching.

I mean, I'm no poacher and he's clearly in love. So that makes him safe. Safe to drool over from a distance. I plan to do just that and create a piece of art worthy of something that beautiful. Fuck, I should probably be paying him for this chance.

My suddenly dry throat and bugged-out eyes have probably given him the wrong impression. I'm scaring him away.

"Maybe this isn't such a great idea. It's just that I want him to know I'm his. Really his. In every way possible. When I look at your paintings, it seems obvious that these men are owned. Like me." The instinctive way he stares at the tips of his shoes as he says it, clasping his hands behind his back, nearly knocks me off my feet a second time.

This man is a dedicated *bottom*? You have got to be fucking kidding me.

I read every cue wrong. For an experienced player like myself, that's a first.

Humbling and intriguing. Downright bonerific.

I hustle behind my counter to hide my inevitable hard-on, choking as I bite my lip to keep from saying something even more inappropriate. As soon as he leaves I'll be taking a jerk break. Not until I fix the damage I did with my arrogant assumptions. A man like him—like I used to be—should never feel less-than. I'm afraid he's reading my shock as distaste. Nothing could be further from the truth.

"Sorry to have taken your time." He clears his throat then begins to turn away.

"No, wait." I somehow manage to roll my lolling tongue back into my face long enough to reassure him. "I'm sure your boyfriend will love your gift. It's just...you're very direct. Assertive. I assumed...um. Stuff that's none of my business. I'm sorry."

The man blinks a few times then grins at me, making me want him twice as bad. "Oh. Yeah, that happens to me a lot. It's sort of like being a superhero. One boring thing by day, another more exciting thing by night."

"You don't have to explain." I wave my hands in front of me, embarrassed for the first time in forever around a guy. How fucking rude could I be?

"Okay then. You really don't mind working on the weekend?" His smile grows. It exposes a wicked set of dimples that do nothing to dissuade my cock from leaking more. "My boyfriend tells me I'm a workaholic when I do that."

Thank God he's easygoing and quick to forgive. I can't believe I put my foot in my mouth like that. It must have been his sexiness rattling my brains. Or maybe some sort of self-defense system that ignored the possibility of a rare guy like him who could turn me on with their tough exterior yet bow to an unassuming top like me. If I believed in romantic possibilities anymore, I'd say that's exactly the kind of man I should be looking for.

"Nah. It's pretty standard for me, actually. People with real jobs aren't usually available to pose nude during the work week. Besides, I'm single. There's no one to give a shit if I don't come home." I shrug one shoulder, as if it doesn't matter.

"It seems as though you have a *real* job." He's quick to correct me with a fascinating blend of aggression, confidence, and humility. Seriously. Hottest dude ever. "I mean, I plan to pay you in actual dollars, not Monopoly money. If I'm an expert in anything, it's businesses. You've got plenty of talent to satisfy the demands of this niche market you've identified and capitalized on. You're a sole proprietor with an obvious lifelong passion for your work. These are the types of ventures I hunt to invest in. You're not looking for a partner to grow your studio, are you?"

Well, I never thought of it quite like that.

"No. I'm not aiming for world domination or anything. This is about me doing what I love." I chuckle kind of awkwardly as his praise sends a flutter of warmth through my chest. He has to get the hell out of here before I actually start to like him in addition to lusting after him.

"I figured, but you can't blame me for trying, can you?" He shrugs.

"Thanks for the vote of confidence." I shake myself, trying to focus on our transaction instead of the weird energy in the room. "What time and where should I meet you?"

He reaches into his breast pocket and withdraws a business card before offering it to me, tucked between two long, fine fingers. Oh, what he could do with hands like those.

Trying to seem far less impressed than I am, I peek at

the name embossed on the cardstock in tasteful gold letters.

Rogan Clearwater III

Doesn't that just figure? His name is as uptight as he first seemed. I wonder how many people never see beneath his misleading exterior.

That's it. I'm going to have to close the shop for a mid-afternoon siesta where I do no sleeping. Instead I'm going to cave to my curiosity, Google the shit out of this guy and his boyfriend in the name of research, then imagine what better uses I could put his fancy silk tie to now that I've developed my taste for power plays. At least I had Cortez to thank for that.

He made me realize how much more fun it is to fuck and fuck over than to be the recipient of all those poundings. If I still find myself jerking off to fantasies of him and what it would be like to recover the courage to submit again someday, well...no one has to know about that but me.

It's pissing me off how twisted up I'm getting. Why does this man—*Rogan*—bring out so many tangled up emotions, especially in such a brief encounter? I thought I was past this shit and here I am having some kind of sexual crisis over a taken man who has no idea how badly his mere existence is confusing me. Making me yearn for things I can't have.

"I usually come downtown to my office for a half day on Saturday mornings. Maybe I'll meet you up at our beach house instead. It's about a forty-minute drive. Is that too far for you?"

"Uh, I don't have a car, but I can arrange an Uber." I refuse to be embarrassed about that. Fuck him and his lavish lifestyle. Who needs *two* houses anyway?

Of course, my drama is entirely in my head. He's not judging me. He's just trying to get what he's paying top dollar for. Maybe I should back out. It's obvious Rogan mashes my buttons without even trying. Except then I wouldn't get to see him again. Besides, no one else will do his portrait justice.

I am the right person for this job. Guaranteed.

"If it's not too weird, I could pick you up since I'll be passing right by on my way out of the city." He waits for my agreement. Patiently. Obediently. Oblivious to the chaos he's churned up in my psyche.

As if my dick is intent on making the worst decisions possible for my sanity, I hear myself agreeing. "Sure. That'll work."

"Email me at the address on my card. I'll have my assistant send you the pertinent information and coordinate the details." There was in-charge guy again. It was incredible how he flip-flopped like that. Now I'd have forty whole minutes, twice, to observe him in addition to the time he's posing. Hopefully he won't detect my fascination.

I nod, brushing my fingers over the fine stationary again.

Rogan checks his watch one last time, his smile fading. "Sorry to cut this short, I've got a meeting."

I bet. Captain of industry and all that.

Maybe he stays late for important crap every day while his poor boyfriend waits for him in some palatial high-rise penthouse. No wonder he's going all out for this occasion. Probably needs to get out of the doghouse for neglecting his duties at home. A guy can only go to bed lonely so many times before he snaps.

I should know.

I guess that's why my fucked-up brain is trying to fabricate some imaginary flaws to make my mental image of Rogan less attractive. It might be the only way I survive this assignment.

"No problem. I look forward to hearing from your assistant." Until then I have a fantasy guy to finish painting. The kind who's everything I hope for and will never disappoint. The kind who lives up to my naughty, misguided thoughts. The kind I can mold into whatever suits my fancy that day. Most important—the kind who's fake and doesn't threaten the sterile backdrop I've fashioned for my existence to keep me sheltered and allow me to learn to function halfway normally again.

Someone entirely opposite of this unexpected, elegant, influential, gorgeous, tempting, and very taken man.

"See you Saturday. Thank you again." He gives me a curt nod then spins sharply on his heel before striding from my shop without a backward glance. Meanwhile, I stare until he's out of sight.

This time the ringing bells sound hollow to me.

Maybe it's time to get rid of them.

3

ROGAN

I drive toward Kaden Finch's studio with enough wiggle room to be comfortably early for our prearranged time even if there's unprecedented Saturday morning traffic. Part of me is as eager as a guy about to pick up a first date. The rest of me still isn't sure I haven't screwed things up royally. It irritates me. I can be so decisive in business dealings, yet I never seem to have the same sort of confidence around my choices in my personal life.

Things are always *complicated*. By my career, by my money, and doubly so by my desires, which make me something of a freak. I don't fit the submissive mold. Most guys I've been interested in have been more intimidated than turned on by me.

Hell, for a while I even convinced myself that Ronaldo and I were wasting each other's time. Except after I'd confided my doubts, he showed me over and over how wrong I'd been and what a colossal mistake I'd almost made by deciding to break up with him. I guess I'd listened to too many of the online tabloid stories that

33

billed us as incompatible from the start then progressed to using completely unsubstantiated cheating rumors as clickbait. It seems being gay and the head of a multi-billion dollar corporation makes the gossip even jucier.

I don't read that trash anymore. Saves a hell of a lot of fighting.

Of course, none of that proves my choice of anniversary presents isn't ridiculous. I'm fairly certain Ronaldo would love to own me however he can. After our rough patch, it's one of the few ways I can think of to show him how committed I am to our partnership.

Lately he seems insecure about the time I spend at work, always questioning me about when I'll be home and glowering when I don't give him the answer he hopes for. I thought the painting might be a physical reminder of how I prioritize our relationship over the wealth or success produced by my career. Those things mean nothing to me without him. I work so that he wants for nothing, even given his lavish tastes, which seems like exactly the sort of thing a dutiful slave should aim for.

The balance in my bank account doesn't give me any illusions about my role in our partnership, although sometimes I think he wishes I would stay at home and clean the house while he goes out and brings home the bacon. Okay, I actually think that every morning while I'm knotting my tie around my neck as he burrows under our pillows and grumbles about waking up alone until I give him a good-morning blowjob to hold him over until the evening.

Maybe instead of a canvas, I should sell the company and give him those papers instead. Is that really what he wants? What the hell would I do with myself then? Truth is, to my business partners I *am* Clearwater Industries.

Without me at the helm, the valuation of our assets would plummet. That's not arrogance speaking; it's business acumen.

I tap my fingers on the leather steering wheel as I glide down the highway at a speed precisely one mile below the limit. Careful, cautious, calculated. That's how I usually am. This impulsive and nontraditional gift might be part of my growing unease. Or maybe Kaden Finch himself is spurring my reservations. Aren't artists supposed to be the sophisticated, enlightened ones among us?

If he hadn't come so highly recommended I'd have turned around and taken my commission right back out the door with me when he judged me on first sight, as so many other people do. If all he can see is what's on the surface, I'm not sure Ronaldo is going to get my message or that my ultimate act of submission—making myself an object for him to own—will shine through the final artwork.

It was either Finch's reputation or his impish charm that had me glued to his weathered plank floor, taking his unintentional abuse and sort of liking it.

How fucked up does that make me?

Oh, come on. Be honest. It was the tattoos clinging to his defined bare chest that had me reluctant to storm out of the place. Not to mention the fact that he, like me, seemed to be something other than he first appeared. Something opposite from what stereotypes might suggest. I know well that assessing scan he raked over me.

Despite his boyish looks and compact stature, that man is nobody's twink. I bet he gets even more riled than I do when someone is foolish enough to make that mistake.

Kaden's hair rebelled against gravity in a spiky disarray and his scruff was somewhere between forgot-to-shave-this-morning and an ungroomed goatee. The mussed look enhanced his creative ambiance, whereas in my corporate existence it would somehow signal a lack of responsibility or authority.

Funny, since it's clear by the way he eye-stalked me—especially after realizing that I'm entirely different in the bedroom than the man I am in the boardroom—that he's a full-on predator.

If I didn't have a man who filled that role in my life already, I might have led Kaden on a wild chase just so I could feel him catch me, take me down, and make me enjoy falling beneath him.

I shiver. Hopefully this session wraps up sooner than I anticipate so I can rush home to Ronaldo. I have a feeling that I'm going to need some relief afterward.

Only because of how Ronaldo will react to my present, I try to convince myself.

Only that.

Right about then, I pull to the curb outside of Kaden's studio. Despite arriving twenty minutes early, he's waiting. Punctuality is another thing I wouldn't have expected from him. Could he be as excited as I am to work together today?

Leaning up against the roughhewn stone façade, his arms are crossed. One booted foot is planted on the rock behind him. For the first time, I really consider what it will be like to be naked in front of the appraising stare he levels through the windshield of my car.

I swallow hard.

Out of habit, I leave the car running when I climb out, round the hood, and open the door to usher Kaden inside. "Let me put your supplies in the trunk for you."

I try not to blush when he nods approvingly before

sliding into the passenger seat where he looks entirely out of place. Instead of studying the contrast between his stained knuckles and the sleek zebrawood veneer of my door handle, I hustle to pack his easel, canvas, a backpack, and two toolboxes full of paints and brushes into the car.

When I return to the driver's seat, I have an instinctive desire to ask if he wants to take the wheel, but even I know that's not appropriate with someone I've barely met. Hell, he doesn't own a car and may not even drive. It's just that he has a way of looking at me that makes me want to yield.

Kaden grins and toys with some of the knobs on the dash without asking, setting things as he likes while I return us to the flow of traffic and head out of town. "Maybe someday I'll trade in my bike for something half as fancy as this."

"You ride motorcycles?" Could the man get any sexier, really?

"Nah, I mean my bicycle. Us hipsters downtown prefer to travel Mary Poppins style. Don't worry, there are no streamers in my handlebars. I'm not *that* gay." He offers me a lopsided grin that makes me fairly sure he doesn't hate me for ruining the planet with my fossil-fuel-guzzling vehicle. It also makes me imagine how simultaneously cute and cool he must look pedaling down the street on a vintage bike. He keeps me on edge. Most people don't. I can't quite figure him out. I guess it's the weird balance between authority and humble self-denigration he manages to strike.

Not that it matters much what he thinks. Except it keeps me from feeling too guilty to enjoy one of my favorite indulgences. I rev the engine and draw a chuckle from him as he's flattened against the Italian leather.

Kaden practically purrs as he settles in, the seat hugging his frame as we slither around tight curves in the road that leads into the countryside and toward the shore. To my beach house.

"So where exactly are you taking me?" he asks.

"Seaside."

"Nice neighborhood. Or so I hear. Never been myself." He picks at the threads on the tattered knee of his jeans. "I'm more of a Jefferson Boardwalk kind of guy."

"Hey, nothing wrong with that. I can demolish a corndog in three seconds flat and the people-watching isn't bad either." I think back to the times I spent there in my younger days before I built my empire from scratch. Too bad Ronaldo wouldn't be into it or I'd ask for a date night. Holding hands, playing the rigged games, being blasted by cheesy music while eating greasy food...nope, not his thing in the slightest.

"If you mean that spot where the bodybuilders show off for the crowds in the open-air gym..." Kaden hums appreciatively. "A definite sightseeing destination."

I hadn't, but now that he mentioned it... "Yeah, there's always great scenery there, too."

He laughs then turns serious again as he stares out at the growing expanse of sea grass and dunes. "Nothing like this, though. This is true beauty. Makes me think about trying a landscape instead of portraits all the time."

"I love sitting on the porch, watching the waves and listening to the birds circling above the shore." It's one of the few things that helps me relax after intense negotiations. Besides sex, of course. Giving up control, even for a moment, is such a relief."

"I can see how a guy like you would need a place to unwind." He shoots me a glance that makes me sure he knows exactly what it takes to settle me down. Not in a weird way either. More like a basic understanding...a camaraderie.

The best tops are guys who've visited the flip side, who understand how difficult it is and how it affects their partners. Maybe I wasn't wrong about Kaden as I thought. He gets me on a level that's hard to explain. Slightly unnerving because there's nowhere to hide, but also comforting because I don't need to.

I'm used to making small talk with business associates, constantly trying to recall their interests, the names of the people close to them or finding out about causes they're committed to furthering. It's a habit. A skill I've honed over the years.

With Kaden, conversation is effortless. Natural. It seems that without trying, we keep gravitating toward topics beyond meaningless bullshit. He lures me in by opening up first, explaining how he fell in love with art as a way to overcome his shyness and study men as intensely as he liked without making himself a target for ignorance or hatred. I find myself rewarding his trust by sharing how I founded Clearwater Industries with an inheritance to gain a sense of security after the death of my parents at an early age. Stuff I don't normally disclose to near strangers.

Before long, I've forgotten about my nerves or self-doubts. I roll up my sleeves and crack the sunroof to let in a few rays of sunshine. A breeze strikes my face with a briskness that brings me fully awake for the first time in a while.

I grin over at Kaden and catch him staring. "What?"

"I'm starting to understand some boys' fascination with four-wheeled toys."

I can't help but press the accelerator to treat him to a wilder ride.

By the time we approach the gated lane leading to my favorite beachfront property, we're both flushed. It feels traitorous to admit that even a sliver of my elevated heart rate might be caused by something other than our trip out here.

Hey, I'm only human. Even Ronaldo would have to admit Kaden is something special, appreciate him like a fine wine. I'll never act on the attraction zinging between us. Loyalty is something I prize above executive power or crushing my competition in the stock markets. Somehow I get the feeling Kaden agrees.

It's one of the reasons I'm comfortable enough with him to go ahead with this plan.

Besides, this entire outing is about showing Ronaldo how much he means to me. Why can't it be as simple to communicate with him as it has been with Kaden so far this morning?

It's been so long since I experienced such an easy familiarity that I forgot what it can be like to simply *be* without considering every possible ramification of my words or actions. How they might be taken out of context or used against me in an argument. Then again, this could be part of what makes Kaden's artwork shine. Maybe he's loosening me up to eliminate any potential barriers during our session, like some kind of artistic foreplay.

If so, it's working.

Wanting for some foolish reason to impress the man, I don't pull around back to the private parking area and garage. Instead, I cut the engine in the round drive that encircles a marble fountain and formal landscaping out front. Garish for my tastes. Ronaldo insisted on the improvements. Kaden's thinly veiled awe makes me think they might not be so bad after all.

Plus, it will be easier to carry his supplies through the front door since it's closer to the floor-to-ceiling windows that overlook the sunny beach, which should provide excellent lighting for his work.

Suddenly, I realize I'm not only going to be naked while he stares at me. I'm going to be staring at him staring at me, with nothing to occupy me other than reading every detail of his expression. Will he like what he sees? It's not that I'm modest. In fact, I sort of get off on displaying the result of the time I've spent sweating my balls off in my home gym. That's sort of the issue.

A stirring in my groin makes me think I'd better keep the air conditioning on full blast and mentally review the facts and figures of my upcoming business deals to keep anything unwanted from springing up. Or is a raging hard-on something that *should* be captured in my painting for Ronaldo?

That could make this afternoon a hell of a lot more interesting, awkward, painful...

All of the above.

Am I supposed to be like those serious complications listed in Viagra commercials? Maintaining a four-hour erection sounded like a good way to end up in the hospital or die from unspent desire. Or it could make for an amazing night if I rush home afterward so Ronaldo can take care of me properly.

Now that doesn't sound half bad.

Kaden looks up at me and catches the wicked tilt of my lips. He snorts as he gestures to the trunk. "I don't want to know what you're thinking about, but remember that expression for when I'm sketching. Let me get my stuff and then I want to see that face again. It'll be perfect for your guy's portrait. I hope he knows how good he's got it with you."

It's been a while since someone complimented me outright. I'm not embarrassed to admit it only increases the electricity humming through me. Sometimes it's hard to say if people gravitate toward me because they genuinely want a relationship—a friendship, partnership, whatever—or if it's my money and what it can buy that motivates their kindness.

With Kaden it's easy to tell.

He's not asking for anything. I discovered him, hired him, and I'm finding that I genuinely like the guy. I'll have to send lots of business his way. Or maybe our entertainment division should follow up with him about doing a documentary on his work. He has star quality that could make us both a ton of cash.

"If you take the canvas, I'll get the rest," I offer. Though I have the urge to handle it all for him, I'd rather not risk messing up the painting. His other supplies are far heavier anyway. If I can make his burden lighter, I want to. Not because of the magnetism I'm doing my best to ignore between us. It's just who I am. Doing things for him or other people I respect makes me happy. What's wrong with that?

I set a couple things down to key in the entry code, then use my chin to gesture toward the living room. When I catch up, I'm shocked to find that a man who idolizes natural beauty isn't riveted by the multi-million dollar view of the ocean, which never fails to capture my attention.

Instead, he's watching me and has totally busted me reacting to the scenery.

Like every time I glimpse the sea, peace washes over me. If I smile any wider, I'm likely to rip open the face Kaden seems eager to immortalize.

He teases me. "You're that excited about getting naked for me?"

"You wish."

He turns away. Either my imagination is playing tricks on me or he murmurs, "Damn straight, I do."

Then louder, so that I can't mistake it, he says, "It's time. Let's do this."

Like a good boy, I peel off my shirt and toss it into the corner.

4

ROGAN

I t's oddly intimate sitting in silence, posed exactly as Kaden molded me. He stalks in an arc around me, judging me from every perspective then tweaking my position until he's satisfied with what he sees.

His assessing stare lasers over me. He hums low in his throat then strides to his supplies.

Professional, yes. Impersonal...not quite.

I'm laid out on my back on a low, tufted leather bench. The outside edge of my left foot rests on the floor while my right foot is propped on the seat, causing my knee to bend. One arm is raised, folded sharply behind my head, flexing the muscles there as well as highlighting the definition along my ribs. My head is pillowed on that palm while the heel of the other is situated low on my abdomen.

This perpetual quasi-crunch is pretty damn flattering even to my untrained eye. Comfortable, well, that's another matter. My fingers detect the beginnings of a quiver where they splay low across my pelvis, nearly brushing the base of my dick. The stiffness and

45

discomfort I'm sure to feel tomorrow will be worth it to look my best for Ronaldo, make him proud to call me his.

The look comes off casually sensual, though each minute detail—down to the angle my jaw is tilted—is deliberate. Calculated to appeal.

I'm staring directly at Kaden now, unable to look away even if I wanted to. Every bit of me is exposed, including my semi, which has naturally flopped onto my thigh in plain view.

"Feel free to add a couple of inches," I joke as I glance at my cock then back toward him in an effort to cut the tension. No sense in trying to pretend it's not on prominent display. The centerpiece of an erotic arrangement he's fashioned out of my body with a firm and unapologetic grip on each of my various parts.

He waves me off. "Anyone who looks at this painting is going to assume I already did."

"Fortunately, Ronaldo knows it's not false advertising. Nobody but him—and you, I suppose—are going to see it until I'm dead." The contract he sent to my assistant earlier in the week gave us the right to keep the portrait in a private collection for the rest of our lives. After that, our estate would bequeath it to a museum Kaden had named as the intended recipient of his oeuvre.

I'd checked out the place online and had been impressed by the institute's commitment to protecting and displaying art by LGBT creators. In fact, I started the process of becoming a benefactor after researching their conservation efforts, their current collection, and outreach programs funded by grants they issue. I'm happy to contribute both now, and later, to their cause. Kaden's life's work deserves to be enshrined in a magnificent hall for everyone to enjoy.

As soon as my privacy is no longer a factor, anyway.

"You could be the world's next David." He eyes the blank canvas as if he can already envision the finished piece. "I have a feeling this is going to be one of my best yet."

With that, he gets serious about his work. Instead of crossing to the pad of paper and the satchel full of colored pencils for the layout-blocking sketch he told me he'd do first, he reaches into a padded black backpack and withdraws a fancy camera from within.

"Wait. You're going to take pictures of me like this?" I shrink from the lens aimed in my direction without ruining Kaden's handiwork. I'm not sure I could stand another round of his unintentional caresses without embarrassing myself.

"Yup." He nods as he fiddles with some dials then peeks at the preview screen on the back. "They're insurance. I always hope I don't have to, but I could work from them alone if you get called away to take over the corporate world or something."

I bark out a laugh then freeze when I see him double-checking to make sure I didn't shift too much. There's an ingrained part of me that doesn't like to disappoint a handsome man who has given me orders.

"I'll also use them to reset your pose when you need a break. It's going to take me at least twenty minutes of drawing before I'm ready to paint. After that, we'll go as long as you can stand it today. A couple hours of me torturing you, maybe?"

In my mind, I treat it as a game. I'll stay still as a statue for him. Beat the record set by any of his other clients. I'm kind of fucked up, I know. But I can't help it. It's just how I am. Competitive. Especially against myself. The fact that my body already feels the strain of this unnatural pose means it won't be easy. Even better.

Kaden is still talking, although he's already pretty much convinced me to be his subject. The subject of his photographs, I mean. I scrunch my eyes and imagine the expression on Ronaldo's face as he unveils my gift to ground myself, before focusing on what Kaden's saying again. "Once I'm back in my studio, putting on the finishing touches, these will give me a good reference for the lighting, too. Is that a problem? They're no more revealing than the portrait will be."

"I know. But it's harder for a painting to accidentally go viral." I balk once more at the idea of being captured like this on film or in pixels, whatever cameras use these days. A single stray email attachment could have resounding implications. "My investors might not appreciate my dick plastered all over the internet."

"If they were smart, they'd use naked shots of you to market every damn product you make. You'd all get rich —*richer*—quick. These go nowhere, I swear. I don't even put them on my laptop that has internet access. And if they somehow were to be leaked, you could sue the shit out of me according to that paperwork we signed, right?"

I nod. There was an ironclad nondisclosure agreement included in the contract we executed earlier in the week. It was one of the only reasons I'd gone ahead with my potentially reckless decision to immortalize myself at my most vulnerable for Ronaldo.

I draw a shaky breath, pause to consider the risks, and realize I trust Kaden. I'm totally comfortable around him. Maybe a little *too* comfortable considering I'm completely bared. Doubly so since he seems like he's looking at me hard enough to see beyond surface features like the shade of my skin or the lines of my body.

He's peering into me. Prepared to capture my essence. It was what made his paintings so captivating and memorable. Would I like the reflection of myself as much as I enjoyed his other paintings? I hope so.

"Sorry, go ahead." I try to relax as he frames me and snaps away.

"Thanks." He rewards me with a lopsided grin then clicks the shutter release a few more times before I can change my mind.

What seems like an eternity later, I'm still hooked on watching him do his thing. My thigh and ass have long since gone numb. The burning in my arm is only eclipsed by the stiffness in my lower back. I think my spine might be permanently deformed. Still, I don't dare budge.

There's no chance in hell I'll cry mercy. In many ways, we're playing a game like the ones I enjoy with my boyfriend. At least, I am. Kaden is blissfully unaware that I'm testing myself. So why does it feel more thrilling than anything I've experienced with Ronaldo in a while?

Because it's secret?

Because Kaden is forbidden?

It must be.

He's in his own world, brush flying from his palette to the canvas and back as he squints, shrugs, and mumbles to himself. Simultaneously adorable and expert in his approach. It's fascinating to observe as I imagine him fleshing out the basic outlines of the pencil sketch he did earlier. I can tell from his intensity that painting gives him the same rush negotiating a business deal brings me.

That's something Ronaldo can't relate to. He doesn't have that kind of passion for a career. He'd been a server when we met, but it was only a job to him. Not an obsession or a foot in the door to something bigger. It hadn't taken much to convince him to quit and spend his evenings with me instead. Otherwise, my hectic schedule would never have allowed us to spend time together.

Every occasion since then that I've tried to not-so-subtly prod him into taking an interest in something, anything, to occupy his time while I'm gone, our discussions have ended up as arguments. Despite his willingness to spend my money, he often equates my ambition to greed. It makes me feel slimy for trying to do better for us and my shareholders instead of simply enjoying the abundance I've already amassed. Maybe that was why he asked when I'd be done with my weekend "meeting" five times this morning. His irritated huffs had escalated each time I reiterated that I didn't have a precise answer to that question until I nearly divulged my surprise to keep the peace.

Guilt adds to my discomfort. My boyfriend is stuck at home, probably bored out of his mind, and I'm here having one hell of a time. At least as much fun as Kaden's having painting me. The bulge in his jeans tells me his work turns him on. It probably floods his bloodstream with a rush of endorphins I'm very familiar with.

What does he see when he looks at me? I'd give anything to peek over his shoulder for a moment. Lost in thought, I don't register the approaching sound of voices right away. They're distant and out of place in the bubble of hushed concentration encapsulating Kaden and me. Distorted by the glass walls of the house that they're passing through from outside.

He pauses and frowns, surfacing from his trance.

I hate whoever is interrupting. Trespassers. Usually I don't mind. Today, it pisses me off.

"Are you expecting visitors?" Kaden asks.

I shake my head, wincing when my neck cracks. Damn it. They made me move. My streak is broken. As if that shatters my self-control, I suddenly have the urge to stretch except I feel like the Tin Man at this point. I might need some help working out the kinks enough to stand.

I'm hoping the passersby don't peek in the wall of windows or they're going to get an eyeful. I glance around for my clothes, which are neatly folded in a stack on the sofa halfway across the room. As creaky as my joints are at the moment, they might as well be in the closet of my main house. "No. People cut through our yard to get to the beach sometimes since they know we're not around much. They'll go away in a minute. If you don't mind, I think I'll take that break now."

Kaden peeks at his watch a moment before his cheeks flame. "Rogan, it's been too long. Why didn't you say something? You must be dying. I'm sorry. I got caught up. Never needed a safe word for this kind of session before."

He rushes to my side and stoops, looping an arm around my shoulders.

Which is right about when I notice that instead of fading, the voices outside are growing louder. Husky conversation and something more filter into my sanctuary.

A moan. A muffled curse.

And...dirty talk?

"Just a little farther. And then I'll bend you over and have you begging for my cock in that tight ass. You need that, don't you? Even though you couldn't wait and sucked me off while we were out there sunbathing where anyone

—including the damn paparazzi—could have spotted us. I should punish you for that. Spank you then fuck your brains out. You want that, huh?"

"Yes, sir. Please, hurry."

"We'll see." A wicked chuckle I know very well, but haven't heard for quite some time—not like that— reverberates through the room.

Ronaldo!

My gaze snaps to Kaden's. He's suddenly become as stiff as I have been for hours. His wide eyes bore into mine from mere inches away.

I should brush him off, jump to my feet, cover myself, prepare for the implosion of my life that's coming in three...two...

Do something other than lounge here like the statue with a heart of stone I wish I was. But I can't. It seems like I'm stuck in some horrible nightmare.

Worst of all is the dawning realization on Kaden Finch's handsome face as his gaze whips between me and the direction the voices are coming from multiple times in a split second. Then I lose track of what he's doing as I follow his horrified stare to the house's glass backdoor. The one off the garage where I usually park, but didn't today. Where two men in skintight bathing suits that hide nothing make it clear they're coming inside and ready to party.

"Oh shit..." Kaden turns toward the door, his hand outstretched as if he can barricade it and keep reality from barging in and crushing me. Nice try. Gallant, even. Except it doesn't work.

Both of us stare as my boyfriend slaps his lover on the ass, shoves him over the threshold, then stuffs his tongue down the guy's throat. He shivers in Ronaldo's unrelenting grasp.

He's cute, I'll give him that. Ronaldo does have good taste in men.

Air flies from my body in a rush along with shreds of my heart, ego, and the last of my misguided loyalty to this absolutely unworthy bastard. It makes some sort of sound between a gasp and a wheeze as it leaves my empty, aching chest.

The guy in Ronaldo's arms stiffens. His eyes nearly pop out of his skull when he notices Kaden and me.

Talk about a willy wilter. I almost feel bad for him.

"What the—?" Ronaldo jerks around. He takes in the sight of Kaden so near, touching my naked body. I've never seen that shade of purple on a person before. Dumbass me, for a moment I think it's caused by mortification. Shock at being caught.

Until he drops his sidepiece, abandoning the man, who stumbles and crumples into a heap. Ronaldo rounds on me and has the gall to unleash his infamous temper. This time I won't let the toxic blend of aggression and rage or the sheer volume at which he projects his animosity deter me from speaking my mind. At least, when I can find my voice again.

"You're screwing me over?" He storms toward me, drawn up short only when Kaden steps nimbly between us. "I guess I know now why you're too tired to fuck when you get home at night! When you bother to come home. Is *he* why you're out of town so damn much?"

All I can do is laugh.

It might be the slightly insane sort of amusement that comes from trying to make sense of the impossible, but I clutch my sore abs and snort as I sit up fully. Goddamn, I hurt. Everywhere.

"I think you've got this twisted around." Kaden's shoulders broaden as his chest puffs up. He's smaller than Ronaldo, but I would bet my entire fortune that he'll kick my boyfriend's—no, *ex*-boyfriend's—ass if I don't intervene.

"Who the hell are you to tell me what to think about my boy fucking some hottie behind my back?" Ronaldo snarls. His hook-up whimpers, then scuttles out the door, letting it slam behind him.

"Thanks for the compliment, but I'm not a sack of shit like you. I don't touch men who are taken." Kaden reaches out and spins his easel so Ronaldo can see the work in progress. It's already obvious that it's me. Here. Looking pretty damn fine, if I do say so myself.

Ronaldo's nostrils flare. "What's that? A souvenir? Pretty stupid to leave proof of an affair."

He must have a system locked down. Knows all the tips and tricks to avoid getting caught. Clearly, I'm an idiot to have ignored my instincts. I should have realized he's been fooling around. I guess sometimes the gossip columns have it right after all. Even I'm not dumb enough to think I caught him cheating the very first time he's strayed.

This is a pattern. A habit he's used to hiding.

Son of a bitch.

"It was a gift. That I won't be selling to him anymore if he plans to give it to a dirtbag like you for your anniversary. You don't deserve this. Or him, for that matter." Kaden cracks his knuckles before his fingers ball into fists.

"No!" I lunge to my feet, pain blazing through parts of

me that are so dead they transcend numbness and throb in agony. I ignore the bolts of lightning zapping my nerve endings and grab Kaden's elbow, tugging him out of Ronaldo's reach. "You're not going to bust up those hands because of me. It's not worth it."

My ex blinks at me, leering at my nudity.

I feel disgusting when his pupils dilate. If he thinks there's any chance he's touching me with his filthy junk ever again, he's insane.

When Kaden comes to his senses and retreats, I do the same. Limping to the sofa, I snatch my pants from the cushion and shake them out. I tip precariously trying to put them on with even a hint of grace. Kaden is there, steadying me.

"*He's* not worth a fight," he corrects me quietly. "I have a feeling you are."

"Why don't you get rid of this loser so we can talk?" Ronaldo shifts gears smoothly, like he has the other times I've reached my breaking point. He paints a half-apologetic, half-pleading expression on his face and lowers his voice a couple dozen decibels. Only now can I see how effortlessly he's manipulated me in past, and how he's trying to do it again.

"There's nothing to say. We're done." I cross my arms and try to keep my shit together. How could I have been so blind? "In fact, don't bother coming home. You can stay here for a maximum of two weeks. By the end of that time you'll need to find somewhere else to live because the locks here will be changed and this place will be on the market. I'll have someone from my staff pack your things and bring them out here tonight."

"What? You can't do that! It's not like you give a shit anyway. You're always so damn busy running your empire, you don't have time for me, the man who's supposed to be the center of your life. Have you forgotten all your promises? Did you ever mean them? Aren't you going to man up and take some of the blame for this?" Ronaldo takes a step forward.

I jerk backward hard enough to give my already stiff neck whiplash. Suddenly he's so repulsive I think I might puke if he touches me. Yet his emotional abuse still has the power to screw with my head. Maybe I should have paid more attention to him. Or cut him loose a few years back, when he persuaded me to try harder at strengthening our relationship instead of calling it quits. I waver the slightest bit in my convictions.

Once again, Kaden is there, coming to my defense. "Stay the hell away from him. Quit spouting that bullshit, too. You're the only person responsible for your terrible choices, asshole."

Ronaldo's mask slips. He roars at Kaden, "It's no business of yours!"

"I'm making it my business." Kaden turns to me and levels his most authoritative stare in my direction. "Put your shirt on, and let's go. I'm taking you home."

Instinctively, I respond, doing as he commands. I shove my arms through the sleeves of my dress shirt and leave it hanging open over my unbuttoned slacks. As I head for the front door of the house I know I'll never return to, I don't bother to look over my shoulder at either the view or the man I used to imagine I loved.

My breathing sticks in my chest. I feel as numb inside as all of my limbs are. Ironically, that doesn't keep either my body or my spirit from throbbing in excruciating pain.

Kaden grabs hold of my elbow, casually supporting me as we make our escape. He scoops my keys and wallet from the bowl by the front entrance then murmurs in my ear, "Stand tall. Don't let him see you wrecked. You can do this. A few more steps and we'll be gone."

I do as he tells me. Trusting him to get me out of this mess.

Funny how it seems only natural.

Maybe I'm reaching for a connection after severing ties with Ronaldo. Or maybe he's the kind of guy my ex-boyfriend was only pretending to be all along.

5

KADEN

Oh shit, oh shit, oh shit.

I tuck Rogan into the passenger seat of his sporty sedan. While I imagined myself driving the sleek Tesla earlier today, I hadn't expected to have the opportunity. And definitely wouldn't have wanted to if I had known why it would be necessary.

Jogging around to the driver's side, I'm glad there's no transmission in this car so I won't embarrass myself by grinding the gears. I'd rather squeal the tires and make an exit worthy of the rage I feel on Rogan's behalf. Either way, I don't think he's going to notice.

The poor bastard is sitting across from me and hasn't made a peep. He scrubs his face with his hands, then presses his knuckles to his eyes. I wouldn't blame him if he broke down.

"It's okay, you know. Completely understandable to be upset after...what just happened." Hell, it even shocked me and I wasn't in a relationship with that piece of shit.

"I'm not over here weeping like a teenager with a

59

broken heart. I'm angry I let myself waste the past five years of my life on a con artist like him," Rogan explodes.

Thank God—I can deal with that much better.

"Do you know how to drive? Have a license?" he asks, his voice still raised, though I know it's not in anger at me. I nod. "Then, please. Go."

I adjust the mirrors quickly, not wanting to destroy his sweet ride after he's already lost so much in one morning, then launch us down the fancypants driveway. I skid a little when I gun it onto the rural road that leads back to the city.

Rogan doesn't freak. He doesn't even flinch. His shoulders slump and he looks out the window with an expression that makes me think he's saying goodbye to his precious ocean. I hate that Ronaldo ruined it for him. As my surprise begins to morph into indignation on Rogan's behalf, I realize why his boyfriend looked so familiar.

Uh oh.

Should I tell him? I mean, it's better to know the full extent of things all at once, right? Plus it might keep him from taking that guy back. Ronaldo doesn't deserve a man like Rogan.

"Hey, Rogan?" I bite my lip and glance over to see if he's lost any of that far-away, dazed look. "You did say the painting was for your fifth anniversary, didn't you?"

"Unfortunately."

"I hate to break this to you..."

He rubs his temples. "What? What now? He's not following us, is he?"

When he cranes his neck then winces, I put my hand on his forearm to keep him from straining his muscles, which have to be knotted all to hell. I can't help myself. I rub my thumb over the ropes of sinew beneath my fingers.

He seems to relax. Until I drop another bomb. "I've seen that douchebag before. There's a club...for people in the lifestyle...a few blocks from my place. Romeo & Julian. I met my own douchebag of an ex-boyfriend there."

"Not a resounding endorsement." Rogan faces me with a wry hint of a smile. I hate to wipe even that off his face.

"I used to see Ronaldo there all the time. Picking up guys. One time Cortez—my ex—and I saw him fucking some guy up against a Dumpster in the alley on our way out. He had a reputation for being especially cruel. Got off on using the inexperienced guys and screwing with their emotions. Eventually he got banned from the bar. The owner had enough of the drama."

"When?" Rogan sounds like he's about to choke on the question.

I hope the glance I shoot him between taking the curves in the road isn't doused in pity. It used to make me feel even worse when I ran into people after my breakup and saw the look in their eyes when I confessed I was single. This has to be *way* worse. "A couple years ago. Two-ish."

"All that time..." Rogan swallows hard then lets his head fall back on the plush leather seat. "Fuck."

He doesn't speak again until I ask for directions to his place. Neither does he shake off my hand, which never leaves his.

6

CORTEZ

I sit in the front pew of this weathered wooden church, nestled on a lush hilltop in Columbia, staring at the stained glass windows. I find myself here often. The bright colors that wash over my uplifted face as I blink against the filtered sunlight from outside make me feel as though I have some piece of Kaden with me. Painted on my skin.

He's untouchable, but still out there. Somewhere. So far from here and what my life is like now. Always a part of me.

It's the only time I allow myself to remember how things used to be. Usually, I try to forget that anything else has ever existed beyond this game of deceit and cunning. Otherwise, I might slip up on my cover.

Here, I'm Father Cortez. What a joke!

A priest I am not. Saintly isn't my style.

In my dreams of making love to Kaden, I hear us laughing and whispering naughty things to each other in English. It sounds so foreign to me. I'm not even sure I know how to speak that language after two and a half years embedded in the South American drug scene. Carefree joy is extinct here.

I've accepted freely given confessions from some of the wickedest men alive. Tortured additional admissions from the black hearts of others, who don't attend my house of worship, under cover of night and the verdant vegetation surrounding the area. I've done my duty. Spied on, influenced, and stopped pure evil however I could.

No man could be proud of these actions or left untainted by the measures necessary to rebel against the worst of humanity. To fight them, I've had to become one of them. Learn to think like them. Ignore civility and my inherent distaste for brutality to stop them from inflicting those injustices on innocents.

I'm so glad I cut Kaden loose before I left. I will never be normal again after the terrible things I've seen and done during this assignment.

Each day it grows more dangerous, too.

Last week, our organization won a major victory. We intercepted a monumental shipment. Busting the main players in that deal means everyone with access to their plans is under scrutiny, myself included.

There are only so many times I can get away with passing along information I overhear within these walls before our enemies will narrow the list of suspects to me alone.

I'm supposed to man this post for six more months. I can't see how I'll last half that long.

I'm tired. Lying like this to everyone about everything is exhausting.

Isolating.

Relentless. There's never a break. Never a chance to let my guard down.

Even now, I hear hushed voices. I creep to the window and peer through a crack in one of the panes. Two men I recognize as leaders in the local cartel are having a heated discussion in the memorial garden outside.

I slip my recorder from beneath my robes and turn it on.

Memories of Kaden, and the comfort they bring me, will have to wait for some other stolen moment of peace.

7

ROGAN

I feel foolish climbing the rickety iron stairs to the second-story rear entry above Kaden's shop. It's after ten o'clock at night—too late for an unannounced visit in my social circles, and far later than I planned to swing by. I got sidetracked by a videoconference with international investors to discuss a complication that supposedly couldn't wait until morning for resolution. Before I realized it, three hours had flown by.

Some of Ronaldo's criticisms were valid. I need to learn how to balance my life better. What I keep wondering is if I meet the right man, will I be as compelled to spend time with him as I am to close deals? I think the fact that I'm here now might be a clue.

The amount of time I've spent thinking about Kaden since I watched him climb into an Uber and roll out of my driveway last weekend is right up there with how often I've checked the stocks or scoured the internet looking for venture capital investment opportunities my competitors haven't caught on to yet.

Hopefully he's less concerned about etiquette than my

usual companions. As it is, I've already delayed this visit for the better part of a week. I at least have to drop off the stuff I brought with me now that I've worked up the nerve to come here.

I wish Kaden had better lighting in this alley. I'll have to see what I can do about improving some of the conditions back here before someone breaks an ankle or gets mugged in the inky shadows between the buildings.

When I reach the landing, I lift my loose fist but hesitate before my knuckles can connect with the crimson door. Am I an idiot for doing this personally when I could have sent someone else during regular business hours instead? Probably.

He's already seen me at rock bottom. Overstepping now probably won't do any more to lower his opinion of me.

Fuck it, I knock.

My heart pounds a half dozen times. I guess he's already gone to bed for the night. With a sigh, I turn to go.

"Don't leave! I'm coming!" A muffled shout echoes from within followed by the pounding of footsteps that make me sure he's in the apartment, running toward me. The rattle of chain follows shortly after.

Kaden's there, unlatching the door. A few inches away from where I'm standing.

Suddenly, my palms begin to sweat. I feel like an animal who's been lured into a poacher's spotlight by the promise of a tasty treat. It's too late to change my mind and run. If I could, I'd vanish over the side of the railing like a superhero.

So when he peeks out and realizes it's me causing a racket so late, I try for a smile and a wave that come out sort of wobbly and super awkward. Great.

"Oh! Hey, Rogan." He seems genuinely surprised, as if I'm the last person he expected to find on his doorstep.

Who had he been afraid of missing then? My cheeks heat as I consider that he might have an entirely different sort of company on the way over. This was stupid. I should turn right around and leave.

As if he can sense my disappointment, he chuckles. "Thought you were the delivery guy. Oops."

"Uh. No, sorry." The mere mention of food practically has me drooling. My assistant ordered me lunch sometime around eleven, I guess. I haven't eaten since. "I brought the stuff you left at the beach house the other day. Let me go grab it. I just wanted to make sure you were here before carrying it up."

"Great, thanks." Does he sound sort of disappointed? If he's half as hungry as me, I can understand.

Too bad he's already made arrangements or I might have worked up the nerve to ask him out to dinner. Yeah, right. I'm not the sort of guy who asks first, but I would have wanted to.

"Here, I'll help." Kaden opens the door wider and joins me on the landing. It's a tight squeeze. The scent I remember from a few days ago hits me—man and something slightly astringent. Paint thinner, probably. On him, it smells great.

After a slightly too-long pause I realize he's waiting for me to get out of the way. I shake my head then jog down the stairs, as if that will make up for my dazed reaction time. I pop the trunk of my car and start lifting boxes out.

I close my eyes briefly as I prepare to explain.

"What's this?" He takes the first one from me and peeks at it. In the gloom back here I'm not surprised he's unsure.

"It's a new camera." I draw in a shaky breath as the image of shattered windows and destroyed furnishings from the police report flashes into my mind. The beach house looks like it's been hit by a hurricane. "Ronaldo took out his frustration on a lot of things, your camera included. I'm so sorry."

"That guy is a serious fuckwad." Kaden catches me off guard by leaning over and squeezing my shoulders in a quick hug. Casual and genuine, he's not uncomfortable in the least. That alone eases my nerves and brings me some peace for the first time since he drove me home the other day. Maybe this wasn't such a terrible idea after all. "I'm sorry you had to deal with that. Thanks for replacing my equipment."

I didn't simply replace it. I upgraded it and had the guy at the photo-video supply store throw in a bunch of lenses and other doodads he seemed excited about, too. Hopefully that would atone for Ronaldo's antics.

"Of course. The old one is in here too, for what that's worth. I couldn't even get it to turn on. Worse..." I drew a deep breath then reached into the trunk again. This one hurt. I hope it didn't upset him too much. "He didn't seem to like his present very much."

Kaden curses violently when he sees the mangled painting in my hands. I hold it out to him as if it were a beloved pet that passed away. After watching him work, I know how much of himself he puts into each of his pieces.

He runs his fingers along a shredded edge of the canvas that effectively split my face in two. He hadn't been anywhere near finished, but he'd done enough that it was obvious it was supposed to be me. Now it's slashed to ribbons.

"Forget   fuckwad—Ronaldo's   a   straight   up

psychopath." Kaden seems more concerned about me than his ruined masterpiece. "I hope you filed a restraining order."

"I did." I look away then. "Things got pretty ugly this week. It's handled. Don't worry."

Despite how I acted when the shit hit the fan, and my preferences for my role in relationships, I'm more than capable of taking care of myself. Once the shock wore off, I'd sicced my team of lawyers on Ronaldo. They assured me he wouldn't bother me ever again.

Thank God.

I pick up Kaden's easel along with his brushes, paints, and sketching supplies, then shut the trunk. As if he understands I'm also closing the conversation about Ronaldo, hopefully forever, he nods then heads inside. I follow him, admiring his tight ass in his well-worn jeans.

Hey, I'm only human and it's right there in front of me. You would look too.

It's a good thing my hands are full or I might be tempted to do more.

When we reach the top of the stairs, he opens the door then holds it for me as he ushers me inside. The single-room loft apartment is nothing like the places I've lived. The exposed brick walls are perfectly imperfect. A tidy kitchenette has the basics to guarantee a bachelor's survival. A sofa and a few tall bookcases delineate the living room space. Beyond them I catch a glimpse of part of a large, mussed bed.

Giant windows reach from the ground floor of his shop up to the living quarters where a spiral staircase ascends from his workspaces. A wrought iron railing decorates the edge of the loft and allows for a two-story open area of about twenty feet between the edge of it and the outside front wall, making his personal space seem larger and less confined. I bet in the daytime it's as bright and sunny in here as the alleyway out back is dingy and dark right now.

Though it's a modest apartment, it has style. Nothing about it is generic or sterile.

Immediately, I feel at home. Just like when I'm around Kaden.

"Nice place," I say as I follow his lead and set my armfuls of his supplies on the kitchen table, which seems to be made of a reclaimed antique door.

He raises a brow at me as if he doesn't believe me. "I've seen two of your houses. Enough to know this is a hole in the wall by comparison."

"It's not what you have that's important. It's what you make of it." I look around, noticing something weird and wonderful everywhere my gaze lands. Artwork, of course, but also refurbished furnishings, original wooden beams, and nontraditional LED strip lighting that highlights architectural details. Everything here has one-of-a-kind character that's been lovingly enhanced.

He seems like he might say more right before someone calls from outside and the door swings open a crack. "Yo, Kaden. Supper time."

With a fist pump, he sprints to greet the delivery guy. His wallet is out of his back pocket before I can offer to cover it for him. The delicious aroma of Chinese food wafts to me and I groan, clutching my abdomen when it cramps.

"You already have company?" the guy asks. "Too bad. I was hoping you'd give me one of those *special* tips again."

Kaden responds too quietly for me to hear.

Am I interrupting? I drop the rest of his things and spin toward the door. "I guess I should be going..."

With a solid shake of his head, Kaden opens it wider as he starts back inside. The crook of his arm is laden with a brown paper bag full of fresh, steaming food.

The delivery guy grins at us. "I guess I can't blame you this time, Kaden. He's smoking. Let me know if you ever update your No Do-Overs policy, though, okay?"

Kaden laughs, highlighting his dimples and his easygoing charm. They're so at odds with the facet of him I'd seen last weekend. The take-charge part, I mean. For a long time I thought I was the only one with two completely disparate sides like that. It's nice to feel like less of a freak. "Will do. See you around."

"Have a great night!" the guy shouts from halfway down the stairs.

I only wish things between Kaden and I actually were how they'd obviously appeared.

He's still chuckling as he clears his throat. "Sorry about that. He's...uh..."

I wave him off. No need to explain how he spends his evenings. If I'm jealous it's mostly of the meal in his hands and not the fun time he's shown the delivery guy in the past.

Sure, that's it.

"I'm guessing by the way you're eye-fucking my dinner that you haven't eaten?" Kaden struts past me as if nothing happened. He sets the paper bag on the counter then reaches into the funky metal locker unit beside his refrigerator and takes out not one, but two, plates.

"Haven't gotten around to it yet." I shake my head. The fact that I'm still wearing my suit is probably evidence enough that I came straight from my office.

"I got carried away with something I was working on, too. That's why it took me a second to answer the door. I ran up from my studio. Join me?" he asks, holding one of the mismatched plates out to me. They look hand-painted with bold swirls of color. Welcoming. Warm.

What else am I going to do?

Spend another lonely night starting at the ceiling of the hotel I've been staying at because I can't bear to crawl into the bed I shared with Ronaldo?

Fuck it. I accept the plate. And the invitation to stay.

Maybe that's what I'd hoped for all along.

Maybe that's why it had taken me days to work up the nerve to see Kaden again. I'm like a bug drawn to the spark of attraction between us. It's been so long since I've felt that intoxicating pull toward another man. But I'm also nervous now that, theoretically, I'm free to explore it. I couldn't stand to get squashed again so soon.

"It's just food, Rogan. Calm down." He understands too much, like he can read my mind. The light skimming of his hand over my lower back as he circles around me to reach the takeout doesn't help me settle my appetites. "Hope you like orange chicken with stir-fried vegetables."

"My favorite, actually." I hold out my plate as he pops open a white box and stabs a fork into it.

"Mine too." He grins. "If I wasn't trying to impress you by pretending to be civilized, I'd eat it straight out of the container while watching Netflix in bed."

Nothing has ever sounded so delicious. "Don't feel the need to change your plans on my behalf."

Kaden steals the plate and instead hands me the chicken, a quart of fried rice, some plastic utensils, chopsticks, and two fortune cookies. "You take that. I'll grab the beer."

This night couldn't possibly get any better.

With a six pack of a microbrew IPA under one arm, he gestures for me to follow him as he leads me to his bedroom nook. It reminds me of some kind of nest hovering over the shop. The pile of assorted blankets and pillows scattered around the mattress, which dips a bit in the middle, only enhances that impression. It seems cozy. Kind of like an adult's version of a blanket fort.

I'm man enough to admit that after the week I've had, it's an appealing proposition.

Kaden plunks the beer in the center of the bed then turns toward me. Instead of divesting me of the food I'm carrying, he drops to one knee then nudges my calf until I lift my foot. He unlaces my shoe and slips it off along with my dress sock, tossing them aside before repeating the process on the other side. Although he's servicing me, it's clear that he's in charge. Doing what he wants to prepare me to spend time with him.

Fine by me. I don't object, letting him do as he pleases when he rises and circles behind me. His fingers slip beneath the collar of my suit jacket. I know what he wants. I transfer the Chinese to one hand and drop my shoulder. He works the sleeve down my arm until my hand is free. Every place he touches tingles as if I've been posing for him again.

I switch the containers to my other hand so he can finish undressing me.

After removing my jacket, Kaden unbuttons my cuffs then rolls up my sleeves. As his fingers trail across my exposed forearms I wonder if he's remembering how the muscles there felt beneath his hand in the car the other day. I'm sure he only meant to comfort me when he touched me, but I haven't been able to forget the weight of his palm or the strength in his grasp since then.

Next he loosens my navy silk tie enough that he can undo the top few buttons of my shirt. I can't breathe any better. Not with him so close. From here the chocolate of his eyes turns molten as he does what he likes with me.

Satisfied, he ruffles my hair, mussing it from the slick style I'd forced the short strands into this morning. "That's better. Come on, I'm *starving*." He hops into bed, sits cross-legged, and pats the spot beside him.

"Me too." And not only for deep-fried chicken bits covered in sticky sweet sauce.

Although, I have to admit, that's pretty fucking great. For fifteen minutes straight, I'm not sure if we say a single word. For my part it's not because I'm engrossed in whatever show is playing on his laptop at the foot of the bed. We take turns alternating jabbing our forks into the containers and stuffing ourselves.

I've never eaten in bed before. It seems dirty and dangerous. What if I drop something on my pressed white shirt, or the sheets?

It's liberating to do something my better sense says I shouldn't. Thrilling because I like it. I guess I should be reckless more often. At least with Kaden.

As our hunger abates, our chewing slows. When I can't stomach another bite, I slump against his headboard.

"One last beer to wash it down with?" Kaden offers.

I probably should stop with two if I'm going to drive home soon. But hey, that's what cabs are for, right?

I nod. Kaden opens the bottle for me before passing it over. He polishes off the final brew himself before letting out a huge belch. I start laughing and can't seem to stop.

"I bet nobody does that at your fancy business

dinners, huh?" He smacks himself in the forehead with the heel of his palm. "Sorry."

"I'm just jealous I didn't do it myself." I rub my chest. Is the fullness there from overindulging in Chinese or spending time with Kaden? Probably some of both.

Either way, if I don't excuse myself soon or find some relief from the pressure, I'm probably going to explode. When Kaden reclines on a mountain of pillows and closes his eyes with a sound remarkably like a purr, I figure that's my cue.

"Thanks for dinner. I really needed that." My voice is raspy as I admit it. I hope he knows I'm not only talking about nourishment.

He opens his eyes again. They lose their sated, dreamy haze when I lift one side of my ass to work my wallet from my pocket.

"You might want to rethink that unless you want me to stab you with one of those chopsticks." He glares at me.

"I'm not trying to chip in, though I would if you'd let me. I...uh...had one other thing to give you before I leave." I clear my throat then slip the check I'd written earlier from my billfold. "I never paid my deposit. You know, before things went to hell. Because I broke our contract and Ronaldo ruined what work you did, I need you to take this. You earned it and then some. I really appreciated your support on Saturday. Thank you, Kaden."

He covers my hand with his and guides it back to the shiny leather in my hands. The check crumples between our fingers as he stuffs it back inside. "I'm going to pretend you didn't just try to pay me for being a decent human being. I think your standards are really low because you've been hanging out with scumbags. And I'm too content right now to ruin my buzz by getting upset."

"We had a deal." I sit straighter. "For all I know, you made plans for that commission when we signed the contract. Fair's fair."

"It's not your money I'm after, Rogan."

I stay still, hoping he means that like it sounds.

Swallowing hard, I meet his stare with my pleading one.

Please make the first move. I need you to do it.

Kaden doesn't disappoint me. He climbs over to my side of the bed so that he's straddling my thighs, puts his hands on either side of my face then draws me toward him. He holds me steady as he covers my lips with his.

Kaden Finch is kissing me.

And it's like nothing I've experienced before.

8

KADEN

Rogan is the most scrumptious dessert I've ever devoured. Beer and the sweetness of our meal enhance the flavor of his mouth. Most delicious, though, is his instant and complete surrender of control. While I was a pretty good bottom once upon a time, I had nothing on him. None of the other guys I've slept with since then do either.

From the moment I take the reins and capture his lips, he becomes the perfect partner, letting me lead. He doesn't resist when I sip from his parted mouth and tease the very tip of his tongue with mine. Neither does he close his eyes or look away from the honest desire I'm telegraphing in my stare.

He lets me see, hear, and feel his reactions to my touch.

It's so impressive and addicting that I spend forever simply kissing him over and over. The last time I locked lips with a guy like this...

I groan to ward off the memory of Cortez and my infatuation with him. I haven't thought of him once this week. Now is definitely not the time to recall the summer I spent with him in this very same bed.

I've wasted enough time mourning as it is.

I cope the only way I know how—by replacing pain with pleasure. My fingers spear into Rogan's hair, tugging some as I move him into the optimal position to accept my deepening kisses. He gasps, then melts into my arms. Sure, the man had a long-term partner a few short days ago, but I'd bet it's been a while since he experienced a connection as electric as this. After years of going without it myself, I plan to rewrite as many awful memories as possible with steamy ones before I let him out of my clutches.

If I only get one shot at making an impression, I intend to do it right.

I shift my lips so that I'm kissing the corner of his mouth then rubbing our stubbled jaws against one another as my hands glide down the powerful column of his neck, over his prominent collarbones, then onto the front of his shirt.

While I'd love to go barbarian and rip it from him, I'm sure it costs more than a month of my utilities. I slip button after button free of the fine fabric and reveal the even finer form beneath.

Dear God, he's as magnificent as I remembered. Easily one of the most classically attractive men I've ever seen, never mind fucked.

Cortez had been gorgeous too. Not in this way. He'd been commanding, rugged, and raw where Rogan is completely opposite. Sophisticated, flawless, and magazine-cover handsome. The kind of guy I never imagined I'd drool over until I found myself staring at his naked body in appreciation while nearly forgetting why we were alone in that beach house last weekend.

And now...

Now everything is different.

For tonight only, he can be mine.

After I shove the shirt off his shoulders, leaving his loosened tie in place for the moment, I tackle his belt and the button of his fly. My intention to take things beyond a make-out session are translated loud and clear to Rogan when I plunge my hand down his pants for a sneak preview of the main event. I snake my fingers beneath the waistband of his briefs to fist his rock-hard cock.

"What are you doing?" Rogan twists his head and refuses to meet my gaze.

I nudge his chin until he stares into my eyes again. "Keeping you from making the same mistake I did after I had my heart broken."

He doesn't respond right away, so I kiss him again, lulling him, hoping he realizes I'm telling the absolute truth. I may barely know him, but I've seen enough to recognize the parts of us that are nearly identical.

When I pause so he can draw air into his lungs, he shudders. "It's...so soon. I don't know—"

His fat cock, pulsing in my palm, tells me his body knows damn well what it needs.

"Don't shut down. Denying yourself the best parts of life won't help. Stop wondering what you did wrong. Physical intimacy doesn't have to be reserved for your forever guy. It can be just for fun, until you're ready for something permanent. Who knows how long that will take? You might never buy in to that fairytale again. Don't keep yourself from enjoying what you can because it's not what you thought you'd have."

If I can use this single night to teach him everything I've learned over the past two years, slowly and painfully, maybe I can save him even more heartache—the self-inflicted variety.

I wish someone had done that for me.

He doesn't tell me to stop when I lean forward and kiss him again, this time while also massaging his shaft. His hips rock eagerly, pressing his cock deeper into my palm as I seduce his mouth. I reward him with short, even strokes until the slickness of his precome coats my fingers. I withdraw my hand, smirking when he groans in disappointment, intent on tasting the proof of his desire on my hand.

When he realizes what I'm about to do, he objects. Horror and regret erase the rapture that had dilated his pupils, making his eyes appear nearly black in the diffused lighting of my apartment.

"Wait!" Rogan slaps at my arm, keeping me from sampling his flavor on my skin.

As much as I would love to sleep with him, I won't railroad him into it. I'm not the kind of guy to take advantage of his obedient nature or the way his ex trampled his confidence.

"Shhh…if you really aren't ready yet then I hope you'll at least take a rain check. No pressure. Just please, don't wait years before you find an outlet again like I was dumb enough to do."

"Huh? *Years*?" He shakes his head, more lust evaporating from his demeanor as the flush drains from his golden skin. "No. Like five minutes. Long enough to find protection. For you, I mean. If Ronaldo was screwing around—"

I grunt at that. "Rogan. Seriously. You know he was. No *if* about it. He didn't deserve you."

My guts clench as I think of all the times I saw him taking advantage of the youngest, most naïve guys at the bar. I should have said something. Stopped him. Even before I understood the implications of his actions for Rogan. Maybe I could have saved this man some of the trouble he has now, because of that prick.

"Fuck." His eyes slam shut. "You're right. We probably should call this off. I need to get tested. What if—?"

More than ever I need to hold him. To make him realize the actions of his disloyal lover shouldn't be held against him. To promise I'll stand by him while he faces the real and brutal consequences of his prior relationship. I might never fuck him again after tonight, or even at all. I promise us both silently right then that no matter what happens I'll be the best damn friend I can be as he recovers from the aftermath of Ronaldo.

Someone I could have used but didn't have when I needed support.

"Hey now. Don't assume the worst. You're right. You need to schedule a doctor's appointment as soon as possible." I kiss him lightly. "I'll even go with you if you want. But there's nothing you can do about that tonight. So why not let me distract you? I have condoms if we get far enough along to need them. If not, then it's a moot point. We're covered. Whatever happens, we'll be careful. Okay?"

He lets out a sigh, sagging into my arms, then nods against my shoulder. "Yeah."

"So why don't you try to relax and let me take care of you?"

He hugs me, digging his fingers into my T-shirt. "Are you for real?"

I laugh into his hair, running my hand up and down his spine. It feels amazing to do this for him, to shelter him and act like I'm strong enough to carry us both. It's taken me a while to heal, but my scars might finally be fading.

"Yup. I'm an ordinary guy. Except I'm fortunate enough to be here with you tonight. No strings, no expectations, no commitments beyond what we can share with each other in this moment. Take whatever you can from me to make yourself feel good and I promise to do the same." I kiss his forehead then wait for him to green-light me.

"Don't go easy on me, Kaden." He peers up at me from beneath long, thick lashes with a laser-like intensity that reminds me of how spectacular it is that he can suppress his usual fierceness in private. With me. "I can handle you. This. Whatever we're doing here. I'm sort of cracked right now, but I'm definitely not broken. I won't give him that sort of control over me. Not anymore."

He doesn't have to spell it out. We both know Ronaldo's mistreatment left him feeling shitty about himself—worthless and used. Weak. Those wounds have barely had time to scab over. I have no intentions of making him bleed again.

No, I want to heal him. Arrogant to assume I can? Maybe. But I'm going to try my damndest to bring him relief. Do something for him that years of self-medicating with drugs and alcohol and casual sex haven't done for me.

When I'm done with him, he'll have no doubt about his ability to please a man.

I can already tell this is going to be epic.

"I promise, won't hold back with you. I'm going to give you everything I've got, Rogan." I reach forward and slip his tie over his head, wrapping it around my knuckles before I ask, "How do you feel about being tied up?"

9

ROGAN

The noise that escapes my throat is partially a groan, partially a whimper, and entirely *yes please!* Fortunately, Kaden is fluent in impatient non-verbalizations.

He smirks then commands, "Give me your hands."

I thrust them in front of me, wrists stacked, so fast I risk knocking the wind out of him when he leans in to whisper in my ear. "If you change your mind, say *Pygmalion*. Will you remember?"

I nod. He *is* bringing me to life again.

Each pump of my heart is flooding my system with adrenaline and hope. The possibility that I might be better off without Ronaldo's dead weight dragging me down is enough to make me euphoric. Kaden and everything he's about to do to me are a hell of a bonus.

"That's it." He kisses my temple before shackling my wrists with his hands, squeezing them in his grip then winding the silk in place of his fingers. It reminds me that my tie is the tool, doing his bidding. Just like I will be soon.

I can't wait.

I shift restlessly on the bed beneath him as he works, securing my bound hands to the headboard above and behind me. I'm desperate for him to hurry. To touch me. To use me.

"See, if you weren't tied down, you'd rush me, wouldn't you?" He pins my hip to the mattress, stilling my unconscious movements. "Tempt me into skipping straight to the grand finale before enjoying the rest of the show."

That doesn't sound like such a terrible thing to me. But I'm game for whatever he decides to do. Here, in the bedroom, it brings me more pleasure to blank out my mind and react reflexively to the stimulation he provides. I don't want to think of the best strategy to achieve our mutual satisfaction or deliberate about what seductive move to make next.

He can have that responsibility.

I love that he's showing me what he wants, taking it, and making us both happy in the process. This is what I crave. Submitting to a skilled lover is a welcome release from my stresses. I need someone like Kaden to provide this venting. It keeps me from exploding under the pressure of my daily life, which is somewhat more intense than the average person's, I guess.

This week especially. I need this. Him.

He can read me well enough to know I'm becoming lost in my own world, teetering on that fulcrum between thinking and feeling. Shutting off my brain and allowing myself to exist on a more primal level. So he doesn't wait for me to respond to his rhetorical questions. Instead, he keeps rambling. His smooth stream of dirty talk pacifies me like an animal tamer praising his captive beasts as he circles them with a whip.

"I plan to take my time. No interruptions allowed while I'm exploring this gorgeous body of yours." He trails his fingers down my chest, tickling the light smattering of hair there, pausing to brush the pad of his thumb across my nipple. "Do you have any idea how hard it was to keep my hands, and mouth, and cock to myself last weekend?"

I do because I also know how close I came to begging him to touch me despite my commitment to Ronaldo. Only my morals had kept my tongue in check and his dick out of my ass. Foolish me.

The soles of my feet rub against his fuzzy sheets in an attempt to convert some of the tension he's building into action. At least the soft cotton dragging against my skin sates my need for more tactile input. Until Kaden realizes I'm cheating.

"Stay still." This time the pressure on my nipple is sharper. A pinch more than a caress. I gasp and wish he'd tweaked it harder. "I decide which sensations you feel from now until I release you or you say Pygmalion. Remember?"

I obey, stilling instantly. If I break his rules he might set me free far sooner than I would like. After Ronaldo, I'd really like to be something other than a disappointment to a sexy, controlling-in-a-good-way man.

"That's right, Rogan." He rewards me with another lazy kiss, this time nibbling on my bottom lip before he withdraws. "It's going to be so much better like this. Full of anticipation. By the time I give you what you want so badly, you're going to be out of your mind with ecstasy."

Not hard to believe given how I feel right now, when he's only treated me to a hint of what's to come.

Kaden shifts his knees, walking them down either side of my legs. With open-mouthed kisses on my abs, he pauses to sample the perspiration beginning to dampen my skin. While he feasts on me, he lowers his pelvis, allowing me to feel how hard he is. For me.

He humps me a few times, rubbing his cock against mine so there's no doubt he's as into our arrangement as I am. The reassurance helps me sink deeper into the sensual spell he's weaving around us.

I think it's safe to say that any person who's been cheated on doubts their allure from time to time. Kaden obliterates my anxiety when he looks up at me and rasps, "I haven't been this hard in a long time. At this rate, you're going to earn one hell of a ride."

"Yes. Please, fuck me." I can't help but ask for what I need. A hard, driving fuck will help me forget all the screwed up shit in my life right now.

He laughs softly. "I like that you're greedy. But no. Not yet. Not for a while. Patience, Rogan."

This is why he's in charge.

If it was up to me I'd already have his cock halfway in my throat. We'd hardly get started before it was over. I need someone like him to draw things out. To force me to savor the moment and extend this bliss as long as possible.

I forget how to speak when he continues his trek, mapping every inch of my torso with his fingers and mouth. As promised, he takes his sweet time, appreciates each ridge of muscle, and laves the divots between them on his meandering path to his next destination. When he traces the contour of the indentation that stretches from my hipbone toward the base of my cock, I moan out loud and shudder.

He's so close to where I need him to be.

Instead of progressing, he lingers there. Tormenting me with swirls of his tongue and sweeps of his palms up my sides until I think I might come if his chin accidentally bumps my erection.

"Need a break?" he asks as one corner of his mouth curls upward. "How about I get rid of the rest of your clothes?"

"Can I see you, too?" I manage to make the request between shallow pants. "Please, you've already seen me naked."

Kaden evaluates me carefully, reading my expression. Although I don't elaborate, I think he understands how vulnerable Ronaldo left me. I love Kaden's intrinsic authority. It's even more special that he wields it in a way that empowers me too. How is he so good at comprehending my unspoken wishes? More than any guy I've ever gone to bed with, he responds as if he knows exactly how I'm feeling.

"Of course." He smiles at me benevolently, running a knuckle across my swollen lips. I part them on instinct. When he dips his middle finger between them, I suck on it lightly, using only the hint of teeth to show him exactly what I'd do to his dick if he fed me that instead.

"Why am I not surprised you're so damn good at that?" He withdraws with a sigh. "You're going to tempt me to shoot down your throat, aren't you?"

"I'd love to taste you." That's the truth. Cock-sucking is one of my favorite pastimes. There's something soothing about it. Thrilling too when you can make someone deliriously happy, even if the rapture is short-lived. I'm pretty sure only another guy can truly understand the impact a great blowjob can have on a man. Then again, maybe I think that because I don't have a clit or experience satisfying women to compare with.

Either way, I'd kill to have Kaden's dick stuffing my mouth right now.

I want it so bad, I forget for a minute that my hands are strapped to his headboard and reach for him. My tie draws me up short, rattling the ironwork it's attached to.

"Only when I'm ready." He *tsks* then turns away. My ego hopes it's because he needs a breather too. "Get those hands back where I put them."

They fly to the headboard. This time I wrap my fingers around it to ensure they don't stray. Let's be honest, I'm going to slip up again. How can I think of anything but how enticing Kaden is, and how badly I want to touch him when he addles my brain, just like I hoped he would?

He takes a couple steps away from the bed. I whimper.

"It's okay. I'm not going far," he reassures me. "Thought I'd give you the show you asked for, since you're being such a good boy."

His hips sway from side to side, as if he's dancing to music only he can hear.

If those liquid rolls are any indication of how smoothly he fucks, I might start begging to fast forward to that portion of tonight's entertainment at any second. I'm mesmerized by the pale skin he reveals as he walks the cotton of his shirt up his rippling abdomen. It makes the perfect canvas for the ink that starts to peek beneath his hem. He wears drawings that migrate across his chest and down his arms.

I'd like to trace every single line with my tongue.

He's a living, breathing work of art.

"Do you like what you see?" he asks, though the flash of his grin makes me sure my admiration is obvious. "That tent in your pants is getting even bigger, Rogan. Are you imagining what it will feel like when I'm lying on top of you, our bare skin touching?"

I hadn't gone there yet, but now I can't dream of anything else.

Except maybe what I might feel shortly after that—the nudge of his cock parting my cheeks.

"Gah!" I drop my head back and stare at the ceiling for a moment, swallowing hard. I can't catch my breath. How is he doing this to me without even touching me? I'd give him an entire division of my company if he'd climb on top of me and grind some more right now.

"Eyes on me. Now!"

How can I look away when he's sliding his belt free of his jeans? With one hand, he snaps it in my direction. The resounding clap of leather startles me. If that's how he likes to play, I'm game. I roll to one side, exposing as much of my flank as possible with my arms immobile.

"Not tonight." He shakes his head. "You've suffered enough lately."

"You're torturing me right now, you know."

"Trying to change my mind about a spanking with that sass?" He pauses.

I wish I could take back the challenge that flew, unbidden, from my lips. I shake my head. "Whatever you like is fine. Just...please...don't stop."

"You want me to get rid of these?" He's back to teasing, tucking his thumbs beneath his waistband and wiggling it lower and lower. The trail of trimmed hair beneath his navel grows darker as he risks exposing himself to me.

"Yes." I can't manage to say more than that.

Not when he's flashing the barest bit of his cock to me, enough to make it obvious he's not wearing underwear.

Shit, I sat on this bed, ate dinner, and got half-drunk with him. The whole time the only thing that separated my face from his dick was a thin layer of denim.

Kaden's drawing this out, rubbing his chest with one hand while the other snakes into his pants. He's touching himself. Pleasing himself as he watches me squirm, tied to his bed.

I can hardly remember not to move in sync with him when his jeans start sliding off his tight ass. He lets them drop. Though he attempts to shield himself from me with his hand, it isn't big enough to block all of the good stuff.

Damn.

He steps out of his discarded clothes then turns, letting me get a good look at his cut shoulders and svelte back, which tapers to a narrow waist before flaring at the curve of his bubble butt. When he looks over his shoulder, I'm sure he doesn't need me to tell him how fucking cute he is. Even his ass has dimples, damn him.

Impish, yet domineering. It's a rare and potent combination.

Maybe someday I'll get to dance with him. I can imagine a club on a hot summer night filled with the pounding bass of house music. I'd undulate against him. Sweat and the crush of other horny guys would only add to my excitement. And when I left with him, every man in the place would wish they were me.

"Payback is a bitch, Rogan." He laughs softly as he approaches. "Imagine how hard I was for *hours* on Saturday. Looking at your fine self on display. Should I make you wait that long before I touch you some more?"

"Fuck no!" I growl before catching myself. "I mean... please, don't."

It isn't usually this hard to keep myself in check.

Kaden brings out things in me I've never experienced before. My desire is like a fever, burning through me and setting me on fire from the inside out.

"That's better." He comes close enough to run his hand over my head, petting me for remembering my place before checking the circulation in my wrists. Standing at the edge of the bed, he puts pressure on my crown until I'm forced to stare at his crotch. One finger at a time, he reveals himself to me.

When you've seen one dick you've mostly seen them all with a few variables—length, girth, color, hair, whatever. Somehow his seems like something legendary to me. Probably because it has the ability to fuck me into what I already can sense will be a lifetime top-ten orgasm. Long and not-too-thick, curved downward a bit at the tip, he's going to feel amazing inside me.

The perfect instrument for bringing me pleasure.

I open my mouth and strain my neck toward his groin.

"Soon." He steps backward, making my mouth miss its target.

It's hard to be too sad about that when I realize he's heading for my own pants, the last of our remaining clothing. His stiff cock bobs between his legs as he moves, making me sure that he's anticipating this moment as much as I am. However, he still takes his damn time.

The man has nerves of steel and more self-control than a Buddhist monk.

He hops onto the bed beside my knees, sitting on his heels so he can drag his palms down my chest and abs repeatedly. I lose track of how long he strokes me, savoring each pass of his fingers. He entrances me, so I'm startled when he finally makes his move.

Kaden unzips my pants fast enough to make me

nervous, the metal teeth making a *zhhip* that cuts through my nebulous thoughts. I lift my head in time to watch him strip me with one efficient yank. My pants and underwear hit the plank floor together, instantly forgotten.

My cock is so stiff it springs onto my abdomen as soon as the downward pressure from my restrictive clothing is relieved. It looks flushed. Veins I didn't even know I had form a distinct web around my shaft. A thin line of glossy precome stretches from the head of my dick to my abdomen, where arousal begins to pool.

"I hate your douchebag ex for making me waste that." Kaden glowers at the proof of my excitement for a moment before reaching over to the nightstand drawer and rummaging around. He fishes out a jumbo box of condoms.

The spark of envy and resentment for the other men he's used them on, and will use them on after this fling has run its course, catches me off guard. We just met. I'm not delusional. This is nothing more than a painkiller. Convenient timing. A rebound fuck.

So why do I care?

I shouldn't.

But I do. Damn it.

10

ROGAN

The instant Kaden rings the base of my cock with the fingers of one hand and sets a condom on the tip of it with the other, I cease to have enough brain cells to keep wondering about anything except how his hands can feel so good on my shaft when all they're doing is sheathing it in latex.

As soon as he finishes, he repeats the process on himself. The moment he's protected himself from me, I relax.

I never thought Ronaldo could make me feel this dirty.

"Hey. I don't want you thinking about him. Only me. We're the only two people in this bed tonight." Kaden grimaces. Could he be coaching himself as well? I'll have to ask him some other time when I can be appropriately empathetic.

As if to prove his point, Kaden moves so he's above me again. He straddles my hips, balancing on his knees and one locked arm while he reaches between us to align our cocks.

When our shafts touch and his balls rest on mine, I swear I nearly lose it.

Kaden fists our dicks and pumps them in unison a few times. His thumb rubs the head of my dick on its way past. All I can do is stare up at him, completely undone. The way he toys with me is new and fresh compared to the rough quickies that have made up most of my sexual experience.

Don't get me wrong. I love that, too. Being forced to my knees so a man can fuck my mouth, then leave me unsatisfied to show I exist only to please him. Or bent over the desk of my home office and plowed until my partner finds release in my body.

But this...

I could get used to this.

A moan breaks loose from my chest. Kaden is there, swallowing it down before he fuses our mouths once more. I missed his kisses. I'd already forgotten how good they were. Or maybe it's just hard to believe I'm not exaggerating their potency in my own mind.

Nope.

He's amazing, manipulating my tongue and lips until I'm breathless as he stares deep into my eyes. He doesn't hide from anything. Completely open, he sips from my mouth.

My balls draw up tight to my torso as his chest brushes mine. I love the heat and pressure of his contact. Face-to-face from head to toe. A little too much—I'm on the edge.

"Kaden!" I shout in warning.

Except instead of embarrassing myself by shooting into my condom without permission, I'm left hanging when he flies off me, leaving me cold and exposed without the security blanket of his warm body covering me.

"Oh no." He's standing at the edge of the bed now, staring down at me. "You're too sexy when you're blissed out on lust for me to let you go so soon."

Why is he obsessed with making the most of this encounter?

I hate him for it. And I love him for it.

My balls ache from the unrelieved pressure. But I get to keep riding this high for a while longer. It's a fair trade, I suppose.

Kaden draws my attention to him by tapping his cock on my cheek. The resulting slapping sound is salacious and does nothing to tone down my arousal.

"You ready to show me what you can do with that mouth?"

I lick my lips and nod.

"Open up, Rogan." He uses a thumb on my jaw to make enough room for his shaft.

He doesn't have to tell me twice. I practically devour him, lunging upward as far as my restraints will allow. His length impresses me as I measure it with my tongue. In fact, he's even bigger than I thought. I choke as my motion rams the head of his dick into the back of my mouth.

"Easy." He withdraws a bit and brushes his thumb over my cheek until my eyes stop watering. Then he's there, like he promised, advancing again. Absolutely *not* taking it easy on me.

Thank you.

I show my gratitude by treating him to the best blowjob I'm capable of delivering. It chills me out to work him over with long sucks and bobs of my head. Finding my rhythm, that's all that I have room to think about.

Keeping it up, not missing a stride, so I please him best. After a while, my jaw has developed a pleasant soreness. I hum when he begins to thrust with involuntary twitches of his hips that prove he's not immune to the flickering of my tongue on the underside of his shaft or the suction I apply to his tip.

Right when I think he might let me finish him off in my mouth after all, he steals my fun. He withdraws his cock and stumbles two steps backward. Bracing his palms on his knees, he draws in several billowing breaths. I can't believe he lasted that long or that he was able to stop.

Ronaldo definitely had never been able to resist.

Before I can wonder if I'm maybe not quite the oral virtuoso I suspected, Kaden lifts his face. His eyes are bright and his cheeks are flushed. "Goddamn, Rogan. I think you missed your calling. Forget businesses. You could take over the world one dick at a time with a mouth like that. I kept hanging on because I couldn't stand for it to stop. You're easily the best cocksucker I've ever met."

"Thanks." I smile as he closes the gap between us, slamming his mouth over mine. This is no gentle foreplay. This is what I've been waiting for.

Kaden is taking things to the next level. All I can do it lie here, tied to his bed, and take it.

Yes.

I honestly expect him to yank the knot free from my bindings, flip me over, and sink inside me in the next few seconds. But he doesn't.

"How are those wrists?" he checks as he slides his fingers beneath my soft tie.

"Fine."

"You're sure? You can still feel your fingers?" He takes one in his mouth and makes me wish I had enough stamina to withstand some of that treatment between my legs. No way. They say it takes one to know one. Well, Kaden Finch is no rookie when it comes to fellatio.

Being with him is like going to one of the best restaurants in the world and knowing you only have enough room in your stomach for one entree, even if you loosen your belt to squeeze in dessert. I want to sample every flavor Kaden has to offer.

But if I have to pick one…

"I'm sure, Kaden. Please don't untie me. I want you to fuck me like this." My eyes are wide as I look up steeply at him. I don't say it out loud, but what I really crave is to watch him take me. To see the genuine awe on his face as my body brings him pleasure.

I hope his thrusts smack my hands and this headboard against the rough wall so I can use that slight discomfort to guarantee I last. Because what I want most of all is to come with him, and know that while my pride might be bruised right now, I'm still capable of finding my own joy in this sort of power exchange.

That Ronaldo hasn't ruined that for me too.

Kaden watches me with something other than desire. Is it compassion, or something deeper, like understanding? I'm not sure. After a moment, he nods solemnly.

"You were meant for this, Rogan." He rakes his fingers through my hair then uses the edge of the pillowcase to dab sweat from my brow. "He won't steal this from you. At least not if I can help it."

I'd like to do more to ease the melancholy I hear underlining his arousal, except I'm too overwhelmed at the moment to puzzle out the root cause of it. It must be the outrageous highs and lows of the past few days making tonight seem so much more momentous than a casual hookup.

When Kaden spreads my knees and situates himself between them, I don't have the ability to focus on anything other than what's about to happen. I must have drifted, lost in my anticipation, because I didn't even see him retrieve the lube he's now drizzling into his palm. He heats the liquid against his own skin before slathering a finger in it.

Then he drops his hand below my sac, hunting for the entrance to my body.

"Plant your feet flat on the mattress." Whatever fleeting emotion had passed between us a minute ago, it's gone, replaced with his obvious intentions. It probably makes me a jerk because I'm relieved. For being able to simply enjoy without worry.

I do as I'm told, leaving myself more exposed to his seeking prods. He dissolves the last of my logic and replaces it with brilliant sensations.

He finds my hole and circles it, transferring some of the slickness from his finger to the puckered muscle there. After he massages me enough to grant me a false sense of security, the ring relaxes.

Kaden takes advantage. He presses inward, breeching my ass.

For the first time in five years, someone other than Ronaldo is tunneling into me.

"Let me in," he instructs. "It's okay. I'm not going to hurt you like he did."

If my eyes sting, I'm sure it's because whatever digits he's opening me with are fatter than Ronaldo's cock and not because of his remarkable instincts or his unexpected kindness. How can I feel safer with a man I didn't know last week than one I lived with for years?

I guess because I never knew my boyfriend like I thought I did.

"Kaden, please." I need him to help me put it out of my mind, to make it go away for a few minutes. This is what I came here for tonight. And he's so close to giving it to me.

"Shhh. I've got you." He slides his fingers from my ass. I hear the snick of the cap on the lube bottle again as he distracts me with another one of his addicting kisses. Except this time, he doesn't stop with one or two.

He keeps entertaining my mouth as he coats himself. I've almost forgotten what he's doing when he returns, fitting himself against me. This time it's the blunt head of his cock attempting to invade me. I push outward as he burrows into me. His flattened hand slides under me, then curls, cupping my shoulder for leverage. He tugs me toward him as he advances. The pressure seems like it might almost be too much. Then, just when I start to wonder if he's going to fit, the fattest part of him pops inside. He sinks several inches deep.

We both groan. Our gazes collide.

There's nothing like that moment. The one where someone penetrates you for the first time. Joined temporarily, it's impossible to deny that link. Though to be honest, there were nights when that corporal bond with Ronaldo wasn't enough to keep me from feeling lonely.

It hurts. Not Kaden's cock in my ass. That stings, sure. But...no. The rest. Remembering how much time I wasted, how fucked up things had gotten. It's too much.

He has to make it go away. Now.

I stare up at Kaden, unable to express myself except by rocking my hips in his direction.

"You need more?" Kaden's uncanny perception isn't derailed by being buried inside of me. I'm not sure if I'm thrilled or upset that he still has that strong of a grip on the situation.

I nod, incapable of any other answer.

"Brace yourself." He puts one hand on my elbow, steadying me until my mind realizes what he means.

I lock my arm above my head, prepared to hold myself in place and keep from getting a concussion. Good thing, too.

Kaden gives me a few tentative thrusts to make sure I've adjusted to holding him within me. When he's satisfied that I'm ready, he picks up the pace. The graceful swings of his hips are every bit as devastating as I thought they'd be when he was flaunting his moves earlier.

Especially when coupled with the roaming of his hands and mouth across the rest of my body. There's no part of me he leaves untouched.

And there it is.

Blinding ecstasy wipes everything from my mind except Kaden and the nerve endings he's stimulating. I'm helpless to do anything but enjoy the moment and wish it could last forever. He does a damn fine job of granting my desires.

Kaden hammers into me, riding me hard. He growls, bites my neck, and digs in.

Sometime later, my arms ache from the punishment of his driving between my legs. Sweat drips from both of us.

I have no idea how long he's been pumping into me, generating enough pleasure to make everyone within three blocks spontaneously orgasm. I absorb every single shove, curse, and moan. The column of his neck is taut as he concentrates on fucking me well, and the set of his jaw tells me how hard he's trying not to lose it in my ass.

Kaden is fucking the shit out of me and loving every second of it.

"Yes!" I shout as I creep closer to the edge of orgasm.

Each time his pelvis approaches mine, it's bouncing my balls aggressively, right on the edge of pain. As he angles forward now and grinds deeper, his abdomen rubs over my cock, which is now sandwiched between us.

"It's time," he moans close to my face as he hunches over me. His pistoning accelerates. It becomes the slightest bit uneven right before he seals his mouth over mine one final time.

I know what he's insisting on.

He wants me to surrender first.

Maybe he even needs me to before he can let himself be that helpless along with me.

There's no stopping it anyway. Not when he's kissing me and dragging his entire body across mine. Not when his cock is tapping my prostate while his pelvis strokes my dick.

Not when something deep inside me recognizes his wounded soul and my ability to grant him even a fraction of the respite he's given me tonight.

"Kaden!" I bellow as my ass clamps around his cock. My nuts gather into a dense rock close to my body. I come so hard I'm afraid I might explode and die right in the middle of it.

But I don't.

Pulse after pulse of come shoots from my cock, flooding the condom I'm wearing. I wish Kaden could have seen it splattered across my chest and abdomen so he'd know how much he's affected me. I want to wear the sticky mess so that he's proud of how well he's fucked me. He deserves to be.

My spasms bring him his reward. The tugs of my ass on his cock send him over the edge.

He pounds the pillow with his fist, roars my name, and rams into me with a half dozen jerky plunges that make me certain he's pouring his own orgasm into the condom I wish he wasn't using.

For the first time, I regret that my hands are trapped. I would have held Kaden as he empties himself into me, allowing himself to be defenseless, if only for an instant.

When that moment passes and he lifts his head to meet my stare with a boyish grin, I pray I heard the delivery guy wrong earlier. Or that his crack about do-overs was a polite excuse instead of Kaden's actual policy on second dates.

Because I already want to do this again.

And again.

And again.

11

KADEN

I should probably say something profound. Maybe I would if I knew the words. But I'm not sure anything I tell Rogan would adequately communicate how this one night with him has impacted me. Hopefully he picked up on that when our bodies were doing the talking for us. He's incredible. A perfect fit.

Temptation like I haven't faced in more than two long years.

When I look into his eyes, I see a reflection of myself. Except he's so much better than me. Stronger. Back on the horse right away instead of wallowing in misery and losing himself over a guy who never deserved him anyway.

It's better if I don't make a fool of myself, gushing over him before I have to throw him back into the dating pool. I quit crushing him and flop onto my back on the mattress. The only sound in the apartment is our mismatched gasping as we attempt to suck down some much-needed oxygen.

I can feel his ribs expanding and contracting against

my arm, which reminds me that his arms are up. He's still bound.

Shit.

I reach over and yank on the end of the quick-release knot. Rogan's tie unravels, setting him free. My stomach sinks as I realize there's no longer anything holding him here. He could get up and walk away in the next ten seconds. I bring the luxurious sapphire silk to my face and inhale his scent. I rub it against my cheek before folding it and placing it neatly on the pillow next to us.

Rogan rolls onto his side, wincing slightly as he does. With a few quick motions, I ditch our condoms and use my discarded shirt to clean us up.

Then, without considering the cost to us both, I deepen the intimacy of the moment by gathering him in my arms. He snuggles against my chest and sighs, making it impossible to loosen my grip.

For the first time, he returns my embrace. His hands press me to him as tightly as I'm doing to him. We're crushed together. Sweaty. Still catching our breath.

Deliriously happy.

For the first time in a while, I'm content.

It felt amazing to pour my frustration into him. To have him absorb it and know it was doing him good, forcing us both to ignore the past and concentrate only on the spectacular present we shared.

Now it's over. Pretending there can be more of this is delusional and reckless.

I know better. Hopefully he does, too.

I clear my throat, wondering if he'll get the hint or if I'll have to escort him out. It's never been this hard to force space between myself and someone I've just fucked. At least not since I became a serial dater.

Rogan looks up and blinks a few times. He shakes his head softly, setting the dark strands of his hair tumbling onto his forehead. "Thanks, Kaden. I really needed that."

"Me too." I taste his lips once more as I brush his hair into place. He doesn't have to know it's a kiss goodbye.

"I didn't mean to crash your evening like this. It's late, huh?" He adjusts his position. I despise the gap he puts between us. Still, I don't reach out and close it.

"It is." Should I tell him I don't care? That it might be past my bedtime but I'll sleep better tonight than I have in ages? Or should I keep those thoughts to myself and make his exit easier on us both?

What I've been doing no longer seems like the right thing.

"Well, uh..." He sits up, cataloging his belongings, which are strewn around my bedroom. When his eyes land on his keys, I know he's about to make his getaway.

I'm confused. There's no time to figure out what the best thing is to do. So I fall back on habit. "Are you okay to drive? I could take you home then order an Uber again. I don't mind if you're too wrecked."

God, the urge to take care of him overwhelms me. Besides, if he says yes I can also spend a little more time with him. He doesn't have to know I'm secretly clinging to something I can't allow myself long term.

"I appreciate the offer, but I'll be fine. I'm not going far." His teeth click as he shuts his mouth fast. Is he, like me, afraid he might reveal too much?

"It's at least a twenty-minute ride out to your place." I should let it go. Stay out of his shit. Uncomplicated. The way I like it.

He hesitates too long. I can tell he's debating what to say next. I don't like him calculating. I much preferred when he was beneath me, reacting honestly, with genuine emotion. This is bullshit. "Rogan?"

He swings his legs over the edge of the bed so his back is to me. His shoulders droop as he confesses, "I haven't been able to go back there. Or to the beach house. Don't think I ever will. They're both on the market."

"Where are you staying if you're not living in either of your houses?" I slide over so I'm sitting next to him, our knees touching as I cover his hand with mine.

"A hotel about a half mile from here. I mean, technically I own it, so maybe it's my place. But...it's nothing like I'm used to. Definitely nothing like this."

Maybe the legendary sex we're still recovering from messed up my brain, or maybe he's blowing my mind all over again. It's too much to process when I'm still drunk on him. "Hold up. You own an entire hotel?"

"More like I own a real estate conglomerate that owns a chain of them. I'll pick another property from the holdings to live in eventually. I guess I just wanted somewhere neutral to lick my wounds in the interim. You know, so I don't contaminate the new place with bad juju. It'll be a fresh start when I move in. Only cheery memories allowed."

"Makes sense." Damn, though. He was even more baller than I'd realized. Yet he submitted to me graciously. Enthusiastically. Despite the fact that I'm pretty much nobody. Wow.

"Maybe there's another property like this in the portfolio. The other half of this building has potential too if it wouldn't be too weird to be neighbors." He sounds oddly wistful. "I'm not the stalker type, don't worry."

Why doesn't that thought horrify me? An ex-lover popping in to borrow my ladder or some shit in exchange for a quickie? It wouldn't really count as a do-over if it was a thank-you fuck between friends, would it?

The rest of my building has been vacant since before I opened my studio. It's one reason I get such a great deal on the rent. I was willing to take it as is and fix it up myself. The quirky space works for me. I've kind of gotten used to the insulation from the rest of the block, too. But what if Rogan was the one living there?

Maybe we could negotiate some kind of fuck buddy arrangement. I'd get to see him from time to time. No relationship necessary. Hmm...

"It must be nice to have so many options. I can't imagine snapping up half a building on a whim." Which, I suppose, is why I'm still renting this place.

"Actually..." He trails off again until I knock my thigh against his. It might make me an asshole to leverage our dynamic for info after we're done sleeping together, but I'm super curious about his hesitation.

"*Actually* what?" My eyes narrow.

It's not like him to be deceptive. Even by a lie of omission.

"I might sort of own this building too." He shrugs one shoulder as if that's no big deal.

"Come again?" My brows practically wing off my face. What if he turns into a jealous prick and he evicts me? I try not to freak out at the thought of another man having so much power over me. Especially one I'm in bed with.

This is exactly the kind of sticky situation I've tried to avoid.

"I would love to, but I'm not as young as I used to be." His deadpan delivery in the face of my potential hysteria slays me.

I burst out laughing. "I hear that, Gramps. But... seriously, you're my landlord?"

"Only in a vague and roundabout fashion. More like I'm your landlord's boss's boss or something. Don't worry, I've already sent a few texts about improvements to the property. You should have demanded lights out back. And better security for your artwork."

I do not need him dictating what I should or shouldn't have done to my own home. I don't give a fuck who owns it. I live here. It's *my* place in the world. "This is my house, not a museum. It's fine the way it is."

"Of course it is. I'm sorry. Didn't mean to overstep. It's just that...I really appreciate what you've done for me and I want the best for you." He stands then, scrunching his eyes closed for a second before opening them and glaring at me. His demure side is usurped by the businessman he is outside of his sex life. There's an entirely new—fiery and steely—man I haven't met yet lurking beneath his calm. I like the glimpse I get, too. A lot. "Ronaldo used to hate it when I tried to take care of him too. I didn't mean it as a slight to your authority. Yeah, okay. I guess I'm going to take off then."

No way in hell. Not when my big, dumb mouth has shaken the foundation for rebuilding his self-esteem that I've worked so hard on laying all evening. Taking care of him is more important than my issues. I obviously struck a nerve.

"Rogan, wait. I'm being an idiot. Thank you for caring." I lace my fingers with his and tug. Hard. He tumbles onto the rumpled sheets beside me again. I break all my rules when I insist, "Don't go. Stay here with me tonight."

Rogan doesn't say anything for far too long. I'm sure

he's about to slip through my fingers. Another regret. Another great thing my hang-ups have spoiled. Maybe it's time to stop making some of these same mistakes.

It might be time to change again. Just a little.

"You really are welcome, Rogan. I'd love to fall asleep with you. It's been a while since I've done that." That's the least I can do. Share a jagged part of myself in exchange for the sting I caused by balking at his well-intended meddling.

"You're sure?" he wonders.

I don't respond automatically, without actually weighing my options. Am I certain?

"I'm positive I'd be upset if you left." I just don't know if it's a good idea. Oh well. There's no way I'm kicking him out, condemning him to flounder in emptiness made more evident by the intimacy we shared earlier.

Or is it myself I'm trying to protect? I can't do it tonight. Sleep alone, I mean.

I'm selfish, I know. But I need him every bit as much as he needs me. If I can pretend I'm hanging on for his own good, even better.

"Then how can I say no?" He settles in beside me. My relief is mirrored in every smoothed-out line of his face. I trace them along his brow and the corners of his mouth with the tip of my index finger before dropping a soft kiss on his cheek.

I have to look away from the tenderness in his gaze before it blinds me, like a person emerging from a pitch-black cave who sees the sun for the first time in ages. Which is when I spot our fortune cookies on the nightstand.

Sweet diversion.

"Hey, we never ate these." I reach across Rogan to grab

them and toss one to him at random. "I could use a midnight snack after that workout."

He moves fluidly and fast as fuck, snagging his out of midair. It reminds me of how capable he is and how fearless it was of him to let me be in charge of managing our pleasure tonight.

Rogan tears open the wrapper and shakes the cookie into his hand.

"Don't forget to do that whole 'in bed' thing," I tease as I slap him on the ass.

After breaking his dessert in half and inhaling the edible parts, he unfurls his fortune. "Huh." Rogan flips the slip of paper around so I can read it.

You're exactly where you're meant to be (in bed).

If I was the superstitious sort, I'd think it was some kind of sign. We grin at each other.

Figuring mine will be a letdown after that, I bust it apart anyway. I scarf the cookie before the crumbs can escape then take a peek at my own fortune.

"What the—?"

"They can't all be winners." Rogan beams up at me with a triumphant glint in his eyes.

Until I show him what it says.

"Wow. What are the odds of that?" He glances from his strip of paper to my matching one then back. Two guys. One fortune. "I mean, I guess they're all made in the same plant. A matching pair could wind up stuck together, but I've never had that happen."

"Me either." Why do I have a feeling there are a lot of things I've never experienced before meeting Rogan? What will I do when dawn blasts through my gallery windows, searing away the fog of intimacy surrounding us?

I pretend not to notice when he tucks his fortune into the pocket of his shirt on the floor for safekeeping. I also act like it doesn't touch me to know this means something to him.

You know, maybe just one do-over might be okay.

Morning sex, for sure. If he hasn't left yet then it doesn't count as a repeat. I can't wait to wake him with pleasure before saying goodbye. For real this time.

Blissfully unaware of my internal debate, Rogan tips onto his side and buries his face against my pecs again. A few inches shorter than me, he fits incredibly well there. He yawns then flings a lazy arm around my waist. Subconsciously, I trap his thigh below mine. Reveling in the heat and nearness of another person as I drift toward unconsciousness, I'm afraid he might disappear if I don't wind myself around him.

It's nice. I've missed this.

Which is exactly why it's so dangerous.

I try to stay awake as long as possible. Soak in the sensations. Because in a few hours, I'm going to have to let him go or jeopardize my sanity and soul.

Again.

If anyone is capable of stealing them without even trying, it's Rogan.

12

ROGAN

Mmm. The first thing I think as I surface from fantastic dreams of lovemaking is that Ronaldo must be hitting the gym harder than usual. His body is a lot firmer than I remember. Smells good, too.

Of course, that's because it's actually Kaden I'm plastered up against.

Holy shit. Those were no dreams. Neither are the sweet aches in various parts of my body phantom sensations. Those are evidence that he used me well. I wonder if he'd approve if I slithered beneath the sheets, nuzzled my way between his thighs, and took him into my mouth again.

The delivery guy's rueful parting remarks keep me from acting on my filthy fantasy. I could tell Kaden wasn't entirely comfortable with me spending the night. Pressing my luck doesn't seem wise.

After all, I've already gotten a fun meal in bed, a fuckfest for the record books, and a night in his arms. Maximum distraction from the steaming pile of shit my life seemed like yesterday. A glimpse of how great my future could be with a true partner.

Hoping for more would be greedy.

So I blink my eyes open, holding my hand in front of my face to shade it from the flood of light pouring through the massive two-story windows across from Kaden's loft. He must be used to sleeping through sunrise. I am not.

In fact, I squint at my watch on the bedside table and wince. I need to hustle if I'm going to make it to the hotel to shower, shave, and change before my first meeting. My morning workout and a healthy home-cooked breakfast are already out.

My phone is completely lifeless on the nightstand. I haven't checked messages in about twelve hours. A record compared to my average of every three seconds. The amount of work piled up probably rivals the tallest skyscraper in the city by now.

What had I been thinking by ignoring the world and sleeping over?

Oh, you know, only that it would have been impossible to leave.

As gently and quietly as possible, I disengage myself from Kaden's limbs, which are doing a pretty great impersonation of an octopus. Regret stabs me in the guts as I cut our time short. It's less problematic this way.

An awkward parting might steal some of the shine from last night's encounter, and I plan to use the memories of our liaison to get me through the turbulent transition period ahead.

I pull on my pants and shirt, without bothering to button them. Then I stuff my socks in my pockets before slipping my shoes on.

My tie is resting in a neat pile on Kaden's pillow. Rather than risk waking him, I leave it. Maybe it'll give him something to remember our perfect night by. Or maybe he'll toss it in the trash. It's his choice.

Finally, I pick up my keys and wallet. It's probably creepy, but I stand there and memorize the way he looks, tangled in his sheets. I wish I could hire him again, this time to paint a portrait of himself. Exactly like this.

Which reminds me...

I reluctantly angle away from Kaden's bed and cross to the kitchenette. Once I'm there, I take the check from my billfold and lay it on top of the camera equipment I deposited on his table last night. I'm not sure if it's the best or worst twenty grand I've ever spent.

Although our meeting had led me to a dark part of my life, I wouldn't take a different path even if I could. At least I know the truth now. And I found Kaden. I hope something positive comes of our crossed paths for him.

You know, other than the sheer carnal indulgence of last night.

With a final glance over my shoulder, I unchain his door and head outside.

I must be staring at the ground, either watching my step on the rickety iron staircase or because my head is tipping forward beneath the weight of my thoughts. Exhaustion plagues me despite how well I slept.

Otherwise, I would have noticed Ronaldo leaning up against my car before he calls out to me. "I *knew* you were fucking him."

Son of a bitch.

I try to ignore his sneer and shove past him to the driver's side door.

Of course, he's got other ideas and blocks my path.

"There you were, acting so damn innocent. Hurt that I would have a little fun on the side. Meanwhile you've been slumming it with this twink." He laughs. "Oh, that's perfect."

"Get out of my way." I almost don't recognize my own voice. It's not the timid tone I've used with him before. It's me. The guy I am with everyone I don't trust in the world. The ones I don't let into my life, heart, or bed.

"I don't think so, pretty boy." He ramps up his tirade, both in volume and intensity, drawing more attention than I'm comfortable with from the early risers, who pass periodically on the sidewalk at the end of the alley. "Where would I go anyway? I'm fucking *homeless*. Because of you."

"Way to take responsibility for your actions, Ronaldo." I try to stay calm, desperate to keep things quasi-civil until I can handle this properly. Legally. My phone is useless, essentially a paperweight in my pocket after being left unplugged all night. "You know you're not supposed to be near me, right?"

"I don't give a shit what some piece of paper says. The cops don't understand our relationship. You do what *I* say."

How could I not have seen this side of him? Sure, he sometimes gets nasty when he drinks too much. The next morning he apologizes and we work it out. At least we had. Now, though...

I can't get the hell away from him fast enough.

This has gone beyond acceptable.

"Not anymore. Last time, Ronaldo. Move." I whip my phone out, keeping it facing away from him so he can't see the black screen, then bluff, "Or I'm calling the police."

"Don't be so dramatic." He rolls his eyes at me then

shoves my arm hard enough that it smashes into the car and my cell goes flying. The sickening crunch of glass makes me sure the dead battery is the least of its issues now. "I'll let you go. Just admit it, Rogan. I won't be mad. We're both guilty. We can fix this if you say it. You were fucking him all along, weren't you?"

"I wasn't. But I am now." Who am I kidding? I did once. I don't think Kaden's going to be asking me out on a real date any time soon. Ronaldo doesn't need to know that, though.

"How does that work exactly?" He tips his head to one side.

I really don't have the patience for this today. Maybe if I'm blunt he'll get the idea quicker and leave me the hell alone. Besides, his threatening posture is pissing me off. How *dare* he think he has any hold left over me? I'll show him that it's over. Really over.

"His cock, my ass, lots of come. From us both. Unlike when I was stupid enough to sleep with you and you'd leave me hanging most times."

"But he's not into that, is he? Fucking you?" At least Ronaldo toned down some of the yelling in exchange for what seemed like authentic curiosity. I'll play along if it means I can escape then unleash my lawyers on his pompous, overbearing, sleazy ass.

Is it so hard to believe someone could get off on fucking me?

My blood pressure skyrockets. I'm not going to let him treat me like dirt. How could I have been so blind? It had happened gradually, subtle insults graduating to relentless putdowns until I didn't even realize how deeply he disrespects me. One night with Kaden reset my standards.

"Not that it's any business of yours but there's no doubt in my mind that he did. If you hated being with me so much, why did you stay?"

"Money?" He thinks I'm an idiot. Of course that's why he hung around. Sometimes I forget about what I've amassed doing what I enjoy. And that some people would prefer to sit on their ass all day rather than make something for themselves or use their advantages to help others.

That's it. We're done talking.

I give him the finger then lunge for the door handle. He slams his meaty hand over my wrist and twists. I shout —partly out of rage and partly out of pure agony. Fuck, that hurts.

He grabs my shirt and uses it to slam my shoulders against the roof. I'm sure that will leave a decent bruise. What the fuck?

Sanity check. At least I'm not even the slightest bit turned on by his manhandling like I have been in the past. That alone is a sign that I'm recovering.

I ball my fist, intending to put my boxing lessons to good use, except a lightning bolt shoots up my arm. Oh shit, did he break my wrist?

And still, he's ranting. Yelling now. Right in my face so that I can smell the stale liquor on his breath. Is he already drunk...or maybe *still* drunk? Fuck. "No, really. How do two bottoms get each other off? Did you sixty-nine until you drown each other or what? You know, I could top you both. Together. Would he be into that? I could make you both like it."

I want to spit in his face. Especially when I feel his meager hard-on jabbing me in the hip.

"You're disgusting. Way off base." Frantically, I look

around. I can't decide if I'm hoping someone will see us or if I'm afraid someone will witnesses the repercussions of my poor life choices. Doesn't matter, there's no one I can ask for help. "Don't judge people by their appearances, Ronaldo. Or you'll have no idea what they're capable of."

Like me. I'm about to lose my shit. Enough is enough.

My hand is screaming, my back throbbing, and I'm man enough to admit this is rapidly becoming a scary situation.

"Nah, I might have done some things I shouldn't have with you, Rogan. That doesn't mean I'm wrong about your playmate. There was no mistaking it when his boyfriend used to parade him around Romeo & Julian. I knew I recognized him from somewhere. It didn't hit me where until after...you'd left. You're fucking Cortez's bitch. Watch out. Now *that's* a guy you don't want to mess around with. He's not here, is he?"

What?

Could that be true?

Is *that* why Kaden understood me so well last night? He's not actually a dedicated top like he'd led me to believe? That's why he doesn't sleep with the same guys twice? Because he only likes taking charge once in a while?

That's not how I operate. There's no chance at a relationship with Kaden if that's true. Not that he insinuated there was anyway. I guess it's my fault that I tend to fall for guys I fuck no matter if they're good for me or not.

Motherfucker! Why was I hearing this from Ronaldo and not Kaden? Furious at them both—irrationally or not —I thrash in Ronaldo's hold. "Shut the fuck up! You don't know Kaden! You don't know anything!"

Not my most intelligent debate retort ever. I'm sure I'll hate myself for this moment later. A new low. I have to get away so I can think without testosterone overload warping my brainwaves.

"Get your hands off him." A low growl from behind Ronaldo startles us both.

My stalker ex obeys Kaden instantly, like an upstart wolf getting barked at by the true head of the pack. Appearances aside, it's easy to see who's in charge here.

It isn't me. And it sure as hell isn't Ronaldo.

He sidesteps Kaden and me, slinking toward the shrinking shadows in the alley like the gutter rat he is, but he can't resist taking a parting shot. "Or what? You'll call that hulk Cortez to teach me a lesson? Sounds like he might have gotten bored of your tight ass and pretty little mouth. I could take care of those for you, you know."

"I'm plenty capable of taking care of myself. *And* Rogan." Kaden steps forward, chest puffed up. Just like at the beach house, I believe he'll tear into the loser like a pitbull. Compact, yet ferocious. Tenacious. Loyal.

If I was the swooning sort, I might fall a little bit in love with him right now despite Ronaldo's disclosures. "And I will, if I ever see you near him again. He has a restraining order. Keep your distance. I dialed 911 as soon as I heard you harassing him. You'd best be out of here by the time they show up. Better yet, stick around. I'd love for them to arrest you."

Faint sirens accompany Kaden's tirade. Thank god he's not conning Ronaldo like I had been. I never imagined I'd be involved in a domestic disturbance call to the authorities. A scandal won't go over well if it gets back to my investors. I didn't mean to put Kaden or his gallery in the line of any gossips either.

But why didn't he deny Ronaldo's accusation?

Could it be true?

Deep down, I know it is. Kaden is a switch. Or maybe he converted from bottom to top. Either way, I'm pretty sure he could never be satisfied with only me. Which is exactly the kind of mess I don't need in my life right now. Even the delivery guy inadvertently warned me about Kaden's inability or unwillingness to stay with one man. I've already been with someone incapable of faithfulness.

He's right to stick to one-and-done affairs if he craves variety in his partners. I don't hold that against him. It's just that we're not as compatible as I'd thought.

I try not to let my disappointment show. I guess part of me was longing, against the odds, that last night might have kindled something between us.

"He's gone." Kaden swings around to face me. I'd already forgotten Ronaldo existed. He's a coward who'd never accept the consequences of his actions. "Are you okay? Jesus Christ! Come here."

I duck his outstretched arms. Right now, they won't bring me any comfort.

"Shit, sorry. Does your back hurt?"

It does, so I don't bother to correct his misunderstanding.

"I saw that bastard knocking you around. Did he do that to you before? When you were a couple?" Kaden gnashes his teeth.

"No. Not like that." Though I'm starting to realize his mistreatment and manipulation had run deeper than I admitted to myself previously.

I'm worn out. I don't give a shit about dirt or appearances when I crash onto my ass, right there on the muddy ground. I gingerly lift my wrist into my lap with my uninjured hand and lean forward, staring at the rocks an inch in front of my crossed legs.

"Hey, it's okay. You're all right now." Kaden brushes his fingers through my hair.

"Don't touch me," I rasp.

He retracts his hand as if burned. "Hang on. Are you mad? About the stuff he told you?"

I grunt.

"Why does that matter? You're pretty judgy about me kneeling for a guy you don't even know when you enjoy the same things." Defensive much?

"Would have rather heard it from you, that's all. You edited out a few details when you told me about Ronaldo's cheating. Intentionally or not, you mislead me." God, could this morning be any more humiliating?

I'm sure if my emotions weren't running sky high because of Ronaldo's attack, I'd be able to hash this out like an adult. Right now, I'm incapable of anything except blurting my raw feelings.

"That wasn't my intent. The past doesn't matter." He clears his throat. "It's not easy to talk about, okay?"

"So you *are* a sub, like me?"

"Did it feel like it when I had my dick inside you? Maybe I would have told you the whole story if we'd done more talking and less fucking last night." He crosses his arms, some of his self-protective instincts kicking in again. We both know that last part's a lie.

It's clear now how he understands me so well. He, too, has been burned by someone who was supposed to care for him. Protect him. Cherish him.

Charred, really. Worse than me, I think.

I'd like to be senselessly angry. It's easier.

I can't be. I feel bad for him.

"Sit with me until they get here?" I peek up at him, offering an olive branch.

He takes it, plopping down next to me. "Rogan..."

"I didn't say anything about talking." I shoot him a side-eyed glare. I've hit my limit.

Wisely, he shuts the fuck up. So when he slides his hand onto my knee and squeezes, I don't stop him. It can't be more than a minute or two before a police car flies into the alley. Lights flashing, sirens blaring.

The next ten or fifteen minutes are filled with questions. Explanations. Uncomfortable realities. Worst of all, my wrist swells up so much it starts to look like I'm smuggling an orange under my purple skin.

Neither the officer taking my statement nor Kaden will listen to my protests when they recommend I seek medical treatment. Here comes an ambulance, squeezing itself into the alley, which isn't designed for this much traffic.

I make another mental note to have the area expanded for emergency access in case Kaden ever sets the place on fire with one of the dozens of candles I spied in his apartment.

More people. More questions.

A few extremely painful pokes and prods.

It's decided. Despite my best efforts, I can't avoid a trip to the ER.

Kaden curses at the verdict. His murderous expression alarms me. I don't want that on my conscience.

"Hey, I had to see a doctor about that blood work anyway." I try to make light of the situation. Play it off. "Kills two birds with one stone. Gets me out of some boring meetings, too."

Shit. What time is it? I need to call my assistant. She

probably has half the company on high alert by now since I've hardly ever shown up late in the ten years she's been employed by me, and never without first calling the office with a valid and unavoidable reason for my tardiness.

"Kaden, can I borrow your phone?" I ask. "I'll have my assistant run it over as soon as she brings me a replacement at the hospital. I need to let her know what's up and—"

"Of course." He shows me the passcode. "Except I'd rather you bring it back yourself when you have a chance. No hurry. I'd just like to see for myself that you're all right. Deal?"

I nod. I'm half-dreading another encounter with Kaden and half-relieved that I'll have an excuse to circle back with him after the adrenaline and wild reactions of this morning have settled down.

He leans in to whisper, "Feel free to check out my image gallery. There are some dick pics in there if you get bored in the waiting room."

Before I can set him straight, or even blush—because, come on, you know I'm going to look—he's out of reach, letting the paramedics do their job.

"Take good care of him, please," Kaden says to the woman guiding the stretcher toward the waiting ambulance when I refuse his company for the thousandth time. I'm not going to waste his day after I've already caused so much drama and imposed on him. The man has rules to keep his sex life simple for a reason.

I keep reminding myself this isn't his thing. *I'm* not his thing.

"You got it." She winks at Kaden. No one is immune to his charm, damn it.

Before I can stop him—or maybe because I don't

really want to—he jogs over again, leans in, and kisses my cheek. "See you later."

Then I'm being whisked toward the nearest x-ray machine, hoping there will be a bottle of pain pills with my name on it somewhere in the near future.

My life is a hell of a lot more exciting this week than it was last week, I'll say that.

13

KADEN

Rogan's pale, drawn face disappears when the paramedics slam the door to the ambulance between us. I consider ignoring him and following them to the hospital. Except... One, I didn't ask where they were taking him. And two, he'll probably be done by the time I ride my bike all over the city searching for him and then I'll miss him when he swings by to return my phone.

So I stomp up the stairs to my apartment. Guys are nothing but trouble. Not worth it.

I glare in the general direction of my dick. *Do you hear me, big guy?*

Then I remember last night.

Okay, kind of worth it.

The sick part of it all is that right now I could really use a solid fuck to blow off some steam. Watching Ronaldo threaten Rogan freaked me out bad enough. Then on top of that, my darkest secret about the man I used to be before I buried that part of me had been shouted into the open. Right in the face of the one guy I care enough about to worry over how that sensitive information delivered so insensitively would alter his opinion of me...

Yeah.

If I ever doubted I still have issues, I don't now.

Just hearing Cortez's name out loud had shaken me. Watching Rogan's eyes cloud with disapproval had nearly gutted me. It's best to keep those parts of me safely locked up. Otherwise, look what happens. It's never good.

I drop into a chair at my kitchen table, trying to calm myself. I count to ten, in a futile attempt at slowing my racing heartbeat or steadying my shaking hands. I press them to the table, coaching myself to relax.

Which is when I feel a crisp, folded paper beneath my palm.

What the—?

I open one eye and see a whole lot of zeros. On a check. Made out to me.

That son of a bitch! I don't want Rogan's money. Especially not after we fucked. I didn't show him a good time because I was after anything other than what we'd shared.

I'm not Ronaldo.

The paper strains in my grasp, wrinkling as it's about to tear in half.

Wait. I stop before it's destroyed, then carefully place it back on the table. I smooth my fingers over it again and again as I think my plan through. When I can't come up with a flaw in my reasoning, I make up my mind.

I'm cashing this bad boy.

Rogan commissioned a painting. So I'm going to paint the man a fucking picture.

I doubt it's going to be what he expected. It's sure as

fuck not going to be what we'd originally agreed on. But that's how life goes. It never turns out like we thought it might at the start.

Getting lost in my work will help sear off some of the anxiety eating me alive. It's the one outlet I have left to rely on, since I'm guessing sex isn't going to appeal anytime soon. At least not sex with strangers.

Without that crutch to lean on, or some idea of what to do next...

I paint.

14

ROGAN

Out of habit, I lift my right hand to knock on Kaden's door before I realize that's going to be hard to do in a big, dumb cast. It might also make me pass out on his doorstep. I've endured enough indignities in front of the man to toss that one on the pile. I blow out a sigh then use the knuckles of my left hand to rap on the solid wood instead.

I wait a while then repeat. Louder, despite how odd it feels. Six to eight weeks of this might drive me nuts. If I didn't already hate Ronaldo, I would for this. A third set of knocks, harder this time because just thinking about that bastard makes my blood boil.

Nothing.

I guess Kaden isn't home. Or doesn't care for my company after all.

Ordinarily, I'd call him. Since his phone—and its extensive library of X-rated pictures—is in my pocket, I doubt that's going to do much good.

More knocking.

More waiting.

Shit. I give up. Probably for the best. I've had a hell of a day. I'm grouchy—emotionally raw and unstable. My arm is throbbing. Worst of all, I'm riled up from browsing through Kaden's sensual selfies. He could hold a world-class exhibition featuring a slew of the artistic shots he's masterfully captured of himself. I'd be tempted to buy every single photograph myself, though.

Hello, creeper.

I can't seem to help it. The attraction between us is irresistible.

If he's not planning to numb my suffering with ecstasy by joining me in another round of steamy sex, then I'm better off going back to the hotel, taking some of the pain medication the emergency room doctor prescribed, and crashing facedown on a bed for at least twelve hours.

So why do I feel like curling up on this uncomfortable landing and hanging around until Kaden gets home instead?

Because he's fun to be with.

Because he made me feel safe last night.

Because he's a talented and motivated leader in his chosen field.

Because he stood up to my ex for me. Twice.

Because he's a phenomenal lover.

Okay, fine. Mostly it's because I want answers about the things Ronaldo said and the questions that have been swirling around my mind since then. I didn't handle the situation well, I admit it. Cut me a break, though. I was shocked, alarmed, and in a considerable amount of pain. Faced with someone I shouldn't have trusted and someone I desperately wanted to, who turned out to be not quite what I'd originally assumed.

My bad.

One I'd like to fix.

I'm here. I might as well inspect the rest of this building. Make sure there's nothing else to add to my memo about improvements. If Kaden happens to return while I'm poking around...well, then it was meant to be, right?

I amble along the rear of the structure, eyeballing the distance between Kaden's portion, which ends right after the staircase, and the outside corner. The rest of the space must be huge. I wonder if he could use it. Expand his gallery?

It might be a win-win situation. The property would easily double in value if it was completely renovated, and he could probably benefit from more room. A makeover could also draw additional customers for him. I'll make some more phone calls about the situation tomorrow. Investing in his studio could be very lucrative.

Or messy.

Never hurts to have data, though.

When I round the building to evaluate the frontage, I realize there's a glow coming from Kaden's side. Hang on. Was he in there? Dodging me?

Could he have changed his mind about seeing me again? Worse, does he have another guy tied to his bed? My stomach churns.

Shit. I should leave his phone and flee the scene.

I march over to the front door of the gallery, prepared to slide his cell through the mail slot, when I realize the lights aren't coming from the upper portion of the windows. They're brighter at ground level, off to the side. In his workspace.

He's painting.

Of course he is.

Half the time when I'm studying financial reports, I lose track of what's going on around me. Engrossed in facts and figures, I've unintentionally ignored plenty of important people, phone calls, and repeated knocks on my office door.

I respect Kaden's passion for his work. It might look like obsession to some people. Even that I can completely identify with.

I knock again, this time on the front door. Still no answer. So I try the knob. It feels weird to grab it with the wrong damn hand.

While the door is locked, rattling the handle bends the entire thing. If I were the brutish type, I'm fairly certain I could kick it in without much trouble.

The motion jostles the bells at the entrance to the shop. I shake my head. That's definitely going on the To-Fix list.

Kaden must be attuned to listening for those soft peals. He calls, "Closed! Come back tomorrow."

Feeling somewhat foolish, I shout into the evening, "It's me, Rogan. I have your phone."

A couple on the sidewalk turn their heads to stare but keep walking down the street. I barely have time to wonder if they're used to seeing men clawing their way into Kaden's territory when he emerges from his studio, wiping paint on his pants.

No wonder they're so...colorful.

"Hey." He smiles as he flips the puny lock and holds the door open for me. "What was the verdict?"

I grimace and lift my encased arm. The cast is relatively short. It engulfs my palm and thumb then extends about six inches beyond my wrist. Enough to be annoying. Impossible to hide. "Eh. Fractured in a couple of places. Nothing time won't heal."

Unlike some other parts of me, which might be permanently scarred after the past week.

"Shit, Rogan, that sucks. I'm sorry." Kaden squeezes me in a quick hug that makes everything seem less awful. I wish he'd do it again. Hold me longer.

"No reason for you to apologize." I can't even look him in the eye. I'm mortified that he witnessed things go down between Ronaldo and me. Again. "I should be the one to do that. I didn't mean to involve you or put you in danger. Please, be careful. I'm afraid he might bug you."

"I kind of hope he tries." Kaden crosses his arms.

"Don't do anything to get yourself in trouble if he does. I know this makes me look lame. That I didn't kick his ass on sight or whatever, but he's sneaky and underhanded. It wouldn't be wise to give him ammunition for a lawsuit. He has nothing. We have things we've worked hard for. Everything to lose." I grit my teeth knowing that's not how other people will interpret my passivism.

"We'll see. So why'd you pick boring white? They have pretty much every color these days, don't they? I'd have gone for something bright. Neon stripes, maybe."

I don't doubt that. He's definitely not a plain sort of guy.

He's trying to make me smile. Unfortunately, it only makes me more self-conscious. "Hoping no one will notice if I also have a few suits special tailored to fit over it."

"Why bother?" Kaden tips his head as he studies me. A painter has to be a keen people watcher. He perceives too much for my comfort. "It's only for a little while, right?"

"Six weeks minimum," I hiss. "I rushed directly to my office and locked myself inside this afternoon, catching up as best I could. Tomorrow...people other than my too-professional-to-ask-for-details assistant are going to see the damn thing and wonder what happened. So I either have to make up something good and lie, which I fucking hate doing, or admit that my ex-boyfriend roughed me up while I stood there like an idiot and didn't fight back so that he couldn't sue me for it later."

"Is that why you keep hiding your arm behind your back?" Kaden wonders. Damn him and his astute observations. "You think people—including me—are going to think less of you for being hurt by a psychopath? Rogan, I'm willing to bet that anyone who knows you and Ronaldo won't be shocked by his behavior. Hell, they'll probably send you congratulations now that he's out of the picture. If they don't...fuck them."

"I wish it were that simple." It isn't. I guess because I'm disappointed in myself for winding up in this situation. It would be easier to dismiss critics if I weren't the loudest of the bunch.

Kaden takes my elbow in his palm, squeezing gently. He uses his grip to lead me toward his workspace. His touch comforts me even though he's not looking at me anymore. He's inspecting the cast. "I have an idea."

"We cut it off and I promise to take it easy instead. What's the worst that could happen?"

"You could end up with a hand that points ninety-degrees to your right instead of straight ahead, making it impossible for you to jerk off properly ever again?" Kaden's wrinkled brow and bugged out gaze is full of *nope*. "That would be a fate worse than death."

He's right.

So I don't argue.

"What if I dress it up for you? Give people something else to talk about?" Kaden grabs a leather pouch off of an ancient built-in piled with interesting stuff then keeps walking me into his lair. "I read an article in *Artists Today* magazine recently about this couple. The guy is some ex-covert-ops soldier who lost his leg while rescuing his wife from some gnarly sex trafficking ring. They started a company decorating prosthetic limbs with tattoo-style artwork so that their owners feel more comfortable wearing them. Show some personality. They turn their clients' artificial limbs into something beautiful instead of a constant reminder of tragedy. Make them something to gawk at for all the right reasons, you know?"

A wonderful concept. Genius, really. I wonder if they need venture capital to grow their operations. Another mental note for my time in the office. Being with Kaden inspires me, breeds new ideas, and reinvigorates me. It was never like this with Ronaldo.

So maybe I should trust him.

What could it hurt? I intend to cover the cast anyway. If I don't like what Kaden does, or it's inappropriate for work, no one will know what exactly it looks like under my bulky clothes. An ill-fitting suit will probably draw more attention than having the thing out in the open anyway. This could be a much better solution. Hide in plain sight.

I stick my arm out at him.

He grins. "This is going to be fun."

Kaden ushers me around a shoji screen to the place where the magic happens. It's strewn with paint, brushes, canvases, half-finished artwork, and an easel with a sheet draped haphazardly over his work in progress. I'd break my other arm to peek under it and spy on whatever had had him so entranced a few minutes ago.

I'd love to see him working here. I'm about to get my chance.

So I don't resist when he points me toward a yellow, plastic bucket chair with rusted legs and presses my shoulders until I sink into it. Then he drags over a stool and sits beside me at a ninety-degree angle, his knees pressed against my thigh.

So close. Too close. Not close enough.

The chemical bite of his supplies blends with his natural scent. It's so uniquely him that it reminds me of how I kept getting whiffs of it in the ambulance and in the ER. They made me feel less alone, even though I knew that was ridiculous. I'm tempted to accidently-on-purpose rub up against him until some of it transfers to my skin again.

Oblivious to my perving out over him, he cradles my injured arm across his lap, holding my hand lightly with one of his while the other runs over the cast. Without looking up he says quietly, "I'm really am sorry he hurt you. Again. I wish you had woken me up this morning. For a bunch of reasons."

"That makes two of us." I relax for the first time since this morning. Hearing that he doesn't regret what we shared loosens something I didn't realize was wrapped around my heart. Each time I'd remembered the night before it seemed like more than a simple fuck to me. Would he say the same if I found the nerve to ask?

Quiet, I watch him do his thing.

It reminds me of our time at the beach house. Before everything went to shit...or started getting unshitty... however you want to think about that.

Today, I'm free to admit his intense scrutiny turns me on without shame.

He extracts a fancy brush-tipped marker from the leather holder trapped between his knees, then gets busy applying pigment on top of the ivory cast. Beige where my hand and wrist would be, shadows around the edges where the plaster extends past my flesh.

I can't understand how he does it. Lines and dots and squiggles are converted into something that looks real enough to fool my eye even though I saw him do it. It's like watching a magic show from behind the curtain and still not having a clue about how the tricks are executed.

Kaden puts a marker between his teeth and yanks, holding the cap there as he alternates between various nearly indistinguishable shades of peach, white, gray, and red. A hyper-realistic illusion emerges from the place where at first there were only splashes of color.

He's creating a faux suit cuff on top of my artificial wrist. The shading and proportions are so perfect I would hardly notice myself that it wasn't my own skin instead of the cast obscuring my hand. Then, he fashions a tear in the "material" of both the suit jacket and the dress shirt he's created to expose the flesh that would lie beneath it. As he climbs my limb, he digs deeper until it looks like a badass tattoo of the inner workings of my anatomy are on display.

Muscles, sinew, and bone.

To me it represents exactly how I feel about the cast. He took my fear and turned it into something stunning. My insides might be bared to anyone who looks, but now it seems deliberate. My choice rather than something that was done to me out of anger, spite, and greed.

I could still wear a dress shirt over this and render the

cast practically invisible. Only the realistic bits of drawn hand and wrist that blend into my actual appendage would be left showing.

But now I don't want to.

Let them look.

Let them see my vulnerable parts.

Kaden made them beautiful. Me. He made *me* dramatic and fierce—badass—when I felt anything but that. The cast will be worthy of discussing now for the right reasons.

People will say, do you see that? How amazing it is?

He sits up straighter, cracking his neck as he assesses his work from afar. Satisfied, he finally shifts his gaze upward and meets my stare. "There. Better?"

"It's incredible. *You're* incredible. Thank you." I lean toward him, praying he'll take my offering.

He doesn't disappoint.

Kaden drops his markers. They scatter and roll across the cement floor as he frames my face with his hands. He pulls me the rest of the way toward him. The initial contact of our lips is light and reassuring. Comforting.

That doesn't last long, though.

15

ROGAN

I close my eyes and savor the gentle kisses Kaden gives me.

Soon they're not enough. A strangled sound escapes my chest when I open my mouth wider in invitation. He growls in response then begins to devour me.

With teeth that scrape over my tongue and press into my lips, he shows me that he's every bit as hungry for me as I am for him. His hands roam from my face, down my neck to my shoulders. He grasps them tight. Holds me steady as he advances.

He's drifting away from my mouth now, biting my jaw then beneath it lightly, closer to my ear. My cock stands at attention when he hits that special spot, right there, making me instantly malleable and compliant.

"You like that?" he rasps.

"Yeah." I let my arms hang by my sides so he can do whatever he likes to me. "Again. Please."

He obliges, while chuckling against my skin. Then he grows serious. He cranes his neck far enough that he can meet my stare. "You remember the word I told you yesterday?"

"Pygmalion."

"You're going to say it if this is too much for your arm. Or too intense after what happened this morning. Right?"

I nod.

"No. Say it, Rogan." He shakes me lightly. Nothing like Ronaldo's violence. More like he's trying to get my attention before I fall entirely under his spell. It might be too late for that.

"If I want you to stop, I'll say Pygmalion." Then I quickly add, "But I don't want you to stop."

"What *do* you want?"

"Show me that I'm okay. That he hasn't broken me. That I'm strong enough to handle a man like you." What kind of man is that? A dedicated top? Is he really? Has he always been like this or is he playing the role for some reason? Will he eventually expect something I don't have it in me to give?

I don't know. He's certainly in charge tonight. That's good enough at the moment.

"I can do that." He sucks on my neck, hard enough to make me wonder if I'll have to hide a hickey before going into the office tomorrow. At least it will be better if people talk about that than my cast. One makes me seem desirable. The other, pitiful.

I reach for Kaden. My wrist bumps his shoulder, and I wince.

"None of that. Keep your hands to yourself so neither of us accidentally makes it worse." He tucks my arms carefully at my sides once more. Is it really for my benefit or is he afraid of being touched? Last night he bound me. Tonight he's using my injury as a convenient excuse.

I suspect that's the case. I don't call him on it, though. Because I need the release he's capable of giving me even if it stems from an unhealthy dynamic. I might have to reconsider that tactic later, when my mind is clear and strong again.

Right now...my dick has other priorities.

If Kaden is willing to indulge me in a quick and dirty fuck, that's fine by me. I've been on the edge all day. If it hadn't been for the critical deal I blew off to make last night's delivery, I probably would have taken my first ever sick day. Then I would have rushed to his apartment straight from the hospital and the show his phone put on for me while I waited for the doctor.

To avoid breaking his rules, I abandon my attempts to grope him. I scoot off the chair and sink to my knees on the floor, where I touch myself instead. I use my good hand to unbuckle my belt. Or at least I try. Fumbling around with my left hand doesn't make it a smooth process. Especially since I can't seem to stop staring up at him.

He towers over me.

I lean forward and nuzzle his groin. I mean, the evidence of his rock solid cock is right there in front of me. How can I not draw a deep breath and remember what he felt like stretching me?

Kaden smiles, resting his hand on the back of my head. "Would you like some help?"

"Yes. Damn it."

"You're cute when you're desperate for my cock." He crouches down and rests our foreheads together. Then he jams his hands between us and rids me of my belt before unbuttoning and unzipping my pants. He yanks them down. "Lucky for you, I've been thinking of you every minute today while I..."

He fades out.

Before I can ask what exactly I distracted him from, he's kissing me again. When he cups my balls and tugs on them, slightly beyond the realm of comfort, I forget every single one of my questions.

"This isn't going to be like last night," he promises. "I won't torture either of us. You need me, don't you?"

"Yes."

"Good boy." He pats my cheek with his open palm. I angle my face toward him like a cat rubbing against its master.

Thank God. I can't wait.

Worst would be if he treated me like I'm fragile. Even though I feel somewhat delicate and I'm afraid I might never regain my confidence in a relationship, at least he's willing to help me try.

Almost fully clothed—shirt and shoes still on, pants and underwear around my knees—it startles me when his fingers wrap around my shaft. His rough touch is everything I crave.

I moan.

"You're ready aren't you?" he asks as he stares at my full erection.

I nod. For a moment, when his lips part and his eyes widen, I think he might be thinking of blowing me, but we both know I wouldn't last. I'd rather still be excited when he fucks me. It'll make me come twice as hard if I climax with his dick in my ass.

"Just a second." He whips his wallet from his back pocket and digs out a condom. I can't help but notice he found my check. And kept it.

I file away my surprise that he didn't argue over it for later.

Much later, I hope.

He rips open his fly while he traps the foil packet between his teeth. I stare as he rolls latex over his perfect cock. I'm torn between wanting to suck him again and needing him filling me, driving away the disgust in my guts and replacing it with euphoria.

I think I'm addicted to him and the high he induces with his seduction.

He curses beneath his breath. "Wait here. I'm gonna grab some lube from upstairs."

"Too long. Fuck me dry. Or spit works. I don't care." Right now I don't. Tomorrow I might regret my enthusiasm.

He holds me at arm's length. "I'm not ever going to hurt you like that. I might be a selfish bastard, but I'm not cruel."

"Then hurry."

Instead of deserting me, he spots something on a shelf behind me and grins. "Hang on. I'm not a Boy Scout or anything, but I do use linseed oil in my mediums. It's food grade. If you can eat it, you can fuck with it. Pretty sure that's how that saying goes."

Kaden takes a few steps in order to grab the bottle. So he won't doubt my willingness, I use the split second he's not by my side to rotate and face the chair I'd sat on while he decorated my cast. I keep my knees pretty far from it, bend over, then fold my arms on the seat.

My ass is presented to Kaden when he turns back around.

"Jesus, Rogan." He spanks me. Hard. A few times, until I'm chewing on my lower lip. Tingles spread up my spine when he rubs out the sting. "You have the best ass I've ever seen."

"So stop teasing me and fuck it. Please."

He chuckles. "You're awfully bossy for a man on his knees."

I huff, attempting to withhold any demands that might lead to a delay.

"Speaking of that, this floor is too hard. Here, put this under your knees." He whips his T-shirt over his head and wads it up before nudging me to lift first one leg then the other.

It is a hell of a lot more comfortable being cushioned by the warm cotton he wore a moment ago. Plus I get a good look at his cut physique.

My cock twitches. He's so handsome. I can't believe he's about to ride me again.

I rest my forehead on my arms so I can close my eyes and focus on feeling. I memorized a lot of the images on his phone, so I have them to recall while I concentrate on the sound of Kaden positioning himself behind me, the pressure as he spreads my legs as wide as my slacks will allow, and the first brush of his tip against my ass.

He rests his erection in between my cheeks while he drizzles oil over us both.

I cry out his name. If he says anything in return I can't hear it over the rush of blood through my ears. Then he's there, blanketing my back. It's so hot when the pressure of his body imprints the seams of my shirt into my flesh. Neither of us could stand to take a few extra minutes to get rid of the rest of our clothes.

He bites my shoulder, keeping me still as he lines up his erection and begins to work it into my unprepared body.

It hurts. I love the burn.

There's no mistaking his presence in my body.

"That's it, Rogan. Let me in." He moves with the barest twitches of his hips, letting me get used to his presence within me.

I grunt and push backward, needing to be completely reunited with him.

"Not too much, too fast." He slows me with a strong grasp on my hips. "You're going to enjoy this as much as me."

I don't care about that in the heat of the moment. My cock is wilting in response to the pleasurable pain. As long as I please him, it will be worth it. It's more important to be fuckable than to have fun.

"Rogan, stop," he commands.

Obeying isn't a conscious thought. It's a reflexive response to his authority.

He reaches beneath us and cups me, finding that I've softened some.

"Look what you did." He *tsk*s his disapproval before massaging my shaft. His fingers wander from my balls, along my length, and up to the head of my cock. He smears the oil on his palm all over me, making his caresses glide across my skin.

My breaths morph into pants. Blood rushes back to my shaft, rejuvenating my erection.

He kisses the nape of my neck and nips my ear before whispering, "That's better, isn't it?"

"Uh huh." I can barely utter those two syllables.

"Ready for more?"

"Please." I lift my ass, shoving it in his direction.

Kaden wraps his finger lightly around my throat, petting my neck as he begins to deepen our connection.

He pushes into me bit by bit, until his abs rest on my ass.

All the while, he pumps me, bringing my cock back to full stiffness before proceeding. And when he does, he makes sure to nibble on that spot he found earlier. The one on my neck that makes me crazy.

I hope he doesn't care that I'm about to blow my load across his hand and his shirt and the floor. It's not going to take very long, either.

He's not gentle or overly patient as he begins to fuck me.

Even more than last night, I appreciate how he uses me.

I might have a broken bone or two this morning, but I survived. I wish I'd done more to fight back, even though stooping to Ronaldo's level would do absolutely nothing to solve my problems.

I rock my head on my arms, trying to shake the thoughts of my ex from my brain.

"Only me," Kaden growls as he picks up the pace, pounding into me faster. "All you should be thinking of is me and what I'm doing to you. Everything else is irrelevant to what we're sharing."

"So good." My voice sounds shredded. Unrecognizable.

"Yes, it is. For me, too. You're gorgeous, Rogan. Any guy would kill to be buried inside you right now." He punctuates every reassurance with several strokes within me. His moans and the long hard-on he shoves into me don't lie. "I'm the lucky one, though. I'm the one about to shoot deep inside you."

Oh God. How is he still talking?

He's blanked everything except pleasure from my mind. Exactly what I needed.

I wish it could last forever instead of a few more thrusts.

When he starts twisting his wrist, squeezing each time he bumps the side of his hand against the ridge of my cockhead, I know my surrender is imminent.

"Kaden!"

"Yeah? You're going to come for me?" He's relentless, hammering into me so I can't prevent myself from falling over the edge.

I can't answer.

"Go ahead. I'm right there. With you." He groans. The rhythm of his hips stutters slightly, then he plunges to the base of his cock so I'm holding all of him within me.

I only last long enough for him to repeat the motion a couple more times.

Then I burst.

My orgasm curls my toes in my dress shoes and clenches my muscles around him. I lift my head as I roar, squeezing my eyes so tight that moisture leaks from the corners. It's either that or fly apart in his arms.

He joins me, cursing and chanting my name as he shudders along my back. The short jabs of his pelvis that accompany each round of contraction during his climax are dead on target, tapping my prostate.

Fuck.

I keep coming. Seemingly endless spasms extract pulse after pulse of fluid from my balls. I'm sure I'm doing my best Pollock impersonation on his floor right now. Hopefully he'll appreciate the passion he inspires in me.

My rapture seems to feed his, drawing out our

releases. When he finally begins to soften, slipping from my grasp, he collapses.

I enjoy his weight bearing down on me. It boosts my ego to support him fully. At least as much as his desire and compliments had. After a few minutes to catch his breath, Kaden shifts. He sits cross-legged on the floor. His shoulders rest against a pile of books. He hauls me into his lap.

He uses his shirt to clean us off, then sighs as I nestle into the circle of his arms. I rest my head on the curve between his neck and shoulder, admiring the taut, tattooed pecs in front of my face.

Content, we sit in silence for a long while.

My mind drifts, free of self-recrimination or worry like it had when I slept, sheltered in his embrace. I think of our cookie fortune, now tucked into my wallet somewhere around my calves. This *is* where I'm supposed to be right now.

I'm sure of it.

Until my damn mind reengages and the questions I had earlier begin to bubble up from beneath the thick blanket of satisfaction Kaden had fabricated around us.

16

KADEN

I sense the moment blissful Rogan checks out and practical Rogan returns with a vengeance. He tenses in my hold and his breathing loses those slow, shallow qualities that nearly lulled me to sleep right here on the floor of my studio.

It was fun while it lasted.

"You okay?" I ask, knowing he's not.

Rogan isn't the kind of person who will ignore the bombs his meddling ex had dropped this morning about me and who I used to be. Or what that means for us. Considering what he's been through lately, I get that. I do. That doesn't mean I'm looking forward to this conversation and its inevitable conclusion.

"I guess." He sighs then shakes his head. "Honestly, no. Not really."

I don't bother to play dumb and assume he's talking about his arm or the rough sex we just indulged in. Neither of us believes that's the problem here.

I try to head him off. "Do we have to discuss this?"

He considers, then says, "I think so, don't you?"

"I'd rather not."

Rogan looks at me then. The disappointment in his gaze hits me hard in the gut. Is it because he thinks less of me now that he knows what I used to be into or is it because I didn't blab my whole sexual history in between getting blown and fucking him last night?

Okay, that's not fair. I'm not very rational when it comes to examining these parts of myself, never mind sharing them with a guy I'm getting uncomfortably attached to faster than the paint on his portrait can dry.

He climbs out of my lap and attempts to hike his pants back up.

"Here, let me..." I reach over and set his briefs in place, zip his fly and buckle his belt. I should have thought about how that makes him entirely dressed and ready to walk right out of my life. Which he might do any second. Especially if this discussion doesn't go well.

And I don't see how it can.

I get to my feet and fix myself before meeting his level stare.

"Are you going to tell me what Ronaldo was talking about this morning?" he asks point blank.

There's no evading. I still give it a try. "Why is it important? That was then. This is now."

"Hey, no judgment. I guess I'm trying to understand who you are and if I'm the right guy to give you what *you* need. For longer than a night or two, I mean. Unless that's not something you're interested in. In which case, I should go." He glances over his shoulder toward the door.

Panic turns my skin icy and makes my heart stutter. "Wait, don't."

"Then explain." He holds his hands out, palms up, his fingers curled around that damn cast. "Please. I'm kind of confused. My whole life, as far back as I can remember, I knew that someday I planned to grow up and marry a boy. In the same respect, I knew I liked it when they took charge. Not in a sexual sense, of course, that came later. But in subtle things. I've always been strong-willed. So when there was another guy around who could challenge that part of me and tame it, it just felt right. It's part of my nature. Something I never consciously struggled with. Fortunately, my family was very supportive and encouraged me to do me. I get that it's not like that for everyone. Hell, probably not for most guys. I understand they like variety. I assumed, since you seemed to be so dominant, that you were like me. A one-way street. I shouldn't have. Is your preference something that changed over time? Or have you always liked to switch things up?"

Is he wondering if those fundamental tenants of his personality might shift because of his disastrous relationship with Ronaldo? It's not right to let my shit plant those doubts within him.

"Everybody's different, I suppose." It's a cop out. Compared to his rambling attempt to show me where he was coming from, my response seems defensive and curt.

Probably because it is.

I debate a deeper explanation, but choke on the words. Especially Cortez's name. I haven't talked about him in years. With anyone.

I don't think I can. It's so much a part of the story that I don't see how I can clarify without doing it. Like a superstitious old lady, afraid of speaking a demon's name out loud for fear of drawing its attention, I'm not willing to drag that pain into the present. Make it fresh again.

Cortez, and thoughts of what I lost, still has the power to harm me. He's better left in the dark recesses of my mind.

That's fucked up.

Admitting it isn't going to make Rogan want to hang around anymore than avoiding the truth. So why bother?

Rogan's face falls. "Hey, it's okay. I shouldn't push. You don't owe me anything. I understand if it's something you're not comfortable discussing."

He edges toward the door. I don't blame him.

It still cuts me. Why? Why do I care? We fucked. It was great. Time to move on.

Right?

Some part of me is shouting, "NO!" *Fuck.*

I've been with enough guys to know that he's different.

I try to offer him something. An inadequate scrap. "You know how you didn't want people to see your cast and assume shit about you?"

He nods.

I raise my hands then let them drop, irritated with him for making me address feelings that are better left buried. At Cortez for making me experience them in the first place. And primarily at myself for being unable to get the fuck over it. "Well, it's kind of like that."

His face softens, losing the hard lines of tension that had been there a moment ago. "It's tough to be so vulnerable. I'm sorry Ronaldo dredged up bad memories. If you want to share with me, I'm here to listen. Maybe even help you get past some of it, like you did for me the last two nights. Like I said, without judgment. It seems like you've found ways to cope with the situation instead of coming to terms with it. I guess that's what I'm afraid of, getting involved—well, *more* involved—and then having you change your mind about what you're looking for. Can you tell me enough to show me that isn't what's about to happen here?"

"I'm sorry, Rogan." I swallow hard. "I can't. It's not that I don't want to. I *can't*. I'm not ready and I don't know if I ever will be."

I can't promise him things I'm not sure of myself. It's impossible to imagine being brave enough to risk kneeling for a man ever again. Is that out of fear, because Cortez killed that desire in me, or because what I want evolved with my need to control the situations I put myself in? What if someday I change my mind again? Would it be fair to bet Rogan's happiness on something I'm not entirely confident about?

No. It's not. So I don't say anything else to convince him to stay.

He crosses to me and enfolds me in the warmest, sweetest hug I've ever been given before kissing me on the cheek. "I'm sorry he scarred you so bad, Kaden. Stole something so important from you. And that there's not a fix as simple as a cast to repair the damage."

Thank God Rogan understands and won't hold it against me.

Except when I go to hug him back, he evades my embrace, retreating several feet away, out of my reach. Probably forever. "That's why you have a No Do-Overs policy, right? To avoid exactly this."

Shit. Fuck. Damn.

I can't deny it because it's true. "Yeah."

"Then I'll stop making this hard for you. Although it's nice to know I tempted you enough to bend your rules for me." He gives me a sad smile that takes the shards of my heart and breaks them into even smaller slivers. "Thank you for everything—for taking care of me, for some great memories, for coming to my rescue, and extra thanks for lending me your phone. By the way, don't ever lose that thing or you're going to be the internet's most famous amateur porn star."

I wish I could appreciate his attempt at levity.

I can't when my spirit is turning to lead and plummeting toward my feet, leaving me hollow inside. Because it's obvious what he's going to say next before the words even leave his sexy mouth, which is still swollen from my coarse kisses.

"Goodbye, Kaden. I wish you the best. Truly, I do."

It hurts so much to watch him leave that I'm incapable of calling him back again.

What would it change? He deserves someone who isn't damaged. Someone who can love him freely and openly without secrets or regrets.

I'm not the man for him.

The bells above my front door toll as another amazing guy walks out of my life. I wait until I hear his car zoom out of the alley before I dash into the gallery, climb on the window casement, and rip those motherfuckers off the wall. They jangle dully as they hit the bottom of the trashcan.

Before I realize it, I'm back in the studio, whipping the sheet off my easel.

The beginnings of the image there taunts me. Haunts me.

There's no point in trying to sleep. I might as well paint some more. It's better than riding my bike around the city at night until I find a liquor store that's still open, or maybe someone who will sell me something stronger.

At least I'm not quite as fucked up as I used to be.

Progress, right?

Sadly, it doesn't feel like it.

17

KADEN

A FEW DAYS LATER

Rogan has ignored my avalanche of texts. The apologies, the questions about how he's doing, the offer for him to sleep over until he finds a place of his own. That one was ridiculous. Transparently desperate. Born of a weak moment. I'm not surprised he didn't respond.

It might be borderline stalkery, but I run my finger over the phone number listed on the business card he gave me the day we met. What the hell?

I dial it. I don't have to wait more than an instant before his assistant answers. Of course Rogan doesn't give out his private line. Sometimes I forget how powerful he really is and how out of his league I am. I still can't believe he let me have him. And that I threw him away.

I'm an idiot.

"Hello?" she repeats.

"Um, yes. My name is Kaden Finch. Mr. Clearwater commissioned a portrait from my studio. I was wondering if I could speak to him, please?" No, really. *Please.*

"Hello, Mr. Finch." Is it my imagination or does she

163

seem frostier at the mention of my name. Uh oh. "He's tied up in meetings and won't be able to accept or return your call."

Well, that answers that. His assistant is clearly under orders to cock-block me. Even if she doesn't know that's what she's doing or why.

Damn.

"Okay, thank you." I sigh, prepared to disconnect and throw my phone against the wall.

"He did, however, leave a message for you," she adds right before I demolish my cell.

"He did?" Pause.

"Yes, sir. Do you have a piece of paper?"

I rush to my sketching table and grab a lilac colored-pencil. "Shoot."

She rattles off an address that I scribble frantically on my pad.

"What's that?" I ask, noting to myself that it's not too far from here. A mile or two at most.

"Where he's staying." Definitely frosty. I wager he's a fantastic boss. Has he been moping around like me? Can she tell it's at least partly my fault? A double whammy. First Ronaldo, then me. I can't believe I piled on to his misery.

So why is he telling me how to find him? "Um, is there anything else?"

"It just says, 'When you're ready.'" She seems as confused as me. "I assumed you'd know what that means."

"Oh, I do." But am I? Ready to lay myself bare? No, not really. Maybe he'll give me a break and appreciate that I'm trying. "Thank you."

"You're welcome. Is there a message you'd like me to return to him?"

Somehow I don't think he'd appreciate the things I'd like to communicate, like, "Sure, tell him I'm obsessed with his ass and I'm dying to fuck it again."

Or, "Make sure he's home at ten. Naked."

Or, "Let him know I can't stop thinking about how sexy, kind, and fun he is."

He'd probably especially hate that last one.

So instead I say, "Nope. I'm good. Thanks again."

About twelve hours later, I'm rethinking that decision. I probably should have had Rogan's assistant give him a heads-up that I was planning to drop by. But I wasn't sure I'd have the guts to go through with it.

Even now, I've taken a couple extra spins around his fancy block. Each time I pass his place, I slow down, peer at the lit windows, then peddle like I'm leading the Tour de France, hoping he hasn't spotted me. By the tenth lap I'm starting to get dizzy.

Probably because of the lack of oxygen caused by my near hyperventilation.

Without him or someone else—except no other man will do—to top this week, I'm stockpiling my anxiety. I have no way to prove to myself that I'm in charge of my world and that I don't need anyone.

Because clearly...I might.

Fuck.

Rogan has to let me in. He has to let me fix us both. Unless he's figured out how to help himself already. In that case, I'm screwed since I apparently have relied on drugs, booze, and finally sex for too long to come up with any other solutions.

Without my final crutch to lean on, things are getting too real in my head.

A flash followed by a giant clap of thunder startles me. Fat raindrops begin to plop around me. One lands on the top of my head and rolls into my eye. The leaves on the trees lining Rogan's street rattle as wind whips through them, heralding a summer storm. This is going to get nasty, quick.

No more time to delay.

I skid to a stop on the sidewalk, less than ten feet from Rogan's door. One booted foot plants on the cement as I pause to admire the array of colors featured in the immaculate landscaping. It would be nice to paint.

The edge of his curtain dips inward before falling straight again.

Shit. He couldn't have missed me. I'm sitting right there, staring at his house like a dumbass. Or worse, an obsessed ex-lover.

Shortly after, I hear the rattle of what sounds like some serious locks turning. Is he always that cautious, or has Ronaldo continued to harass him? I don't like the thought of him being alone.

If things go right, he won't have to be tonight. Neither of us will.

When he steps onto the small porch at the top of three slate stairs, I can hardly breathe. He's even more handsome than last time I saw him. His hair is a tiny bit less sculpted and his posture is more relaxed.

I can't say the same. In fact, I don't think I can even bend my leg enough to swing it over the seat of my bike. So I sit there, gripping the handlebars hard enough I think I might bend them in half.

"Hey." Lame. Why don't I know how to talk to him

anymore? From the moment we met, that hasn't been a problem.

"Hi." Seems like he might have the same issue now, though.

He also doesn't invite me in.

"I, uh, came to see how you're doing."

"Fine, thanks." He swipes the slightly longer strands of his hair back from his forehead like he styles it when he goes to work. I guess it makes him more confident.

I hate it. I like it tousled and soft. Sexy.

Staring at him, I forget I should say something else.

"I have to be honest here, Kaden. You look like you might be the one struggling tonight." He peers through the intensifying rain at my bedraggled ass. No kidding.

I roll my bike back a few inches, tempted to leave and pretend I hadn't come crawling over here like this. Is this how my hookups felt when they tried to proposition me into tossing them another sweaty bang?

Ugh. I don't want to think about that.

"Are *you* okay?" Rogan leans forward a bit then, putting his hand out toward me.

"Yeah. I just needed to tell you that..." I scuff the toe of my boot on his sidewalk and stare at his socked feet on the welcome mat, feeling decidedly unwelcome. Especially since he doesn't make a sound. Instead he's staring at me as if there's not much I can do to bring back the guy I've spent two of the hottest nights of my life with.

The emptiness inside me actually hurts. My stomach cramps, making me spit out part of the truth. "I miss you."

"Miss *me*? Or miss *fucking* me?" The fingers of his good hand are about to crush the edge of the door. He hasn't let go of it or allowed it to close behind him, as if he might need an escape hatch from this discussion. It doesn't appear he's about to ask me to come inside even though it's pouring now.

What the hell?

At least he's warm and dry beneath the overhang covering his porch. I'm getting soaked. My fingers are turning blue. I could lie my way into his sanctuary. But I won't.

I guess I thought he might need me too. Enough to relax his standards and slum it with me one more time. Clearly, that's not the case. Coming here was a bad idea.

Except now that I have, it pisses me off that he knows I caved first.

"What do you want from me, Rogan? I swallowed my pride. I'm here. Begging like I haven't done for a guy in years. You have no idea how hard this is for me." Rain drips down my spine through my soaked clothing. I'm cold. Freezing inside.

"If you want to discuss why that might be, you can come in." Golden light spills from his temporary home onto the sidewalk at my feet. It's so tempting to crawl into his shelter.

Until I ruin even that glimmer of hope.

Talking isn't what I have in mind. I blow out a huge breath and shake my head.

I still can't.

Rogan doesn't budge. I admire him for his resolve even as it crushes me. "I'm not going to chase you like those other guys did. Or settle for something less than what I really want from you. At least I'm being honest about how I feel when we're together. I'm not trying to trap you or pressure you into a relationship you're not interested in, so please show me the same respect."

Well, shit, when he puts it like that... "I'm sorry. I shouldn't have come."

"No, you shouldn't have. I mean, it was *you* who reminded me I'm worth more than that. I don't deserve to be used. If we keep sleeping together even though you're not looking for something that lasts out of bed, I'm going to get burned. You're not that selfish." Rogan shrugs. "It's bullshit that you forced me to face my fears when you're still running from yours, whatever they are, and that you're stubborn enough to reject what comfort I could bring you. Not only for as long as it takes to blow your load, but potentially forever. I thought you were smarter than that."

Well, that's frank. The man chooses to submit. That doesn't make him a pushover. My mistake for forgetting. It makes me more amazed that he gave me the reins, even for a little while.

He didn't raise his voice. He didn't need to in order for his insults to hit home.

Rogan couldn't have stunned me more if he pulled out a sledgehammer and swung it at my head. It might take something that drastic to get through my thick skull. But I can't dispute his claims. He's right. Absolutely.

When I don't say anything, don't budge despite the storm raging around us now, he tries again. "Tell me about Santiago Cortez. I did some research, called in a few favors. There's not a lot to find, though. Is he in the military? Has some kind of special assignment that called him away from you? Is he coming back? Is that why you're trying not to get attached to anyone else?"

Sadly, I don't really know. He didn't disclose much about his career to me. That alone stings. How could I have given my soul to someone who didn't share such important things with me?

I doubt everything I felt. And the things I'm starting to think I could feel for Rogan. They're too similar. Exposing the flaws in one makes me think I could be repeating my mistakes.

Why can't it be enough to share physically? Why does he have to keep peppering me with impossible questions?

I shift my gaze until I can watch the puddles growing on the sidewalk. Rings spread outward from drops that splash into their depths, disrupting the still, calm surface. Just like Rogan did to my life when he cannonballed into it.

"I just....not tonight." Besides, what would it mean for us if I did confront those demons? Would our power exchange still work for me or would I crave what I had before?

Everything is so fucked up. I don't know what I want anymore.

"That's what I thought. Well, now you know where to find me if you ever want to take me on a real date. One far away from a bed, where we discuss how we make sense together going forward." Rogan smiles sadly. "I hope you figure things out, Kaden."

He doesn't say *before it's too late*. I hear it anyway.

Have I blown my chance at something spectacular?

What I really want is to crush him in my arms then fuck him until I stop feeling so damn much. I look up, staring straight into his eyes. He'd have to be blind not to see the fanatic desire burning there. For him.

He shakes his head, echoing my own words: "Not tonight."

Then Rogan grimaces as if it hurts him as much as it

hurts me before he steps inside and gently shuts the door in my face.

I tumble to one side, ditching my bike in his yard before dropping to my knees on his soggy lawn. It takes a minute or two before I can lever myself to my feet again. Then I stand there hunched, with my hands jammed in my jeans pockets, rain plastering my hair to my face for a while. I have no idea where else to go. My vacant loft doesn't appeal without Rogan waiting for me.

I could grab a drink at the bar I passed on my way here. Only I wouldn't stop at one or even a half-dozen. Rogan wouldn't respect a guy who blacks out in the bathroom of a shady hook-up joint.

Suddenly I realize what he thinks is pretty fucking important to me.

What have I done?

I draw the hood of my saturated sweatshirt up then shuffle a few steps down the sidewalk, my boots squelching as I retreat.

Until I hear the door crack open behind me. My pulse races. I'm afraid to breathe.

"Kaden?"

I grunt as I angle my shoulders slightly to glance over my shoulder at him. That's all I'm capable of, my heart in my throat.

"Do you want me to call you a cab?" Rogan asks, smashing my misguided hopes.

I don't answer. Just stand blinking away raindrops and who knows what other moisture while I steal one last look at him from beneath the drenched black material shielding me from his concerned scrutiny.

"Hey, at least take my umbrella..."

I face the street again. With my back to him, I raise my

hand both to ward him off and wave farewell before wandering away. If he says anything else, I can't hear it over the booming of thunder. Violent and uninhibited, nature thrashes me as I stagger through the city streets.

It doesn't bother me at all. I couldn't possibly end up deader than I already am inside.

So what exactly am I so fucking afraid of?

18

CORTEZ

"Father, your time is up," one of my "parishioners" whispers to me in Spanish where we hunker together in the shadowy confessional of my candlelit church.

"We're not finished here."

"You are. The war will never be over, though you've certainly won this battle by assassinating the cartel leader. It's not going to take them much longer to realize you were the last man to see him alive. He trusted you. You betrayed him and so many of his plans that it's becoming impossible to deny. If you don't leave, you'll end up shipped back home. Assuming we can find your body."

I scrub my hands over my hair, trying to counteract some of the pressure in my skull.

"You've done more here than the prior three agents we had together. Two new assets have been embedded in the cartel ranks recently. One is likely to be promoted to second-in-command under the new regime. Go home, Father. Leave knowing how many lives you've saved and with the thanks of the countless people you've protected, even if they never realize it." He puts his hand on my knee. "You're done. You're free. Collect your pension and find the boy you were rambling about when you were ill with that high fever last summer. See if he's still as in love with you as you are with him."

Doubtful. I'd made sure Kaden wouldn't cling to hope that I'd do exactly that. For his own good.

I've lost track of the number of times I nearly lost my life in this tangled web of lies and sin. Half of the cartel's own members don't last three years. When there's this much illicit cash involved, there's an equal amount of backstabbing, greed, and immorality.

It's a miracle I'm still alive.

"What's the plan?" It's not like I can stroll out of here and hop on a plane. That would draw attention. Every inch of this town is watched, including the airport. Father Cortez has no reason to travel, especially internationally. The flight would never make it off the ground.

"I'll come back for you after dark. We're going to drive into the mountains so you can perform last rites on my grandmother. While we're there, a landslide will put an end to the good Father and explain why we can't return your corpse. A chopper will fly you over the border to Panama, where you'll catch a military flight back to the states."

It seems surreal. The thought of a place far away from here and the mess I've been embroiled in for years. A simple place, where the toughest decisions I had to make were what movie to watch on Netflix and which guy to pick up at the bar on a Friday night.

Can I be that person again?

I'd like to try. "I'll be ready."

Hell, I think I'm ready now.

"Cortez. There's something else." It's not like my handler to make small talk. Extending our conversation is unwise.

"What?"

"The guy you asked me to keep an eye on..."

"Kaden Finch? What's wrong?" It's like a wormhole to an alternate galaxy. The time I spent with him seems so distant and bright compared to what my life has become.

"Is he the one?" The informant waves me off. It's obvious he is and that I'm about to lose what little cool I have left if he doesn't spit this intel out. "His name came up in the system. Domestic violence incident at his residence about a week ago."

"Shit!"

"Shh..." We look around the intentionally half-drawn curtain. Locking ourselves in where anyone could approach unnoticed would be a death trap. No one has noticed the good father's uncharacteristic outburst. Nothing other than a priest counseling one of his lost lambs. I've gotten used to wearing this robe. It's great cover for an agent and it also explains why I never took a lover. Not in three long years.

If I can't have Kaden, I don't want anyone.

I knew I loved him before I left. But I hadn't realized how profoundly that love had changed me. How permanently it was inscribed on my soul.

And now someone had hurt him?

I'll kill them.

Yeah, my time here has altered me, too. Will I figure out how to be a normal person again? One who doesn't take justice into his own hands daily?

"He's okay, right?" Please, please let him be fine.

Perfect. Or the anguish I caused him when I walked out was for nothing. I understand how bad it hurt, because I inflicted the same wound on myself when I chopped us in half.

"I think so. The only injury reported was a broken arm. They're looking for a guy named Ronaldo Pires for questioning. Sounds like this might be good timing for you to return."

I bolt to my feet. Why would Kaden mess around with that loser? Pure scumbag, that one. Sure, he hid it with a pretty face, smooth talk, and fancy clothes, but I'd seen firsthand how he treated guys he played with. So had Kaden.

He should know better. It doesn't make any sense.

Unless he's as fucked up inside as I've been since I left him.

Maybe he needs me after all.

"Can we leave now?" My gaze whips to the handle.

He's staring at the rear of the church. His eyes grow wide.

I see the reflection of flames in his pupils before I spin around. A barrage of Molotov cocktails bombard the church's interior from the rear and side doors. Something else, larger and heavier, bounces onto the floor nearby.

I shout for people to run. It's too late. They're pounding on the doors, which must be barricaded from the outside. None of them budge.

I don't make it more than a step or three before the world erupts with an eardrum-rending boom.

So this is what it feels like to fly. Huh.

My back slams into something, halting my motion with an instant deceleration that jars me more than the initial force. It knocks me half unconscious as I slide down a wall to the floor. I tip onto my hands and knees and crawl despite white-hot pain that shoots through my hip. When I look down, I'm pretty sure I see bone sticking out from somewhere it's not supposed to be, so I look away and keep moving.

Acrid smoke makes it harder to breathe. I lift my head and spot my handler, skewered on the wrought-iron cross on the opposite side of the room. His neck and head are lolling at such an unnatural angle there's no sense in trying to reach him to check for a pulse.

His eyes are still wide open, locked in the blank stare of death I've seen too many times during my stay in Columbia.

For the first time since I got here, I pray. Not for myself.

I beg for the souls of the blameless people surrounding me and even the ones of the men and women I recognize from shady dealings. They're as doomed as I am. Nothing I do can save them from meeting the being they've spent so much of their life devoutly believing in. I hope the answers they're about to discover are the ones they've always sought.

Then the only thing on my mind is Kaden. I hope he's safe. Happy. That whatever went down with Ronaldo was a one-off deal.

If I die now, fearing that's not true or— worse—that he's in danger...that's the purest hell I can imagine. If it weren't for that info, I would gladly lie down and join my handler and the rest of the parishioners screaming as they literally return to dust and ashes.

The world around me is scalding hot. Flames lick the

dry boards, igniting them as if they were tissue paper. A mixture of red, orange, and black flickers around me.

Maybe I'm heading straight to the devil's playground for letting down the one person who needed me the most along with the others here today who will die because of me.

Though it seems impossible, I have to try something, anything, to make this right.

The sacristy! I stuck a Bible in the side door of the little-used area to encourage a cool breeze earlier. A lighter patch in the inky smoke makes me think it's still ajar.

I bellow to the people around me, directing them toward salvation.

Those who are able stampede toward the exit, tumbling into the fresh air. A few walk across my back to get there. I don't hate them for bolting, even when they don't stop to help me in return.

I have one purpose left. A single reason to keep going.

I lever myself toward the sacristy, except I can't feel half my body. Probably better that way, since it no longer hurts. I'm reduced to worming along the ground, planting my elbows then using my upper body to drag myself forward. My legs dangle behind me.

Flames lick my toes. The door is too far away.

There's no hope.

Kaden will have to save himself. He's plenty capable of it. I would have liked to do it for him anyway. If only he could hear me, and know that I never erased him from my soul.

"I'll always love you. I'm sorry I'm not there."

Timbers creak ominously before they give way and plummet to the floor around me. Maybe on me, too.

Pressure compresses my chest. I can't draw the scalding air into my lungs anymore. I'm not sure if that's a blessing or a curse.

I gasp, suffocating. Burning. Melting.

Then I remember nothing else.

19

KADEN

A WEEK LATER

After a solid week of no showers, barely eating, and a hell of a lot of work, I stare at the painting in front of me. I was right. It's the best one I've ever done. I just didn't expect it to look like this. I guess sometimes life doesn't go as planned. This time I believe it can be a twist for the better.

If I haven't ruined my last shot.

Ah, shit.

I finish packing it so I can deliver it safely. It's going to be a bitch to ride my bike—which Rogan had hired someone to wash, tune up, and deliver to the gallery the day after my breakdown—with the unwieldy parcel strapped to my back. I'll make it work.

I can't wait to see Rogan's face when he unwraps it.

After wrestling it into place and strapping it to myself, I take off. Every intersection I zip through on my route to his new house amplifies my excitement and electrifies my nerves. This time I don't take the long way around. I roll right up his sidewalk, then hop off my bike as gracefully

181

as possible given the package I'm wearing like a turtle's shell.

I jog up the stairs, slip my arms out of the straps I'd fashioned out of duct tape, and set my offering on the ground beside me. I rest the top edge against my hip then take a deep breath. Touching my palm to the door, it seems like I might detect his heart beating through the room and across the space dividing us.

Of course, I don't.

If this doesn't work—if he doesn't see what I see when I look at this portrait—I'm afraid I might end up where I was a couple years ago. Drowning in an even deeper abyss that I won't surface from.

Please tell me I haven't fucked this up beyond repair.

I tip my head back and whisper, "Come on, universe. Do me a solid."

Then I knock somewhat louder than I intended. Oops. Nerves.

It doesn't take long before I hear him right there on the other side of the door. I'm glad he pauses to check the peephole. Except that it's just enough hesitation to convince me he's about to slink away and pretend he's not there until I give up and shuffle off.

Little does he know, I'm determined.

So I give the peephole a self-conscious wave.

The lock turns. He pokes his head out. His face seems slimmer. Has he been taking care of himself?

"Kaden?" He seems surprised to see me. I mean, why wouldn't he? He doesn't have a clue that I've been planning this precise moment for a week. Ever since I found my way home, waterlogged and distraught, after he banished me.

My priorities shifted that night.

"Hi." I clear my throat, which is suddenly parched. "I... uh, have a delivery for you."

His brows draw together. "Did I leave something at your place? You could have mailed it to me."

Ouch. "Not exactly." I gesture to the brown paper rectangle leaning against my thigh. "May I bring it inside for you?"

It feels foreign to phrase a question like that. I used to do it a lot, but I admit I'm rusty. It's stressing me the fuck out to put myself in a position where I could be rejected. He's worth the risk. Hell, I spent every night of the past week sleeping fitfully in my studio near the spot where we fucked. I couldn't bring myself to crawl into my bed without him.

If this didn't go well, I was going to need a new plan. I'd try as many times as necessary to convince him I'm ready.

I'm *finally* ready. I think. Mostly.

Rogan stares at me as if my intentions are written on my face, then nods. He opens the door and steps deeper inside.

I follow. "How's your arm?"

"Much better, thanks." He smiles then, even if it's a weak facsimile of his full-on grin. "Your modification is a huge hit. Several of my employees have suggested I get it tattooed on me when this thing comes off. That might not be a bad idea. If you'd approve my use of the design, of course."

He stares at his wrist. Something flip-flops in my chest when his mouth widens a bit, turning into a legit smirk instead of dimming as he considers the cast.

I guess we're both quite a bit different from the last time we saw each other.

At least I did something right by him. "Yeah, that would be cool. I can recommend a couple artists who've worked on me, and I'd be happy to go with you to get it done, if you want."

"I'd like that."

"Me too."

"So..." Rogan glances at my offering. "What's that? I mean, I know what it looks like."

"Yeah, the shape kind of a gives it away, huh? It's obviously not a drum set or a chocolate Easter bunny, sorry 'bout that."

"I would have loved to see you on your bike while giving a giant rabbit a piggyback ride." He laughs, and this time it's real. "You're pretty impressive with that thing."

"I used to moonlight as a courier before my art took off. You should have seen the shit I had to lug around." I roll my eyes.

He hums. The icicles that have been dangling off my heart since last week—hell, since Cortez left me—melt the barest bit. "Did you wear a sexy uniform? I bet you'd look hot as hell in tight pants and some kind of official hat. Damn."

"Sure did. It's still hanging in my closet." I'll wear it for him all day every day if he'll come home with me. The last thing I want is for him to assume that's why I've come. Flirting and fucking would be amazing, don't get me wrong. They're not the only prize I'm after, though. I've learned that lesson. "But...I'm not here to seduce you with my fine ass."

He frowns. "Oooookay. So, why are you here?"

What if he hates it? I mean, I'll gladly issue him a refund and keep the thing myself. It's worth a hell of a lot more than twenty grand to me. I'm dying to see if he loves it as much as I do.

I haven't been this anxious about unveiling one of my pieces since I started doing caricatures on the boardwalk for extra cash the summer between my junior and senior years of high school. When my aspiration to become a self-supported fulltime artist still seemed impossible.

He's standing there patiently. Waiting. Giving me a chance to explain.

"I'm here to give you your painting."

Duh.

He's blinking at me like he doesn't understand.

"The one you commissioned," I continue. How does a man spend that much money and forget about it like it's nothing? Well, honestly, I know he didn't expect me to make him anything.

How could I not?

"What the hell am I going to do with a nude portrait of myself?" He swings his arm toward his fireplace. "Hang it up there and think of what a moron I was every time I look at it? Ugh."

He has no idea what I'm holding. What if he feels the same way after he sees it? "If you hate it, I'll take it and go. But I'd appreciate it if you'd look at it before you decide."

"Fine." He holds out his healthy hand.

I shoo him and carry it to the monolithic ebony dining table nearby. I'm sure it's expensive as fuck. It's also impersonal and cold. Not like the Rogan I know.

He isn't meant to be here.

My distaste must be evident. "My assistant picked out

this place and furnished it. It suits the man she's familiar with. The one I am at the office."

"I'm sorry she's never seen the side of you I have." I hold the edge of the wrapped frame so that it's standing upright and gesture for him to do the rest. He strides over and stands beside me, close enough that I can smell his aftershave. I'd love to turn my head and lick the exposed column of his neck.

I don't.

Doesn't it figure? Rogan is a neat unwrapper. Kill me now. With his left hand, he picks at the tape holding the paper closed, driving me insane. If I were him, I'd be ripping and tearing it like a mini-tornado to unearth what's inside.

He freezes when he reveals the top left quarter of the image.

It's my face peeking through, not his.

"Wait, what?" Rogan comes alive, attacking the packaging. About time! Bits and pieces scatter on the floor around us like confetti as he realizes what I've done. When the image is fully revealed, he pulls out a chair and plunks onto it. "Oh, Kaden. This..."

He clears his throat and swipes a discreet knuckle along the corner of his eye.

Is that a good thing or a bad thing? "You hate it?"

He doesn't take his eyes off the painting for a moment. His response is emphatic enough that I know what I'd see if he faced me. "Are you crazy? Kaden, it's amazing. Perfect. Are you sure it's mine?"

"Absolutely. So am I, if you want me." That finally does it.

Rogan pries his adoring gaze from the picture of him

and me, as we must have looked after coming together that first night, though I painted the scene entirely from my recollection. The perspective makes it seem as if I'd had a camera attached to an exposed beam in my loft, looking straight down at us as we slept tangled in each others' arms and the rumpled sheets. Both of us peaceful and relaxed after granting and receiving solace. The clench of my splayed fingers on his shoulder and the possessive hold he has on my waist are hints of the passion we'd exchanged before exhausting ourselves.

Even our shared fortune is there, lying on my bedside table. If you look close, maybe with a magnifying glass, you can read it. *You're exactly where you're meant to be (in bed).*

I would do anything to hop into that canvas as if it were a time machine and shake myself awake to explain what an awful mistake I was about to make. I'd do everything different.

I'd stay up all night watching Rogan sleep then rouse him with another round of sex, this one more affectionate and less demanding. Then I'd explain how I got so screwed up in the first place and how being with him was mending me.

I know his ugly secrets. He should know mine.

"Rogan, I'm ready to talk about Cortez."

"You don't have to," he back peddles. "As long as you're ready to move past what happened between you two, I don't mind you keeping that stuff in the past. I let what happened with Ronaldo make me afraid you'd be like him. I know you're not. You don't owe me an explanation. Just reassurance that you're comfortable going on from here like we have been so far. That's all I ask."

"No, it's important that you understand some things before you decide whether or not to kick my sorry ass out again." I cut him off when he begins to apologize. "You did the right thing. It's not a criticism. "

"Then I'm here to listen." He takes a huge breath then confesses, "Because, Kaden, I missed you too. A lot."

20

KADEN

I take the seat across from Rogan so I won't be tempted to stop the flow of my words or stem my sadness by kissing him. Neither of us would be able to keep that from turning into lovemaking. I'm sure of it. I'm about to prove to him that what he asks of me is important.

I'm willing to confront myself and share the most damaged parts of me with him. I'll stop hiding in the microcosm of my studio, my gallery, and my loft. There's more of the world to see and share with him out here.

Rogan scoots closer to the table and lays his hand on top of it. I'll take it to help with the telling. I press my palm to his and savor his warmth. We wrap our fingers around each other's wrists at the same moment.

I smile at him then inhale shakily. "I assume you're expecting me to explain what went wrong, and why he left me. If it's okay, I'd rather start by sharing the everyday stuff. What he's like and how we were together. How confident and cocky he is. How strong. How everything fell into place when we found each other. All the reasons I loved him so much, despite not having very long with him. So maybe you'll understand why it hurt so bad, absolutely ripped me apart, when he left and told me he didn't plan to come back."

It could take hours. Days even.

I haven't let myself think of the good times for a while. There are so many things I adored about Cortez. Still do, if I'm being honest. He's not mine anymore. That doesn't mean he's not still an incredible person. Even if I wasn't man enough to keep him.

It's hard to admit it now, after hanging on to my rage for years, but I wasn't wrong in my one-sided love. It's just one of those things no one's to blame for. I hadn't been as critical to his happiness as he was to mine. I hadn't completed him as perfectly as he did me, or he never could have walked away. Stayed away.

The truth I've been ashamed to share is that it was me who hadn't been good enough for Cortez. Worse, I'm terrified I might not be good enough to hang on to Rogan, either. He's every bit as extraordinary in his own way. Rich, handsome, compassionate, and amazing in bed.

That's what I'm so fucking afraid of.

We talk for hours. About the elaborate surprise party Cortez threw me for my thirtieth birthday, and how he supported me through the loss of my father, and how it felt to give myself to him completely. About the millions of tiny things that added up to a heart full of love.

Sometimes we laugh, sometimes we're on the verge of crying.

When I finally run out of positive things to say about Cortez, I figure it's time to fill in the rest. I tell Rogan about the call I got that beautiful summer day. How the asshole on the other end of the line had threatened to throw the man I loved in a dank military jail after a brief tribunal where he'd have no shot at innocence or escape.

It's not that Cortez left that bothers me. I understand his obligations and that he incurred them before he met me. It was how he'd stamped himself indelibly on my soul before going with no intention of returning that destroyed me.

Cortez loved me that final perfect time, then cut me loose. For a man in a submissive role, it was the equivalent of being left floundering in rough seas, drowning.

I relied on him. Trusted him.

Finally, I admit to Rogan how I'd begged Cortez to return to me. Promised to wait. And how that hadn't been enough. I wasn't everything to him like he was to me.

It was the greatest failure of my life.

Then it gets even harder. I have to disclose the horrific way I treated myself and those around me while I was suffering. The dirty deeds I relied on to numb my pain. I also confide how Rogan had burst into my life and stopped that cycle cold.

"So here I am. Different than I used to be. I'm never going back. I can't let someone else have control over me. Because I'm not as strong as you or as courageous. And because, honestly, Cortez will always own that part of me. I hope that's not a deal-breaker for you."

"Kaden." Rogan's hand is trembling in mine. "I'm so sorry you went through that. I admire you for your loyalty. Those are positive traits, not ones to be ashamed of. I can't understand how he didn't cherish you as much as you do him. I appreciate how much you hate Ronaldo right now. To me, Cortez is every bit as foolish and unworthy of your dedication."

"They're nothing alike, Rogan. I promise. Remember

that couple from the magazine I told you about? The soldier and his artist wife? I guess it was reading that article that finally made me begin to realize I was being selfish. Deep down, I know Cortez is out there doing things like that guy talked about. Saving people who need him more than I did." I swallow hard. Even now, it costs me to acknowledge that. Our sacrifice will never be easy. At least I can finally say I believe he did the right thing and mean it. How can I hold his heroism against him?

"Of course he is. You wouldn't have fallen so hard for him if he wasn't a great guy." Rogan squeezes my hand.

"Right. Then what's Ronaldo's excuse?" I huff. "Sometimes we don't see when a person is rotten inside. Or maybe they change over time. I don't know."

"Actually..." Rogan looks away then back. Good thing. I won't let him hide after I've laid myself bare. "I've been doing some soul searching myself. I think *I'm* ready to come clean too. I never loved him."

The guilt and relief that washes over his features when he says it out loud makes me sure it's the truth.

"So why'd you stay together?" I brush my thumb across the inside of his wrist.

"I wanted to love him. And I felt horrible, because I didn't. Like I wasn't capable of that kind of emotion after being a coldhearted businessman for so long or some shit like that. If he treated me badly, it seemed like a fitting punishment for my apathy. I did try to leave him once, a few years ago. But..."

"He's a manipulative bastard and he twisted your feelings around then used them to keep you trapped," I sum up, helpfully.

He nods. "It's also hard to know what love is. How

consuming it is and how impossible to identify until you've experienced it for real."

As if he doesn't want to scare me away, he doesn't make any claims. He doesn't need to. I understand that he's telling me he's only recently gotten a taste of what the full-blown thing might feel like.

I, on the other hand, recognized it immediately.

It's overwhelming and terrifying.

Neither of us admits the strength of the emotion pulsing between us tonight. It's obvious. It could become something legendary. If we don't fuck it up.

I don't say that, settling for this instead. "I'll tell you one thing. You and Ronaldo were together for years. Cortez and I only had a few months together. Time isn't what makes that magic happen. It might make it stronger, or give it the chance to fade away, but how long you've known someone isn't a critical factor in how much you love them."

We leave it at that.

"I understand now, Kaden. What you want, and how that can work for us. Don't take this the wrong way, but I'm glad you loved Cortez and that your relationship with him opened you up to a future with me. That doesn't mean I forgive him for trampling on your heart, though."

That makes two of us. Could Rogan be any more perfect? "Every minute I was away from you sucked. I have no intention of making that mistake—the same fuck up Cortez made with me—again. So whatever you need from me, I'm here to give it."

"In that case..." Rogan lifts his chin and dares me to take action. "My bedroom is down that hall over there."

21

KADEN

"Yeah?" I can't believe this is actually happening.

Though I dreamed it might, I was too afraid to trust it would.

It's the best reward I could have imagined for ripping myself open and showing Rogan the gory bits inside me. Instead of shrinking from them and my admission that I still love another man, he's embracing them.

I have to show him how I feel. Words are no longer enough.

Shooting to my feet, I almost knock the fancy chair onto the exotic-hardwood floor. Instead of wasting time circumnavigating the table, I hurdle over it, skidding on my hip until I fly off the far edge and land at Rogan's feet.

He stares at me in shock then bursts out laughing. He's still cracking up when I put my hands on either side of his strong jaw and draw him toward me so I can crush our mouths together.

I should say thank you for his patience and empathy. Promise that I appreciate a second—or is this the third?—

chance. To do that I would have to stop kissing him, though. And I'm not about to do that anytime soon.

Instead, I glide my hands down his neck to his shoulders then beneath his arms. I pull him toward me until he has no choice but to wrap his legs around my waist to jockey close enough to satisfy my urging. I cup his ass in my palms, still eating at his lips, swallowing his moans.

His erection is palpable where it mashes against my abdomen.

We could fuck right here on the floor, like we did in my studio. That's not quite what I have in mind. I'd like to show him another side of me, one that I've withheld from each of my casual flings for the past two and a half years.

Reminding myself of my intentions, I gentle my caresses and slow the glide of my tongue against his. Carefully, I walk us in the direction he'd indicated, toward his room.

I don't have to ask which it is when I see the soft glow of LED lights splashing onto the wall behind a chocolate leather headboard. It's exactly the place you'd imagine a corporate mogul would sleep. Not *my* Rogan—the man behind the Clearwater empire.

His skin deserves to be bathed in candlelight, not this synthetic glow.

I advance until my knees hit the mattress, then lean forward, placing him carefully on the soft, if sterile, stark-white bedding. He blinks up at me when I finally separate us, just long enough to rid him of the socks, T-shirt, and sweats he must wear to bed.

I'm thrilled to see he's not wearing anything underneath. Dressed down, Rogan is mouth-watering. Naked, he's even more scrumptious.

"Kaden?" he asks, peering up at me. His arms and legs are spread, open for the taking.

I won't be able to deny anything he requests. "Yeah?"

"May I undress you? Touch you?" He lifts his good hand toward my abs. Instead of shrinking from his tentative exploration, or pinning him down as I would have in the past, I lean in.

Where his fingers slip beneath the hem of my polo and make contact with my skin, they thrill me. I let him investigate.

Rogan sits up. He kneels on the bed and inches closer. I clench my teeth against the onslaught of pleasure as he worships my body. He follows his fingers with his lips, kissing my torso as he walks the shirt up, up, up.

When he finally pulls it over my head and tosses it aside, he starts again at my navel then glides downward instead.

I spear my fingers into his hair and guide his mouth to the places I crave his touch most. He moans against my body before nuzzling my cock through my pants.

"Go ahead, get rid of them."

Rogan uses a combination of his teeth and his free hand to strip me. He doesn't stop there. He opens his mouth, warm breath tempting me to plunge inside.

Not before protecting him, first.

I bend over and retrieve my wallet, then withdraw the condom from inside. I hand it to him. "Put it on me."

Rogan fumbles the packet as he struggles with his injured hand. I'm not cutting him any slack. He's plenty capable.

"Use your mouth if you have to."

"God, yes." He tears the foil with his teeth then sets the latex on the tip of my dick with his left hand before covering it with his lips. His tongue nudges the rolled up condom, encasing my shaft.

It takes a painfully long time. I enjoy every moment of his efforts.

When I'm completely sheathed, I use my grip on his hair to direct him. "Good job, Rogan. Now suck it. Deep."

He groans then slides down my cock, gagging only a tiny bit when I press against the back of his mouth. I shift, prepared to retreat, but he isn't deterred, taking me down his throat and swallowing around me.

I reach for his good hand and draw it toward my crotch. He cups my balls and rolls them gently between his fingers.

Rogan needs no instruction. He's an all-star cocksucker. I let him play as much as he likes, until my thighs are quivering from the effort it takes not to shoot right here and now. No, I have other plans for him tonight. Ones I need my erection for.

I indulge him in a few last licks and sucks before I place my hand on his collarbone and hold him in place while I withdraw. He smacks his lips and practically purrs as he stares up at me.

I can't keep myself from leaning down and kissing his lush mouth. I get lost in how he sucks my tongue as skillfully as he did my dick. Eventually, I remember my intent.

I bite a trail along his stubbled jaw before growling in his ear.

"Turn around. Get your ass up in the air." He obeys without question as I climb onto the bed with my knees between his thighs. "Now put your face flat on the bed."

He does, the angle making his cheeks part, granting

me access to every bit of him. Cock, balls, and the hole I want to fuck so slow and deep it drives us both insane.

"Yes, please fuck me. Kaden I need you inside me."

"Not yet." I spank his firm ass a few times, simply because I can't get enough of the tightness against my palm. "I'll fuck you when I'm ready. Understand?"

"Mmm. Yes." He shivers beneath me.

Since he can't see me, I grin. He's so damn cute like this, I can't stand it.

Time for his reward.

Hopefully, I remember how to make this good. I haven't done it in nearly three years.

I bend down until my face is an inch from his freshly showered skin. I can smell the soap on him still. Then I grasp his cheeks, tug them apart, and bury my face in his ass.

Rogan groans. He collapses forward, sprawling on the bed.

"Get up if you want me to eat this ass." I spank him again, sure he's loving every second.

After all, his cock is rock hard as it hangs low beneath him when he repositions himself.

I dive in, using my tongue to spread spit around while I prod and tease the clenching muscle there. While I entertain myself with his wild groans and curses, I sneak my hand around his hip to play with his dick. He rocks, thrusting back against my mouth then forward into my fist.

I love bringing him pleasure in every direction.

Slickness coats my hand as it leaks from his cock.

"Kaden. Kaden," he chants. When the pitch of his voice changes, I know I'm pushing him too close to the edge. So I lower my mouth to his balls and suck on his sac while I reposition my hand to take advantage of the natural lubrication from my saliva and his precome.

I press my finger against his opening and wait until he relaxes before tunneling into him. He's tight and hot, just like I remembered.

I can't wait until it's my dick burrowing into that paradise.

"Do you have anything to make this easier?" I ask.

He grunts and points toward his pillow. Curious, I peek beneath it and find not only a partially used bottle of lube but a small anal vibrator as well.

"What's this?" I withdraw the toy and wave it where he can see it. "Have you been taking care of yourself for me?"

He groans, incapable of verbal communication now that he's lost to desire. Good, I like him like this.

Plan B. Ditch the fingers, use the right tool for the job.

I grease up the vibrator before fitting it to him. The instant it touches his sensitive flesh, Rogan cries out. He thrusts backward, lodging the tip inside him before I make a conscious choice to insert it.

"Settle down." I lean over his back, keeping him still. "I'll give you what you can handle. No more, no less."

He quiets, waiting like the good boy he is for me to take care of him. Shit, he's perfect.

I run my finger along the edge of the toy, checking the fit before pressing it deeper. It doesn't take long before he's swallowed the entire thing. So I begin to swirl it inside him. I can tell when it nudges his prostate because he clenches and moans.

Of course, that means I do it over and over.

Until he's gasping.

Then I turn on the vibrator.

"Kaden!" He rakes the sheets with his good hand. A

long strand of pearly fluid drips from his cock onto the bed between his legs. "Please, stop!"

I freeze. "Are you saying Pygmalion?"

It seemed like he was enjoying himself, but I'll never jeopardize his safety or satisfaction.

"No. God, no." He shakes his head against the bed. "Going to come. Don't want to. Not without you. Fuck me. Please, fuck me."

"When you ask so prettily, how can I say no?" I slip the vibrator from him, switch it off, then toss it to the floor on top of my jeans.

I could easily plunge inside his loosened hole.

But I don't.

I'm angling for something more intimate. Something more *romantic* than to pound into him from behind like this.

I tap his hip then half-lift, half-scoot him so he's lying on his side, his head on his pillow. I cradle him from behind, holding him close to me from the tips of our toes to the tops of our heads. He turns his face toward me, and I capture his mouth.

I'm still kissing the shit out of him when I reach down and guide my cock to his ass.

Rogan inhales sharply as I join us, but he never flinches or removes his lips from mine. He looks into my eyes as I fill him while embracing him.

I lift his thigh and put my top leg between his, finding the leverage to fuck him with long, slow strokes that embed me balls-deep inside him then allow me to withdraw until I nearly slip out of his grasp.

He squeezes his ass around me, never letting me go too far.

I splay my hand over his chest. His heart pounds

against my palm. I relish the sensation before rubbing his nipple with my thumb. Then I wander lower.

Once I touch his cock, our time will be limited, so I draw things out, examining every inch of his flat stomach before wrapping my fingers around his steely shaft. All the while, I glide in and out of him. Steadily, thoroughly, lovingly.

I hope he understands what I'm trying to show him.

The liquid warmth in his gaze tells me he does.

Rogan's cock bulges in my fist. I pump him in time to my fucking. His ass tightens on my dick, making it harder to move within him. But not impossible.

When two people are as committed to each other's rapture as we are, nothing is unattainable.

He begins to tremble in my arms.

"You're ready?" I ask against his mouth. Rogan nods. "Good, then show me. Come all over these gorgeous abs while I fuck you." The more I talk, the more I get into it. "Do it, Rogan. Do it now. Shoot. Hard."

He writhes in my grasp then arches. His body tenses and explodes around me.

Come blasts from his cock, coating not only his stomach but also his chest. He decorates himself for me even as his ass massages my cock. I continue to thrust into him.

He looks up at me, stunned. Still coming, though in smaller pulses.

It awes us both to know I do this to him. That I have the power to drown him in passion.

So I swipe some of his seed from his body onto my thumb. Then I lift it to his mouth.

He stares straight into my eyes as he swallows the evidence of desire I feed him. He sucks on my thumb as greedily as he did my cock earlier, laving it with his tongue as he licks it clean. That's all it takes.

I press my forehead to his and slam against him with a few more jerks of my hips. I call out to him as I release the pent-up fear, desire, and affection our connection has created. I threaten to overflow the condom I'm wearing as I come hard and long in his ass.

When the strongest spasms finish wringing me dry, I relax but never let go of Rogan.

I never will.

His eyes flutter open, still dazed. Then he smiles, bright and wide. It's the most beautiful thing I've seen in a long time. "Thank you, Kaden."

"No, thank you, Rogan." I kiss his cheek and settle him against my chest.

We lie quietly until long after my softening cock slips from his body. Neither of us ready to let go of the moment. Our hands roam over each other lightly as if we're reassuring each other that this is real and that the other person is here. To stay.

If this was my loft, everything would be perfect. I can't fall asleep here. And I don't want him to either. Stronger than ever, I don't believe this is where he belongs.

"What are you thinking about?" he wonders, breaking our magical silence.

I don't mind taking the opportunity to make my pitch.

"I can't believe you own another place so close to my building." Maybe the location explains why he picked this one. My ego can hope.

"Uh..." He blushes, forcing me to make out with him some more. When we come up for air, he said. "Actually, there were quite a few to pick from in this neighborhood."

"Exactly how many properties are in that portfolio of

yours?" I shake my head. It's kind of intimidating to think about, and I can't afford for him to get the wrong idea. I'm not asking because I intend to freeload or anything like that. "You know what, I don't want to know."

"It's a nice enough house to live in for a while." He shrugs his top shoulder.

"You haven't set any roots down then, huh?"

"No. I thought about trying a different one next week. There's one property I keep going back to in my searches, but it has some...issues." He clears his throat.

I'm sure he's got enough money to take care of whatever the problem might be. Secretly, I'm happy he hasn't settled in. Because that might make it harder to ask him the question I've been mulling over since before I arrived. "Well, I realize my texts were out of control the past week. But I meant them. You're welcome to stay with me until you can work out the problems with the house you like. Or, you know, until you get tired of me leaving my laundry on the floor."

Or, hopefully, never.

Okay, so it wasn't a question, but there it was. I've never asked a guy to live with me before. Cortez had followed me home from Romeo & Julian one night and never left. Sort of like a stray mutt you can't say no to.

"Are you asking me to be your roommate?" He stiffens in my arms. Uh oh, too soon?

"Yeah. Sort of." I smile, hoping it's not too awkward. "Look, I didn't come here tonight for a meaningless fuck. I came prepared to pour my heart out to you. Show you the not-so-sexy sides of myself. Be honest. And hope that's enough to keep you in my life. I did that because you're important to me. I'm not going to dick around here. I want to be with you, Rogan. So please say yes. Move in with me.

Not as some generic roommate either. Be my lover. My boyfriend. Please?"

It's been a long time since I begged.

He reaches for me so I go to him, unable to deny him anything at the moment.

After a tender, sensual kiss that does nothing to calm my racing heart, he stares straight into my eyes. Still he says nothing.

"I get that things are happening quickly. It's only been a few weeks and if you need more time—"

"Like you said before, it doesn't always take a long time for love to grow. What I need is for you to help me pack. I'm not much use with this thing." He lifts his cast then shrugs. "I don't have a lot here anyway. Most of my stuff is in boxes in storage."

I look around, noticing it's pretty stark.

"You think I could knock it out in a couple hours?" I ask him seriously. "I don't want to spend another night without you."

"It will probably take twenty minutes, tops."

"Then let's get started." I crack my knuckles and hope he knows I'm talking about more than just the packing.

22

CORTEZ

What the fuck is that beeping and why won't it shut the fuck up?

Each *bleep* stabs into my brain and rouses me from unconsciousness, the only thing that can stave off pure agony for a while.

It's been like this for so long I can't remember anything else. Not how I got here. Not where *here* is. Nothing except the fact that Kaden is hurt and he needs me. Were we in some kind of accident?

I have to get better so I can find out and make sure he's okay.

That's the only thing I think about. The only thing keeping me alive some days.

I'm pretty sure, anyway.

Voices murmur in hushed concern around my hospital bed. I've heard prayers that seem awfully familiar, weeping, and instructions from what must be nurses or doctors. Everything jumbles together.

Skin grafts, broken ribs, pins in my hip, and brain damage.

None of it matters.

"Kaden?" I ask. Or try to. Only a gurgle emerges from my throat.

"Shush," a kind woman says as she pats my hand. "Sleep, if you can. You're scheduled for another round of surgeries in the morning."

"Kaden?"

More reassurance, though not the kind I'm looking for. "It's okay. You can do this. You're obviously a fighter. You're beating all the odds. Improving every day."

"Ka-den?" I try one more time. Even to my own ears, his name is unintelligible.

"It's going to be a long, difficult road. I'm sorry for that. But I believe you're going to pull through." She sniffles then. "Any man who can literally walk through a burning building to save himself must have somewhere important to go."

I nod the slightest bit then instantly regret it.

Everything hurts. Stars burst behind my closed eyelids.

Fuck me.

"Kaden." This time it's not a question. His name alone comforts me and ensures I dream of sweet things when the darkness claims me once more.

23

KADEN

FOUR MONTHS LATER

It turns out the "issue" Rogan was having with that property he was stuck on was that it was the other half of my building. Well, really more like the other two-thirds. The space is gigantic compared to my original cozy loft and the combo gallery-slash-studio space below it. You know, the one I've squashed myself, my belongings, and my work into since I was a bona fide starving artist.

It hadn't taken more than a few weeks from the time he moved in until he'd admitted it, then showed me some design proposals from his team. I could see why they're the best in the business. Each possibility seemed more spectacular than the last. Although it kind of freaked me out, because I could never afford to make those improvements myself, I agreed to allow him to go ahead with renovations. So we've been living in a construction zone since.

I went all in on this roll of the dice.

Why not, since I'm already gambling my heart?

There's no doubt about that. Rogan and I are stupid in love, though neither of us has been foolish enough to admit it yet. It's like we both agree that if we say the words, we'll curse our relationship.

I'm not going to pretend we've resolved every one of our issues. We're both still haunted by our pasts, which can lead to one or both of us doing something dumb that sparks an argument. Like me worrying about whether or not he's going to leave me someday. Or Rogan getting jealous, which is kind of adorable but also occasionally annoying. Half the time I don't even notice other guys, especially not when he's around to hold my attention.

Nothing serious, though, and nothing we haven't been able to fuck out of our systems after a brief cool-down period. We're chiseling away at our insecurities and have gotten better at keeping them from getting the better of us, hashing things out when our emotions are triggered.

We both work hard, and play harder. Sometimes he'll come home and find me still painting. Instead of nagging me about it or making me feel guilty, he grabs his laptop and sets up shop at my sketching table. He's always got a million things of his own to tend to. Emails to send. Calls to business partners on the other side of the world to make in the middle of the night. Charities to hustle for when his own affairs are in order. The man does everything.

When we're finished, we turn to each other for entertainment until our bodies are as exhausted as our minds. Hanging out—relaxing watching movies or working out in our brand-new home gym or checking out restaurants and attractions around the city—helps us recharge. We're even planning a real vacation to some tropical island Rogan owns land on in the Caribbean for a few weeks this winter.

For the most part, this is working for us.

It's crazy to think I've been with him longer now than my affair with Cortez lasted. Apparently it takes three months before I'm really sure I've met the one. Or...the *other* one.

I'm ridiculously pleased. Utterly content.

It shows in my art. Rogan is the best muse I could've asked for. My output has skyrocketed. I'm stockpiling paintings left and right. Quality shit, too. The canvases are heaping up. Rogan said he'll help me put together a business plan for a traveling exhibition and create an online store to expand my gallery sales.

My new stuff is different from what I've painted before.

Frantic. Intense. Yet still highly sensual.

Understandably, instead of painting different subjects every time, there are a hell of a lot of portraits of Rogan mixed in with my commissions and the spare work I create for my shop. They're stacked neatly next to the mound of discarded canvases featuring Cortez.

It disturbs me that I haven't painted over any of those yet.

Tomorrow. I'm going to do that tomorrow. I swear. It's time.

Right now, I'm about to greet my boyfriend, who just made it home after a very long day at the office. I love nothing more than relieving him of the heavy mantle of responsibility he wears while on tycoon duty. I glance at my watch, shocked to see I've painted into the night and didn't even realize it. Another late dinner awaits us.

Chinese in bed with orgasms for dessert has become a favorite bad habit for us both. At least we burn the calories off together.

On my path through the studio to the new living

quarters we share, I pass the painting I gifted Rogan with months ago. I pause every day to admire how we look together.

So right. And yet...

I shove the niggling thought in the back of my mind away when it whispers that something is missing. *Nothing* is missing. We love each other. We have an amazing sex life. We enjoy the time we spend together out of bed. We're supportive of each other's careers.

What the hell else is there to life than that?

I can't put my finger on the exact adjustments I'd make if I smuggled that canvas into my studio for a touch up. And I don't dare take it off the wall since Rogan is as obsessed with the damn thing as I am. Sometimes I catch him staring at it with the dreamiest expression on his face.

Still, my fingers are always itching to make some revisions.

The curse of an artist, honestly.

Nothing is ever finished. Nothing we produce is ever good enough in our eyes.

That must be it.

I forget about my reservations when Rogan waves at me from our opulent new kitchen. It's open to the living and dining areas as well, keeping the airy ambiance of my original home. I swear this area alone is bigger than my whole loft used to be. It's gorgeous. Full of wood and bright colors. A blend of my funky style with Rogan's more luxurious tastes. Exactly what I would have done myself if I'd had unlimited resources.

Though we haven't touched my old loft yet, and lived in it while this section of the house was built out, that's phase two. I'm no longer reluctant to let him transform it into a more useful space that doesn't duplicate the purpose of the rooms down here.

If it makes him happy, it's fine by me.

"I picked up some orange chicken on my way home." He holds up a brown paper bag with a few grease spots and shakes it in my direction. It smells delicious.

I can't wait to eat.

The food.

And him.

24

KADEN

I scrub my knuckles over my eyes a few times. When I blink, I'm shocked at what I see. I finally started painting over those canvases of Cortez like I promised myself I would, filling them with image after image of Rogan instead.

Except the medium I mixed up must be bad. It's not thick enough, or sticking right. Hey, I'm not a chemist. Plus, I'm often caught up in my vision and forget to measure things super accurately. Shit happens.

The repercussions of my distraction are eerie today.

A ghost image of Cortez is seeping through the black background I'd attempted to cover him with. That wouldn't be so odd if it wasn't a new painting of Rogan and me in progress.

I'm trying to work out whatever kinks keep driving me nuts about the first one.

So now I'm faced with a picture of Rogan standing behind me, sweetly kissing the spot between my shoulder blades while Cortez stands in front of both of us. Is he watching or about to make out with me while Rogan cheers us on?

Whoa.

Insta-wood tents my pants. Guilty as hell, I try not to stare. Or drool.

Did I do this subconsciously?

To destroy the evidence, I rush outside intending to toss it the Dumpster. Even that doesn't seem sufficient. I won't risk hurting Rogan or making him feel like he's not enough. He's already wrestling with an inferiority complex—compliments of his douchebag ex—which sometimes makes him suspicious of me and whether I'd cheat on him or go after another man.

That's never going to happen. I don't want anyone else.

If I've experienced a stray desire a time or two for what I used to have—or woken sweaty from a dream about the days when I used to be Cortez's pet—it's only because committing myself to a relationship with a definite power exchange in the bedroom has stirred up some shit in my psyche. I think that's normal.

It could come off greedy as fuck. I freely admit that.

Rogan and I have so much together. I would never jeopardize it.

So I jam the painting in a steel barrel that contained some building supply or other for the renovations. Then I douse it with alcohol from my outdoor supply shed, another recent addition thanks to Rogan, and light it on fire. Only when the smoke clears and I confirm the errant painting has been reduced to coals do I spray its sooty remains with the hose then trudge back inside.

I'm still standing in my studio, kind of in shock, when Rogan comes up behind me and wraps his arms around my waist. "Hey, there."

I jump.

"Sorry, did I startle you?" He chuckles against my shoulder blade. The uncannily similar position I so recently eradicated from existence has me on edge. It's not as easy to erase the scene from my mind as it had been to torch the canvas.

"Kind of." I'm not going to lie, I'm completely freaked out.

"You're tense." He rubs my shoulders, unknotting some of my muscles. Meanwhile, he kisses my neck. I act like my raging erection is entirely in appreciation of his efforts and not because of the lingering memory of the phantom threesome I'd seen.

I mean it's not like I haven't gotten it on with two guys at once before. Hell, even more than that in the days of my bad judgment and wild parties. But something about seeing those two particular men with me sandwiched between them.

It rattled me as if I lived in a snow globe possessed by a hyper child.

"Kaden?" Rogan asks quietly.

"Hmm?"

"Are you all right?"

"Yeah. I just..." I turn and kiss him violently, then practically drag him through the studio toward our new bedroom. Maybe it's the changes that are unsettling me. I really do like them, I swear. But they're drastic. And the loft is next.

Could some part of me be upset at letting that final piece of my life with Cortez go?

I'm sure I should confide in Rogan, share my suspicions. I still have weak moments, where exposing my inner workings is tough. This is one of them. Besides, I don't want to take anything away from the effort he's put in to the plans or his excitement at watching them come to life.

He's proud of what we've accomplished. I'm not going to ruin that for him.

We tumble onto our gigantic new bed. It's like bouncing onto a cloud. Not a single dip, tear or stain in sight. It doesn't quite feel like it's mine. Ours.

The definite upgrade provides plenty of real estate for mattress gymnastics.

Can't complain about that.

"How much do you like that suit, Rogan?" I growl as I pounce on him.

"It's one of my favorites." He doesn't move to stop me from ripping it off him if I choose.

I can see why he prefers it. It's perfectly tailored to showcase his fine form. It makes him seem sharp, classy, and indomitable. One look at him and his competitors must run the other direction.

Not me.

"Then get it off before I tear it off." I sit on my heels and enjoy the show as he strips out of first his jacket and then his pants. When he unbuttons his shirt and peels it down his arms, my breath catches as always.

My straight-laced corporate king now has a hint of rebel badassery inked up his forearm.

It surprised me when he went through with it. Especially because he'd been so worried about what people would think of his cast. Now he didn't care who saw his tattoo. Hell, he often showed off my design. Even at fancy benefit dinners I escorted him to. My art would ride his skin for the rest of his life.

That was one hell of a commitment. A statement that

had touched me, while satisfying the sudden possessiveness I'd developed over him.

"Now undress me."

His cock continues to grow. He gets off on servicing me, nearly as much as I do on letting him. He crawls to me, naked, then eases my shirt up my torso. The entire time kissing, licking, and nibbling on the flesh he exposes.

Rogan was built to bring men pleasure. For some reason I'll never understand, I'm lucky enough to be the recipient of his talents. Night after night.

His skilled touches relax the part of me that was turned on by my accidental fantasy depiction even while they enflame the part of me that lives here, in reality, with my incredible lover.

I'm not sure when he finished removing my socks, the last thing I'd been wearing. Long enough ago that he's massaged my feet and calves and is progressing up my quads. I crash onto the mountain of silk pillows in an array of blues then tug on his hair until he skips to the good stuff.

Rogan blows me, employing every trick he's learned to please me best.

He reaches for my balls as I lift my hips to fuck deeper into the moist heat of his mouth. His fingers slip off target and nudge my ass instead.

I groan, a deep and feral sound.

He freezes and looks to me for permission, his mouth stuffed full of my now twice-as-hard cock. Although I don't explicitly grant it, I don't stop him either when he turns his accidental brush into a deliberate prod.

The tip of his finger rubs my hole. Strictly forbidden territory.

I'm on the verge of shooting, forcing him to drink me

down now that we've gotten our medical all-clears. I usually have much better self-control. What the hell is going on today?

When Rogan correctly reads my arousal, he proceeds nudging the barest bit inside my ass. And that's when everything goes to hell.

My cock wilts.

I hear Cortez in my mind, declaring that I could never go three years without something in my ass. Fuck him. I can and I almost have. I'm not going to break that streak now when I'm so close to proving him wrong.

"Stop." I grab Rogan's wrist, preventing him from impaling me.

"Sorry. I just thought..." He blushes. "You seemed to like it."

"Don't apologize." I loosen my grip, rubbing his poor arm where I'd abused it. I don't want to be like Ronaldo, lashing out for something my boyfriend isn't responsible for. "You didn't do anything wrong. I—changed my mind, that's all. I'm really not into it anymore."

"But you're still into blowjobs, right?" He distracts me from the uncomfortable situation I've landed us in by stroking me and licking my shaft until I regain my erection.

If I'm thinking of the times Cortez used to ride me hard and fast while Rogan sucks me off, that's not a sin, is it? What if they double-teamed me, forcing these rogue thoughts from my head so I could simply enjoy the effort they were putting into pleasuring me?

Oh shit.

"Rogan!" I hardly have time to warn him before my climax crashes over me. One tiny thought is enough to bring me down. Hard.

I throw my head back and shove my dick deeper, pouring jet after jet of come into his throat. I jerk and spurt until I'm sure my balls are completely empty. He drinks it all except for a dribble that overflows his eager mouth.

Even then he continues to suckle my spent cock, bathing it with his tongue until every bit of my seed is cleaned from me. "Fuck, yes. I needed that, Rogan."

He smiles then places one last kiss on the head of my dick. "I noticed."

"Roll onto your back." I shake my head, trying to sort out what just happened while I remember to take care of my guy. He hasn't come. His stiff cock is jabbing my hip.

"It's okay. You don't have to." Rogan smiles sheepishly up at me. "I kind of like going without sometimes. Knowing I pleased you without taking anything in return."

I pet his hair, not entirely comfortable with that. I respect his needs, though. And I recall feeling that way myself sometimes.

It will make his release twice as potent when I wake him with sweet morning loving tomorrow. I nod, then pull him to me, horrified to see my fingers shaking when I reach for him.

What the hell?

As if he can sense my discomfort, he snuggles in tight and lets me rub light circles on his back to soothe myself. After a long time, when his erection has finally faded and I'm floating in this mammoth bed, staring at the ceiling, he whispers, "Kaden? Are you still awake?"

"Yeah. Change your mind about that orgasm?"

"Nah. I was wondering..." He clears his throat, removing some of the extra-husky tone from his voice.

"What?" I put one finger beneath his chin and tip his face toward mine so I can see his expression better. "Go ahead. You can ask me anything."

"Are you starting to miss what Cortez gave you?" He squeezes my knee, which only makes me feel more like shit. Why is he so fucking compassionate? Why can't he get mad? Scream at me to forget that crap and learn to be satisfied with everything he gives me?

"No," I snap, trying to end this discussion before it begins.

Rogan has other plans. He sits up. I don't like him looking down at me, not while we're talking about this.

"Is the reason you won't let me play with your ass really because you're so stubborn that you took Cortez's parting shot as a challenge, or is it because you're afraid that if I do it and you like it, you'll need more? Things that I can't give you." Well that's obviously what *he's* worried about. Am I?

I should be. I'm not sure. It's...confusing. Frightening.

So I lash out. Because that's better than the alternative.

"You're not listening!" Oops. I didn't mean to yell. I also can't seem to stop shouting. "That part of me isn't unsatisfied, it's missing. Gone. I gave it to a guy who didn't give a shit and threw it away. It's destroyed. I can't ever get it back. Just like I'll never recover the part of my heart that belongs to you. I'm sorry it's not the whole thing, but it's everything I have left to give. You don't have to worry about me suddenly deciding I need a cock up my ass again tomorrow then going out to find one to do the job, but you'll have to be happy with the parts of my heart that are left, which are all I have to give you. I hope that can be enough."

My racket fades by the time I finish my speech, which drains my energy.

"Of course it is, Kaden." He kisses me then, comforting me.

I sigh against his parted lips and rub his cheek with my thumb. "Sometimes you're so fucking perfect I kind of hate you."

"Do you, really?" He swallows, then stares at me. "Because I'm pretty sure I love you. Don't flip out, okay?"

There it is. Out in the open. Where neither of us can deny it any longer.

I wrap him in my arms and hold him tight to my chest. The full weight of him rests on me, just like the responsibility of honoring his affection does. "I love you too, Rogan. Even if I shouldn't because I'm too fucked up to do it right."

"Let me be the judge of that." He kisses my jaw, then murmurs in my ear, "One more thing, and then I'll let it go for tonight. I promise. I love you for who you are. Not who you used to be. It scares me when I notice that you're not as settled as I am. And...honestly...sometimes it makes me feel like shit because it seems like you don't believe our life is good enough to blast the shadows from the dark corners of your mind."

"I know. I'm sorry." I deflate, miserable that I'm letting him down. "I'm working on it. That's the best I can do."

"Maybe we should see a counselor. Together." He bites his lip, as if unsure of how I'll react to that suggestion. "I'm afraid if we let these unresolved issues fester, we're not going to make it to our first anniversary. I'll do anything possible to make sure we celebrate that milestone and a lifetime more. Please. Let's get stronger together."

At first I don't say anything, because I can't. I'm overwhelmed by his generosity and patience.

He frowns, his face falling at the pregnant pause between us.

So I scrub my hands over my face and look directly into his eyes. "I'll do anything to keep you. Set it up."

He collapses against me and hugs me tight.

If we're both willing to fight, I have to believe we can make this work. Isn't that what a true partnership is— lifting each other up when one of us is struggling instead of letting us both fall together?

25

KADEN

The next morning, I decide to get up early and make breakfast in bed for Rogan. I'm pretty much never awake first. I usually roll over and find him ruling the universe from his laptop while lounging against our headboard. Sometimes he already has a tray of coffee and a bowl of my favorite cereal with fresh fruit set out for me. He's the best. Seriously.

Rogan deserves something special for putting up with me in general and double for weathering my temporary insanity last night, grounding me in the love we now officially share.

I can't believe he said it. And that I nearly fucked it up again.

I collect ingredients for pancakes, bacon, and eggs from the refrigerator, thinking I can always help him work up an appetite if I cook too much. Whipping the batter together, I flip on the bazillion-burner gas stove, jumping out of the way of the bonfire-worthy flame that shoots out of the professional-grade appliance. It's going to take a while to get used to the differences between my mini-cooktop and this beast.

After checking my reflection in the fancy stainless steel microwave mounted on the wall nearby to make sure I haven't singed my eyebrows, I tap into my creativity. Food coloring, a half-dozen squeeze bottles Rogan had insisted on buying for condiments we never use, and a couple of test runs later, I'm perfecting my pancake art game. This one is a multicolored heart with our initials in it.

Cheesy, yup. Do I care? Nope.

After a few more creations are stacked up and slathered with syrup—which I hope Rogan gets on himself so I can lick it off—I step away from the last two, which are finishing cooking. There's got to be a tray in here somewhere. Digging through the endless row of cabinets, I search for something to pile my edible masterpieces on.

When I peer into the very back of the corner cupboard, I notice a brown paper sack similar to the one Rogan brought the Chinese food home in the night before. What's that doing wedged between a toaster and a stand mixer in their never-before-opened boxes?

Curious, I peek inside.

What. The. Fuck.

It isn't some secret stash of fortune cookies or the gobs of duck sauce packets we never use. Does anyone, really?

No, it's fat stack upon fat stack of cold, hard, cash.

I slide the bag out of the cabinet and drop it on the table as fast as possible, as if I'm afraid to leave DNA evidence on it or some shit. We have a monstrous safe in our bedroom. Rogan insisted on it, along with a host of other security upgrades for my art, the shop proceeds, and times when he brings his business home with him.

So why the fuck is this here?

I use a spare chopstick lying next to the takeout menu on the table to poke the bills. They're fucking hundreds.

Dizzy, I stumble to a chair and sink into it.

As a former user, drugs are the first thing that comes to mind. Except if Rogan had a habit that required this kind of money, I'd know about it. You can't get that high and still function normally enough that your live-in lover could be oblivious to your addiction.

It takes me a few minutes of straight-up panic before I notice the corner of a manila envelope poking through the green bricks. What's that?

I pluck it from the paper bag and undo the brass clasp on the back.

There are photographs inside. Large, glossy, pictures of Rogan. Nude. Posing for me at the beach house.

"Son of a motherfucking bitch!"

I bolt to my feet, knocking the chair over, then whirl toward the bedroom, the damning images in hand. The smoke alarm chooses right then to go off since my forgotten pancakes are starting to char. Two seconds later, Rogan comes flying in, naked as he is in the photographs, nearly crashing into me as I march in that direction.

"What the hell?" We both shout at the same time.

When he sees what's clutched in my fist, and the dirty money scattered across our table, he stops dead. His face blanches. For a moment, I think he's about to pass out.

I should go to him, but I can't.

Instead, I drop the damning evidence on the floor and stomp over to the stove. I use a towel to grasp the griddle skillet and fling it into the enamel sink. I switch on the

JAYNE RYLON

hood fan then stand there, hands on hips, trying to decide if I'm angrier at Rogan for hiding whatever the fuck this is or at myself for taking those photos in the first place.

"It's Ronaldo, isn't it? He stole the memory card from my camera before he smashed it."

"Yes." At least Rogan doesn't bother denying it.

"How much is he blackmailing you for?" I should at least know the going rate for my work.

"Fifty-thousand, this time." He sounds like a stranger to me, his voice shredded and hollow.

"*This time*?" I spin around, waving a spatula like my mom used to when we were kids and had fucked up royally. "Have you paid him before?"

Rogan nods.

"How long has this been going on?" Do I know Rogan at all? Sure, he's submissive when it comes to sex. In other aspects of his life, not so much. I would have thought he'd crush Ronaldo like a fly. I don't get this. At all.

"About six weeks." He stares at our ruined breakfast, smoking in the sink.

My head throbs. I'm fairly sure I'm going to stroke out, right here and now. "Six *motherfucking* weeks? And you didn't think it was important to share that tidbit with me?"

"I'm sorry." He inches toward me. I step back. "I should have—"

I cut him off, uninterested in excuses. "You fucking hypocrite. You strong-armed me into opening up to you, being vulnerable and trusting you implicitly, but when you're threatened...fucking *blackmailed*...you didn't come to me! What kind of bullshit is that? I'm supposed to take care of you. You obviously think I'm incapable of it. Probably since this mess is my fault in the first place. I should never have left that camera behind with those

228

images in there. All I could think of was getting you the hell away from him."

My scalp burns as I yank on my hair. I can't believe I've been so irresponsible. I could cost Rogan his career. If those pictures leak...

I swore they wouldn't. I let him down.

He's going to leave me for it. He should have already. For some reason...he hasn't.

"Kaden, hang on. Please. You're not the one threatening me. You took those pictures with my permission, which is something Ronaldo can't say. He stole them. From us both." He shuffles closer. This time I don't retreat. *"That's* why I didn't tell you. I was afraid you'd blame yourself and...react badly."

Like I am right now. Shit. "Well, I can tell you that finding out you covered it up isn't improving my response to the situation."

He clasps his hands in front of him, bows his head, and takes my verbal lashing before simply saying, "I'm sorry."

The fight leaches from my core. This isn't about me.

He's the one in danger. Threatened by his ex. Again.

I cross to him and smother him in my arms. "Rogan. Shit. I'm going to fix this."

He hugs me back. Thank God. "I'd be lying if I said I'm not worried about Clearwater Industries and the impact this could have on business. But, I promise, I was way more worried about the impact it would have on you."

I smooth my hands down his back. "Never do that again. We're a team, right?"

"Right." He relaxes in my hold. "At least I look hot in the pictures."

"Damn straight you do." I stare at the one facing up on

the floor. "So quit paying Ronaldo. Who cares if the world sees how good I have it with you? Don't reward him for being a deplorable fuckface. Let's go after him. Have him arrested. Get rid of him for good. The right way."

Before Rogan can assure me that we'll take care of this together, permanently, a banging from upstairs startles me. It's coming from my old loft.

"What the fuck?" Immediately, I assume the worst. It's Ronaldo. Perfect. I have a few things I'd like to say to that dickhead. With my fists.

I look at Rogan, he looks at me. "Kaden, wait..."

Then I'm running, taking the spiral stairs two at a time. Rogan is a tiny bit slower, dashing toward our bedroom. Probably for some pants.

Another round of pounding rattles my backdoor. I flip open the locks and nearly rip the thing off its hinges. Except, instead of Ronaldo's disgusting mug staring back at me...

It's a ghost.

Cortez.

He blinks at me. I blink back at him, wondering if I created him as if I really am Pygmalion. Did he sprout from the ashes in the burning barrel overnight?

The entire world has gone insane. It's too much to process.

All I wanted this morning were some goddamn pretty pancakes and an epic fuck.

Instead I got a blackmail scandal, a massive fight, and the return of the other half of my soul, who could ruin everything I barely salvaged once today.

Fuck this. I'm going back to bed.

I slam the door in Cortez's face.

By now, Rogan has caught up to me. In fact, I assume

he got a glimpse at the man ramming his fist into my poor door some more. Twice as loud this time. While shouting for me to open up.

"Is that..." Rogan asks.

"Uh huh," I mumble as I stagger past like a zombie who's overdosed on brains. I wander to my old bed then curl up under the familiar, rumpled covers as if I'm five and it's a trusty hiding spot.

I can't even. I'm over it.

"Kaden?"

I don't answer.

"He's not going to go away until one of us talks to him."

I still don't answer. Instead, I fling my arm over my eyes and pray this has all been some insane nightmare. But when I count to ten and peek from beneath my biceps, I see light spilling from the cracked-open door and hear Rogan sternly telling Cortez this isn't a good time.

It will *never* be a good time.

The three of us are so fucked.

26

CORTEZ

Kaden is apparently still not much of a morning person.

Though it was only for an instant, and obviously not well received, it was so great to lay eyes on him, alive and well. For the most part.

Some of my anxiety about the Ronaldo incident I heard of months ago vanishes. A deeper worry sets in, though. I hardly recognized him. Shocked by how much he seemed to have aged while I was gone and how much... rougher...he looks, I wasn't able to say anything meaningful before he slammed the door in my face.

Oh no. That's not how this is going to go down. I fought too hard to be dismissed so summarily.

I have a lot to make up for and I plan to do precisely that.

I bruise my knuckles, knocking louder and louder. He will not ignore me.

To my surprise, the door actually reopens. This time, though, it's not the guy I've been waiting months and thousands of miles to see. It's a man with impeccable posture and superhero-quality abs. Thinly veiled hostility is etched into his sneer, and his hands are balled into fists.

One of them sports a tattoo that's drawn in a style I instantly recognize. Kaden's technique. This isn't some sleepover guest or a random pickup. Kaden is protective of his art. If he gave some to this guy to wear...

I'm jealous. He never drew me a tattoo. Why hadn't I thought to ask?

At least I'd have that part of him with me still.

There's an air of command surrounding the newcomer. His short-cropped chestnut hair and clean-shaven jaw contribute to his authoritative aura. In addition, he's handsome as fuck. Exactly the kind of guy Kaden would fall for.

Oh.

The man I'm in love with belongs to someone else. This guy.

Shit.

Why didn't I really consider that possibility? It's what I'd hoped for him when I left.

Maybe because I thought...like me...

It doesn't matter what I thought. It's clear I'm not welcome.

"Cortez?" Great, he knows who I am. That probably means he also knows what a loser I am and that I didn't treat Kaden with the respect he deserves. My biggest regret.

"Yeah. And you are?"

I don't expect him to answer such a direct inquiry without pushing back. He does, immediately. "Rogan Clearwater."

He doesn't tell me what his relationship is to Kaden. I'm too afraid to ask. "I need to talk to him. Give me five minutes. That's all I'm asking for."

"He's not interested in speaking to you." The guy spreads his legs and folds his arms over his chest. Even with the damage to my body, I could easily shove past him. But I won't. I appreciate his protective instincts.

"Is he happy?"

The guy gives a kneejerk nod, then hesitates the barest bit before saying, "Hell yes."

It's that glimmer of uncertainty that sparks my hope. I fish my wallet out of the back pocket of my jeans, then slip one of my brand-new business cards from it. "Here. In case he changes his mind."

At first I don't think Rogan is going to accept it.

"I'm not trying to poach. I just need to know he's okay. That's it. I swear."

And if he's not, I'm going to make things better for him. Rogan Clearwater isn't about to stand in my way. He grudgingly sticks out his hand. I drop the card into it, trying not to notice how sexy his long fingers are. Who has sexy fingers?

It's this place and even the barest glimpse of Kaden that have me thinking crazy shit. Plus the fact that I haven't had sex in far too long to be healthy.

Kaden fucks with my system. He's always had this effect on me. I'm never going to be free of it. It sucks that I'm too late. He's gone.

Lost to me.

Without another word of thanks, or parting, or anything, I limp down the metal stairs, hating that Kaden's new man witnesses my weakness. Despite the burn in my hip, and the needles stinging my fresh skin, I push on until I'm out of sight, around the corner of the building.

Only then do I sag against the bricks.

Now where am I going to find the strength to keep going?

And what's the point?

27

KADEN

It's late afternoon when I wake up. Rose and gold rays from the impending sunset filter into my loft. I reach out beside me. The sheets are cold.

Rogan isn't here with me. Neither is Cortez.

I'm alone again.

Will it always be this way? If I don't do something, I'm sure it will.

I sit on the edge of the bed—knees spread, elbows on my thighs—and cradle my head in my hands. Time to put on my big-boy boxers and figure this shit out.

When I trudge through my studio and into the main living area, the familiar tap of Rogan's fingers on his keyboard settles my queasy stomach. He's still here.

He looks up from whatever he's doing as soon as he senses my presence, and smiles. "Have I ever told you how handsome you are when you're sleepy?"

"No, but thanks." I kiss the top of his head then sprawl beside him on the comfy couch. "I'm sorry for bailing on you."

"It's no problem. I wish I could have joined you. There was too much to think about for me to doze off, though."

"It knocked me out. Ronaldo, the blackmail, Cortez. Being afraid of losing you then being reminded of how bad that hurts. Everything." I rub my chest. It doesn't do much to calm the tripping of my heart. I'm having some kind of palpitations. I tug Rogan toward me and tuck him against my side so I can put my arm around him. "What did he say to you?"

"Not much. But he gave me this and I've spent some time researching it." I'm coming to recognize that deceptively casual tone of his. It's like the one he used when breaking the news to me about his plans for this building. What is he up to now?

Rogan stretches over to the side table and grabs something. He holds it out to me.

"What's this?" I take the benign white rectangle and read it.

In simple navy text—not all that different from the font on the business card Rogan had once given me —*Santiago Cortez, Cortez Security Services* is printed, along with an email address and a phone number.

Rogan glances at me. "Looks like he only started it recently. The address on the company registry isn't too far from here. I'm thinking about—" He hesitates.

"What?" I stroke his shoulder. It bites that my inability to deal with this morning's chaos meant I couldn't be here for him after reaming him for not sharing his problems with me. Not one of my finer moments.

"Maybe I should hire a bodyguard." He swallows. "Until the Ronaldo situation is resolved."

It's hard to explain the rush of emotions that slams into me. Mostly relief. That someone far more capable than me will have Rogan's back. "That's a great idea. Get on it."

"So you wouldn't mind if Cortez did the job?"

"Wait. What?" I rear back. "I thought you meant seeing his card put the thought in your mind. Not that you were actually going to call *him*. I don't know about that."

My optimism was short-lived. Irrational fear dampens it. Will Rogan realize how much better Cortez is at taking the lead than I am if they spend too much quality time together?

A dash of jealousy is tossed in the mix too. What would it be like to catch up with Cortez? Have the perfect excuse to hang out all day, every day, for the foreseeable future. Rekindle our friendship, if nothing else.

I shake myself. None of that is important.

Rogan's safety comes first.

"You're right. It's dumb. I'll have my assistant set up some interviews. It's just that he seemed like he'd be really overqualified, if anything." Rogan sighs. "If I'm going to put my safety in someone else's hands, I would prefer they be ones we know and trust. Maybe he could recommend someone else?"

Why is he making sense? Damn him. I'd like nothing more than to dismiss the thought and move on to a risk-free alternative.

Except...he's right. I think back on the nights he walked me home after I'd had a few too many or whisked me out of a crowded party when the heat and crush became oppressive. Hell, once he even stopped a robbery at a convenience store we happened to be buying condoms at in the early morning hours then acted like it was nothing.

I never once doubted he'd protect me.

Rogan should have the best. That's Cortez.

What if we hire another company and something terrible happens? I'll always wonder if it was my insecurity that got Rogan hurt.

Fuck. There's nothing else to do. "No. You're right. It should be him. He won't let anything happen to you."

"So that means you still trust him." Rogan touches my cheek, drawing my attention to him. He's leaning in, peering into my eyes as if to be sure of my answer.

"To do his job? Keep people safe?" There's no denying it. Cortez prioritizes that above everything. Even love. "Yeah, without a doubt."

Would I trust him with my heart? Hell no.

"Then if it's not too weird, could you call him for me? I'd still like to meet with him first. To make sure it feels okay. Not weird. You know?" Rogan looks at me with his big brown eyes. How can I say no?

Assuming I can convince that selfish asshole to take the job.

"Fine." I reach out to Rogan, tugging him into my arms. "I must really love you to do this."

"I know." He kisses my neck, then sinks to his knees to show me his appreciation before I make up for leaving him hanging last night, and again for this morning.

28

KADEN

Why the hell did I tell Rogan I would do this? There has to be someone else. Anyone else.

Maybe I'll call Cortez and ask for a less personal recommendation. He's got to know some other qualified beefcake who'd make an excellent bodyguard for Rogan.

I would insist on that if I didn't believe Cortez was the right choice. He's familiar with Ronaldo. Didn't think much of him. And no matter how things ended up between us, he still cares for me. He wouldn't have stopped by if he didn't.

I'm not sure how I feel about that. I've been trying not to think about it, honestly. Except for one thing: Rogan is important to me. This means Cortez will make his safety a top priority.

It's fucked up, but it's true.

Cursing under my breath, I dial his new number. I can't decide if I love or hate that it's not the same one I have memorized. He's not the same person I used to text

241

dick pics to—hey, they were of the arty variety—every moment of the day. Neither of us are.

"Cortez Security."

"Um, hi."

"Kaden?" It's deathly quiet on the other end of the line. Is he even breathing?

I'm not. "Yup."

"Jesus. How are you?" He doesn't ask it casually, as in a typical phone greeting. It sounds more urgent than that. Like he expects me to be torn up. Over him?

"Perfectly fine. Amazing, actually." I fudge a teensy bit. What does he expect, for me to admit how long it took to pull my head out of my ass after he ditched me? Or how seeing him again yesterday for even an instant had triggered a lot of those old emotions, which are still bubbling to the surface? Screw that. "You met Rogan, didn't you?"

"Mmmhmm." You can say a lot with two hums. His are filled with appreciation, envy, annoyance, and regret. Score. "I've been building a file on your boyfriend. Do you have any idea how loaded he is?"

"Generally. Pretty damn loaded." I don't hold back. If it hurts Cortez to hear me say this, he deserves it. "I don't love him for his money."

"He's that good in bed, huh?" Cortez curses. "Don't answer that."

"Wasn't planning on it, asshole. Our private life is none of your business."

"Agreed. Don't go, okay? I was asking if you're all right because a while back I heard there was some kind of incident at the gallery with Ronaldo Pires. What the hell was that about? Were you tangled up with guys taking advantage of you before Rogan came into the picture? Did that jerk put his hands on you?" His anger fades then, leaving him sounding...weary. "I've been going crazy since they told me he hurt someone at your place. I tried to get to you sooner. I—I couldn't."

"Calm down, Cortez." His outpouring of information might not seem like much to someone who doesn't know him well. To me it proclaimed Cortez was nearly hysterical beneath the stony mask he's been trained to wear.

"Have you ever noticed that telling someone to calm down does everything *except* make them calmer?"

I try not to laugh. It's impossible. I've missed our banter and my uncanny ability to frustrate him. My mischievous streak used to adore toying with him until he forced me to behave.

Shit. Focus.

"Ronaldo is a steaming sack of shit. He didn't do anything to me directly, though." I clear my throat, wondering how much to disclose. Truth is, if he's going to protect Rogan, he needs to know it all. "It's Rogan he's bullying."

"So you're saying that Ronaldo broke *Rogan's* arm?" He pauses. "I'm confused. Were they fighting over you? Maybe that dumb fuck saw his chance after I left and came on to you or pressured you like he used to do to the guys at the club. Your new man wasn't having any of that. That's what happened, right?"

"Uh, no." Awkward. "Ronaldo and Rogan used to be a couple. Lived together and everything. For years. Even during those times we saw Captain Douchebag screwing around on Rogan with anyone naive enough to suck his cock or bend over for him at Romeo & Julian. And since Rogan caught on to his shenanigans and cut him off,

Ronaldo decided he doesn't like being poor very much. The incident in the alley behind our house...well, that's kind of related to why I'm calling."

"Sorry, Kaden, can you back up?" Cortez is speaking slowly. I can hear the gears in his mind turning. "Rogan and Ronaldo? How does that work? Seems like they'd tear each other apart."

"It's unwise for you to assume you know what went on in their bedroom. Or what happens in ours, for that matter. Rogan isn't what he looks like. He's a dedicated bottom, okay?" I snap, pissed that I have to divulge any of our secrets.

Pause.

"And you..."

"I don't kneel for anyone anymore."

Longer pause.

"Hang on. You top *that* guy? Are you shitting me?" His voice turns gruff. It reminds me of the times we used to jack off together over the phone.

"What, you think I'm not capable of it?" I'm equal parts irritated and worried. Sometimes I wonder if I'm worthy of Rogan's submission. Do I provide everything he needs? He hasn't complained yet, but it's relatively new to me, being on this side of the fence.

"I—uh—it caught me off guard, that's all. I have a very different picture of you in my mind." He practically purrs then. "Damn. That's hot as fuck, Kaden. I'd give my left nut to see you like that with your pet."

"Look, if we're not capable of keeping things professional, maybe you're not the person I need to be speaking with." I can't let anything he says soak in or it'll turn me on. And then I'll feel like I'm creeping around behind Rogan's back. Exactly what he fears most. I need to get him help then hang up the fucking phone before I ruin the best thing in my life. "Cortez?"

"Sorry, I'm trying to wipe my mind clean so I can concentrate on what you're saying."

At least that was honest. I could respect that. I'd be lying if I said it doesn't build me up to know I can still affect him.

So why did he throw me away?

Ugh. Who cares? "Anyway, I didn't call you to talk about me, us, or what we used to have. There is only one thing I want from you."

"Anything, Kaden."

"Apply for the personal security position Rogan is hiring for. Ronaldo is blackmailing him over some pictures I took and Rogan doesn't plan to give in to that piece of shit's demands anymore. I won't let him. This has to stop. Once and for all."

"Hang on. You want me to guard your boyfriend's ass for you? That's fucked up."

"Is it? You need a job, he needs protection from a dirtbag ex-boyfriend. I need to know he's safe. Can you do it or not?"

"I'm in. But just so you know...I've got some issues of my own."

"Will they interfere with guarding Rogan?"

He curses softly. "Probably not, but I do have kind of a bum leg. I'm on some heavy-duty pain medication for that and a bunch of burns that are still healing. Every day is better. So I'll try not to take it when I'm on the clock. Sometimes there's no other choice. In a really rough situation, it could matter. I'm not as fast as I used to be. But I'd take a bullet for him. Same as I would for you.

Things between you two must be serious or you wouldn't have reached out."

Do not let the distress in his voice make you feel bad about that! I caution myself.

"What happened?" I ask quietly before I can tell myself it doesn't matter. It *does* matter.

Despite how things ended up between us, I still care for him. Shit, love him. I've never lied to Rogan about my inability to sever our connection.

"Long story. Got blown up and toasted around the edges as a going away present at the end of my assignment. I'll be fine. I just thought you should know in case you want someone...undamaged. Nothing to worry about, okay?"

Ha! The three of us are more alike than different. Hell, maybe everyone on the planet is cracked and barely glued back together. Living is hard. The alternative is worse.

"I'm not sure I believe you. But, okay. For now. Even injured, I'm sure you can squash Ronaldo without breaking a sweat. Keep him away from Rogan. Please?"

"I will. I'll head over to his office right now. I won't let anything happen to your guy."

"Do whatever it takes to get that job. And...thank you."

"You're welcome. You know why? 'Cause it means you still trust me, Kaden. With the most important thing in your life." He sighs, then murmurs, "I still love you, too."

Well, it didn't take long for both Rogan and Cortez to see right through me.

That's the problem with being attracted to strong, intelligent guys.

"Fuck you. Don't let me down this time." I hang up on him.

I'm not as mad as I'd like to be about his audacity.

Those three tiny words still have the power to touch me. Something inside my core stirs as though it isn't actually dead but had only gone dormant when Cortez left me three years ago.

Uh oh.

29

ROGAN

TWO WEEKS LATER

How the hell am I supposed to concentrate when Santiago Cortez is like a vacuum, sucking the air out of my office, making me sweat? Sure, he's sitting quietly in the corner with his bad leg propped on an ottoman. Not interrupting. Not drawing undue attention to himself as he scrolls through news articles on his phone, but *damn*.

Kaden severely understated how fucking attractive the man is. The more I get to know him, the more appealing he becomes. Quietly confident, serious about taking care of me, and unexpectedly chivalrous. He opens every door we walk through, insists on carrying my briefcase despite his physical impairments, and has developed a habit of resting his hand on my lower back as he ushers me to and from the car, my office, and places I travel to for work. For my own safety, of course. Seriously, he doesn't do it in a pervy way. It's just the kind of man he is. It's part of his nature. Like submitting is part of mine.

No wonder he tamed my headstrong, willful, and not-at-all meek boyfriend. Whew. I fan my face with the folder of contracts in front of me.

Physically, Santiago is imposing. Fierce, solid, and sexy with those craggy features and "fuck off" vibe. A current of something deeper runs underneath that tough façade. He keeps it carefully dammed. I've seen ripples at the surface, though. Mostly when Kaden is around. Or when we trade stories about him.

I peek at him over the top of my monitor, imagining what I would have seen if I could have spied on him and Kaden getting it on. I loosen my tie and tug at the collar of my shirt before tapping the intercom button and asking my assistant to turn the air-conditioning on high for the third time today.

Santiago looks at me, one of his brows raised. "You're awfully hot-blooded. Why not take your jacket off? I won't tell."

I don't think Kaden would approve of me stripping in front of his ex. "I'm fine."

He shrugs, then rises, ambling to the full wall of windows that overlooks the city. He moves slowly to disguise the worst of his limp. Clasping his hands behind his back, he spreads his feet wide and stands super straight despite the taut patches of waxy skin visible on the back of his neck, the side of his face, his hands, and... well...pretty much everywhere.

Heaven help me.

The man is even more damaged than Kaden— spiritually, mentally, and physically. By now, we know how much that makes me want to love him. To fix him.

I'm going to have to come clean to Kaden tonight. Tell him we need to hire someone else. Anyone else. Because every day that I'm cooped up in here with the other man my boyfriend adores, I start to understand why.

"You plan on staring at my ass all day or getting some work done? The sooner you finish, the sooner you can go home to Kaden and occupy him appropriately. He tends to get into trouble with no one around to keep him in line."

I whip my gaze from Santiago's magnificent glutes to my spreadsheet. It's too late. He must have seen me gawking at him in the reflection of the window. Damn it. "Or the other way around, you mean?"

"Huh?" He angles his thick torso toward me so that he can stare at me directly.

"Kaden's a lot different now than he was when you left." I try not to hold it against him. It's tough not to be indignant on my boyfriend's behalf. This was the man who crushed his heart. Sent him into a tailspin that could easily have claimed his life. It's wrong to rub Santiago's face in what he sacrificed. Sometimes I can't help it anyway. "*He* keeps *me* very happily occupied when we're together."

"Sorry. I forget sometimes. It's a trip to watch you kick ass in your meetings, wringing more and more of your demands from your competitors. You're a tough negotiator. Hell, my old bosses could have used someone like you when we were dealing with bad guys." He squeezes his eyes closed for a moment, as if warding off terrible memories. "I think of Kaden as I knew him. That pairs up nicely with the side of you I see here. So it's hard to remember things are flipped at home. I didn't mean to insult you. I respect men who give everything to their lovers like that. Appreciate them."

I nod, accepting his apology. It would be impossible

not to when he's looking at me like a diabetic drooling over a gourmet triple-chocolate cake. No amount of air-conditioning is going to cool me off if he keeps staring at me, practically licking his lips.

"It must be such a relief for you." He wanders closer, perching on the edge of my desk.

Of course he gets it. "It is. Completely freeing. I don't have to strategize—debate what move to make next, muster bravado, or carefully weigh my options. I only have to respond and trust Kaden to take care of me. He knows what I need. Maybe because he needs it too. Or... used to, I mean."

"Wait, you think he still might?"

I don't answer. Where's the line between Kaden's confidence and Santiago's curiosity? If I don't talk through this with the one person who might be capable of understanding, maybe we'll never iron out enough wrinkles in our relationship to make it last.

"Rogan?" The command in Santiago's tone is absolute. The part of me that responds to direction stands at attention. My loyalty keeps me from divulging my suspicions. Stuck, I can't prevent my gaze from dropping to my folded hands when he scrutinizes me with that exceptional intensity that dominant guys have.

My reaction is instinct. Ingrained. Reflexive.

Answer enough for him.

"Holy shit." He shocks me by putting his fist beneath my chin and tipping my face toward him. "You really are lovely. Kaden has something special."

I feel exposed, naked in front of him, as he really sees me for the first time.

"Wow," he exclaims in awe. It's almost worth my embarrassment to catch him flatfooted. "I'm not trying to take advantage of your nature to dig into your personal life."

I don't back talk him. Nor do I believe him.

It's second nature for him to twist me up and discover my inner workings so that he can exploit those idiosyncrasies either to give pleasure or withhold it. "Not intentionally."

"We are who we are, right?" He shrugs, then staggers as he puts some distance between us. He settles onto the couch, stretching his arms out along its back and letting his legs fall wide open, as if his cock and balls are too big to be confined by a more polite set of his knees.

I can't speak. The room is spinning and I'm not sure what to do. I wish Kaden were here to tell me how to react. Reassure me I'm not doing anything wrong by having this frank conversation.

"I don't blame you for hating me," he says then. "Either of you guys."

"You broke him." The accusation flies out before I can swallow it.

"I know." He drops his head onto the tops of the cushions and stares at the ceiling. "For the record, I broke myself at the same time."

"You *don't* know. He fell into a horrible depression. Turned to drugs, alcohol, and reckless sex with pretty much every guy in the city to nurse his wounds." Every time I think about how he abused himself, I'm simultaneously furious and dismayed. And so damn glad he's still alive. "It took years for him to claw his way out of that hole. Even now, I'm not sure he's all the way there."

"Son of a bitch! What else was I supposed to do, Rogan?"

"Tell him you'd come back for him, no matter how

long it took."

"Are you kidding me? How could I promise that? Look at me!" He barks, making me flinch. "And this is just the stuff you can see. The invisible scars are a helluva lot worse. I can't walk down the street without checking over my shoulder. A can of coffee fell off the shelf at the grocery store yesterday. When it hit the ground with a bang, I nearly demolition derbied someone's granny with my cart. I envisioned smashing a glass jar and slicing her throat in self defense before I could convince myself I was safe in a neighborhood shop, where she wasn't actually some kind of nefarious secret agent wearing a gray wig and wire rimmed glasses as a disguise so she could end me. I didn't know if I'd ever come home or if I'd be suitable boyfriend material when I got here. I wasn't about to doom him to waiting indefinitely. At least this way he moved on and was free to love you."

Well.

Okay. The man has a point there.

As if talking about his injuries makes them throb, he rubs his hip.

"That really hurts, doesn't it?"

"Standing a few feet from an exploding bomb leaves an impression." He shrugs. "It could have been a lot worse. Believe me."

The unshielded agony in his stare nearly shoves my chair back. This is a side of him he doesn't show many people. Maybe no one, now that he's lost Kaden.

I can't ignore his suffering. It's not who I am, even if it means I might have some explaining to do to my boyfriend later.

Santiago is drawing me in, whether or not he means to.

"You lost someone that day...when you got hurt, I mean." I rise from my desk and join him on the sofa. I tuck one knee under me and sit sideways, my other foot still planted on the floor, so I can face him. "I'm sorry. Truly. Do you want to talk about it?"

"Haven't you realized by now, I'm not the chatty sort?"

Deflection isn't effective on me. Not after years of high-stakes deal making. "Too bad. I've been told I'm a good listener. I promise what you say will stay with me unless you give me permission to share."

"A persuasive fucker, too." He wipes his palm over his mouth. "I'm only telling you this because I want you to understand. I didn't hurt Kaden on accident. Or because I didn't care. I loved him. Not with a Hallmark card, once a year on Valentine's Day, flippant, throwaway sort of love either. I mean the kind that scorches because it's so bright and hot. Eternal. That's not a surprise to you, is it?"

I shake my head. Nor is it unfamiliar. He's describing exactly how I feel for Kaden. I imagine what it would be like if I had to give that up. For the first time, I pity Santiago as much as I do my own boyfriend.

"I can't tell you where I was or why. I'll say this. My cover story...I acted as a priest. The entire time I was gone, I lived that life. In every way."

My eyes grow wide as I consider how unsaintly Kaden was while they were apart. It seems like they went in opposite directions after their paths diverged. "Are you saying...?"

He grunts. "Yup. If it wasn't for my hand, my cock and balls would have fallen off from disuse by now."

The bulge of his package, which constantly distracts me, broadcasts that he's still in possession of his important parts.

"Anyway, my mission came to an abrupt end when some guys I'd pissed off blew up my church. My handler, the person who had been my only connection to the outside world for years...he didn't make it out."

I put my hand on Santiago's knee and squeeze, lightly enough not to cause him any more discomfort.

"If it wasn't for Kaden, I wouldn't have either. I'd just heard about the domestic violence incident at the gallery. I was scared something had happened to him and I wasn't there to save him. I realized as I dragged myself out of the burning building that my priorities were fucked up. I was never going to let the person I loved most be unprotected again. I spent every minute between then and the moment I knocked on your door in hospitals and rehab doing whatever the doctors told me was impossible to get back here and fulfill the promise I made to myself in that moment. So as much as this stuff hurts." He waves at his leg and the rest of his body. "It's nothing compared to the fear and regret I lived with. I'm so grateful you found each other. And that you take such good care of him."

Why does it suddenly seem like maybe I'm not doing what's best for Kaden by standing between him and Santiago?

My stomach churns. I've spent a lot of time worrying that Kaden will ditch me and go back to Cortez. Maybe he should. Am I being selfish by keeping him to myself?

"Oh no. Get that look off your face," Santiago snarls as he leans toward me. "I came clean. You can't use that as an excuse to find yourself lacking somehow. Whatever you're thinking, stop it. Right now."

Easy for him to say when he doesn't understand my concern. He confided in me. Can I do the same? I take a huge, shaky breath, then decide I need his advice.

"I'm only telling you this because I want to do right by Kaden as badly as you do." I bite my lip and fidget as I consider carefully what I'm about to divulge. Kaden will be livid if he finds out. Like Santiago said, if we love him we should do what's best for him despite the repercussions for ourselves. "Even though he slept around —a lot—he hasn't let a guy control him since you."

"I know, he told me."

I relax. I'm relieved to have the green light to discuss something that's been bugging me for a while. "So you think it's normal that he doesn't let me touch his ass and hasn't been fucked in three years? You don't think it's dysfunctional or that someday he'll snap and need those things again? Crave more than I can give? What if I'm not enough?"

Santiago doesn't respond. His chest rises and falls more rapidly as he absorbs my questions. His pupils dilate. "Ah, Rogan. He wasn't quite that explicit. That's...he never...? Really?"

Shit! I put my face in my hands.

"Hey, it's okay. Look at me." Disobeying is not an option. "I appreciate you leveling with me. I won't say anything. It makes perfect sense to be afraid of losing him. It's devastating." Santiago leans forward, staring at me. "But I'm telling you right now that he loves you every bit as much as he ever loved me. He wouldn't have asked me to guard you if he didn't. You leaving him 'for his own good' wouldn't solve your problems. Trust me. I've been there, done that, and don't want the T-shirt."

"So what do we do? What's best for him?"

"One thing that would probably help is if I get out of your hair and quit reminding him of how things used to be. If we force Ronaldo's hand, you won't need me anymore. Either of you. I'll disappear again, and you two can get back to normal without me interfering."

Isn't that what caused this issue in the first place? Although I'm not sure I agree with his assessment of what's best, the cowardly part of me that is still scared Kaden might leave me for Cortez doesn't object. I do agree that having Ronaldo hanging over my head is complicating matters and distracting me from what should be most important. Kaden.

"Why do I get the feeling you could have tracked down Ronaldo and put an end to this mess weeks ago?" I ask. I suspect Cortez hasn't enacted this plan earlier because then he'd have no reason to hang out here with me and, by proxy, would lose his connection to Kaden.

To be honest, I've known that all along. So why haven't I minded his company despite the fact that his presence also makes me nervous?

For the first time, he doesn't hold my stare. He looks away. "Because that's true. Except I don't think you'll like my plan very much. I didn't think you trusted me enough before to suggest it out of the blue."

"Try me."

"I recommend you leak the pictures yourself."

"*What?*"

"See what I mean?" Santiago chuckles. "Ronaldo's got them. I highly doubt he's going to toss them in a drawer and forget about them, digging them out only when he needs something to jerk off to. If he can't squeeze money from you anymore—and each day he fails makes it more apparent he can't—he's going to sell them to a gossip site. Guaranteed. Sure, you'll sue him and win whatever he hasn't blown in damages. But then you're right back at this point with a disgruntled ex who has more reason to despise you than before. So steal his power. Force him to lose his temper and do something rash. When he comes crawling out of wherever he's holed up to confront you, I'll take him down."

As a business executive, I often rely on experts. I've learned it's best to recruit someone who knows what they're doing onto my team and then take their advice. Otherwise, why bother wasting money on their services in the first place, right?

This is one of those times where I need to have faith that I've selected the right person for the post. Because I'm going to do it.

"You went really quiet." Santiago is peering at me nervously. "Are you about to kick me out?"

I laugh. "No. I'm trying to think of the best way to do this."

The gaze he levels at me then is full of heat and intensity. "Thank you for trusting me."

It's a little too intimate, reminds me too much of how a relationship with him might be in the bedroom. Extreme. Nothing held back. Risky. And worth the reward.

So I don't respond. Instead I start speaking out loud as I come up with a plan. "I have the login information for the backend of Kaden's website. I built his online shop. What if I use the photos to advertise for him? Draw attention to his art? He shot them. He deserves credit."

"Friendly advice? Be prepared for him to rip you a new one if you expose yourself for his benefit. But secretly, I think he'll love it." Santiago smiles. "He's proud of you—your accomplishments and how hot you are. You make him look like a stud."

In the midst of such a shitty situation, I never expected to find myself having fun.

It takes less than ten minutes for me to load the image and set a ridiculous, five-figure price for each of the one hundred limited edition prints I place into Kaden's inventory. It's not like anyone is going to want a life-sized picture of me hanging on their wall anyway.

To set things over the top, I prep a press release and email it to my usual contacts at the major news agencies. Same as any other big deal I announce to the media. They'll probably ignore it. If even one or two niche sites pick up the story, which we've spun as a "meet an up-and-coming artist's muse" piece, that will help.

It shouldn't take long for Ronaldo to realize he's screwed.

"I have a few other things I need to finish and then we can get out of here. An hour or two, tops. Okay?"

Santiago nods then returns to his post, settling into the chair in the corner. I have a whole new respect for him and I think he would say the same. Though it's difficult to concentrate at first, I lose myself in my regular business for a while.

Until a knock comes at my office door.

"Mr. Clearwater? I realize you've got your phone muted, but I need some direction on how to handle all these calls." My assistant pokes her head in my office. It's not like her to be sheepish. Still, she seems awfully interested in the carpet for some reason.

"It's fine. I'm about to wrap up. Who's calling?" I stand.

She clears her throat. No doubt about it. Something's going on. "Everyone, pretty much. You're going viral. Well...um...your photo is."

I glance at Santiago. He doesn't seem nearly as surprised as I am.

Our plan might have worked a little too well. Huh. "Give us a second, please?"

My assistant nods then hauls ass back to her desk. Probably to answer the phone, which I can now hear ringing off the hook.

Santiago glances out the window and curses. "The paps are swarming down there. Time to go, Rogan."

I collect my belongings, shoving everything into my briefcase without organizing it first. Right then, my personal cell starts to buzz in my pocket.

I grimace and answer it immediately. "Hey, Kaden."

"What the fuck, Rogan?"

"Sorry, I should have given you a heads up. I didn't think anyone would notice before I came home tonight and had time to tell you about the idea Santiago and I came up with to get rid of Ronaldo for good."

"*Santiago?*" he roars. "You mean Cortez? I should have known this was his fault. I don't care if he is practically one of the X-Men. I'm going to kick his ass when he drops you off."

"I can explain..."

"No, *he* will do the talking and take the heat for corrupting you. You were so adamant that those pictures not be seen by anyone except us when I took them. And now you're whoring yourself out to my customers. For what? I thought that's exactly what we were trying to avoid!"

"It looks like people noticed my press releases. That should be enough to accomplish our goal. We can take the photos down from your site before anyone buys one. Okay?"

"Too late!" His shout rattles my phone speaker.

"Ah, shit. I'll refund that person and explain the

261

situation. I'll offer them additional compensation so they don't leave your gallery a negative review or bad mouth you online." How else can I make this right?

"I don't give a fuck about that. I just don't want strangers staring at you if you're not comfortable with them knowing what a lucky bastard I am. You're *everywhere*. The entire world has seen you naked. And, by the way, we're not talking about a single customer here."

Dread settles in the pit of my stomach. Just how viral is viral, exactly? "We're not?"

"Seventy-two of the prints are claimed. Oh, wait, no. Three more orders have come in since we've been on the phone. These are going to sell out in the next hour. My online banking account is about to explode. I didn't even know there was room for seven digits in the balance field. It was the credit union's frantic call that tipped me off. They thought there was some kind of scam going on."

"Oh. Oops." There was no putting this cock back in the barn, so to speak.

"Can you please come home so we can figure this out? I...I don't like it. I feel like Ronaldo is going to be pissed and unpredictable. I don't like this at all."

"Of course. We're on our way." I clear my throat—better to say it now and give Kaden a chance to cool down before we get there. "And yes, that was the point. Bring things with Ronaldo to a head. So make sure you have the security system engaged and stay inside until we arrive, please."

"Cortez better hope he's wearing a cup. I'm going to knee him right in the balls when I see him. I swear I am."

"I love you, Kaden."

Grudgingly, he puts aside his fury for what's most important. "I love you too, even if you have earned yourself one hell of a spanking for this stunt. See you soon."

I slip my phone into my pocket. Santiago is already there, taking my briefcase and clasping my elbow. Before I can even give my assistant additional direction or help her out, he's hauling me toward the elevators and barking instructions.

I do exactly as he says.

We slip out a side entrance in the food services area of the building. I see now why he parks my car over here by the Dumpsters lately. Despite the short walk behind cover, we barely make it to the vehicle before we're spotted.

Santiago tucks me into the passenger side of my car then cuts a swath through the reporters mobbing the vehicle. Flashes blind me. They hurl yelled questions at us. So many, and so loud, I can't hear any of them clearly.

Before we're surrounded entirely, Santiago sternly warns the paparazzi not to stand in his way. I'd listen if I were them. Then he slides into the driver's seat and gets us the hell out of there.

It's quiet in the car as we escape.

"So Kaden's even more pissed at me now, huh?" His expression doesn't change. Still, I can tell it's another blow. One that pains him more than his physical injuries.

"I'll make things right with him."

He glances over at me somberly. "It's better if you don't. Let him give up on me."

We're on the highway, headed toward home, before I can manage to say, "Thank you, Santiago."

Instead of replying "you're welcome", he dodges the tough stuff again. Or at least he tries when he asks, "Are you ever going to call me Cortez?"

"Nope."

"Come on. It's a mouthful and it sounds weird. Only my mom calls me that."

"Your mom and me, I guess. Get used to it." It feels strange to speak so directly to him. I'm not budging on this one.

"Can I ask why?" He grips the steering wheel. Tight. Muscles knot along his cut arms.

"Because Cortez is the bastard who broke my boyfriend's heart. Santiago is a guy I consider a friend. I hope however this works out that you'll keep in touch. Not only for Kaden's sake, but for mine. With time, maybe things will get easier between us. I still think that's a better option than you vanishing again. Repeating your same mistake with him."

"Oh." He's pensive for a while. His only movements are his eyes flicking between the road and the rearview mirror. I'm sure I've finally pierced his armor when he breathes deep, then exhales in a long, shaky sigh that makes me wish I could hug him. "In that case, can I make a suggestion from one friend to another?"

"Why do I have a feeling I'm not going to like this?"

"Because you're not. But you're a reasonable man. So you'll take every precaution to ensure your safety so that Kaden doesn't have to go through losing another partner."

I groan. "Of course I will. Hell, I already flashed the entire world for him. What more can I do?"

"Now that Ronaldo has lost his only asset, he's temporarily more dangerous than before. It's imperative that we catch him before someone gets caught in the crossfire. Fortunately, I don't think it's going to take long before he makes his move. When he does, I'll get him. I promise you that."

I nod somberly. "I know you will."

"Rogan, I'm not saying this to make you feel guilty. Normal people don't think about things like I do. I've seen... Anyway, you know if Ronaldo comes after you, Kaden could easily become collateral damage."

The thought alone is enough to make me shiver. "Should I break up with him?"

"As much as I'd like to be selfish and encourage you to do something stupid like that so I can have another shot with him...no. Like I said before, I only care that he's happy, settled. That's all I've ever wanted. He is with you. But he also needs to be protected."

"What do you suggest?"

"Convince him to let me move in to your spare bedroom until this is over."

I laugh. Until I realize he's not joking. It's actually an order, one he expects me to obey.

"Son of a bitch." I squeeze the bridge of my nose between my thumb and forefinger.

"Yup. Right now, buddy, I'm glad he's your boyfriend and not mine. Good luck with that."

"How am I supposed to do this?"

"I recommend you butter him up with one hell of a blowjob first. Always worked for him when he'd done something to piss me off."

I knock my head against the car window, mostly to get that image out of my head before I spring a hard-on that would be difficult to explain to my already agitated boyfriend. Fortunately, when we arrive, he's too busy going off on Santiago to notice my lingering arousal.

How we navigate the next few days is going to make or break us.

Please let adversity be the force that fuses us together instead of the one that tears us apart.

30

KADEN

Rogan is snoring softly, crashed out in my arms.

Apparently he's not bothered by the fact that everyone on Earth is discussing his junk. He's already been declared the hottest man alive and the city's most eligible bachelor.

It also didn't faze him when I freaked the fuck out over the piles of undeserved money in my bank account. Instead, he suggested I trade the cash he'd earned by looking so sexy in exchange for this whole building. When I reluctantly agreed, he printed out one of his standard real estate contracts and made it official right there at our dinner table.

This place is now mine, free and clear.

He offered to do both, deed me the house and let me keep the money. He's nuts.

Of course I declined. He's already given me something more important than wealth. No matter what happens between us in the future, I'll never have to leave my home.

I'm embarrassed to admit that alleviated some anxiety

I hadn't realized was gnawing at me. I'm oddly relieved on that front.

Other fronts are an entirely different story.

How the hell am I supposed to sleep when I'm lying in bed with my boyfriend and the other love of my life is right down the hall, also under my roof? If Cortez is anything like he used to be, he's naked in between our fancy sheets.

I must have been temporarily insane to agree to this.

Except we all know Ronaldo is going to show his hand soon. He's too stupid and desperate to let this go now. I'd rather have Cortez as close as possible when the shit hits the fan.

Add to that the fact that my outwardly reserved lover showed his most private parts—quite literally—to anyone with an internet connection today, for me, and there's no possibility I can doze off.

I should go paint.

The only images that come to mind are ones I'm too afraid to put on canvas, though. Remarkably similar to the one I burned a few weeks ago. Having Cortez and Rogan around at the same time is pushing my libido into overload. I heave a huge sigh and prepare to suffer, restless and turned on, through the night.

"Can't sleep?" Rogan murmurs as he rouses and snuggles against me. He strokes my chest with his hand, my shoulder with his cheek, and my shin with his foot.

I run my fingers through his hair and hold him close. "I didn't mean to wake you. I can go out to the living room or my studio and leave you alone."

"Please don't." His fingers wander lower, toward my rigid cock.

I put my hand on top of his and trap it, keeping it from

reaching his destination. Has he forgotten Cortez is nearby? We're not the kind of guys who keep quiet while fucking. Although that could make for well-deserved payback. I'm still fuming at Cortez, even if my anger is unfounded. After I calmed down, I could admit his plan had some merit. God knows I could use an orgasm or twenty to release some of this nervous energy.

Maybe I'll gag Rogan. With my underwear. Even better.

I still owe him that spanking, too.

"Kaden, I'm so horny," he whispers.

"Hanging out with Cortez all day will do that to a man." I caress his back then cup his ass, squeezing so he knows I'm not upset. Denying my ex's sex appeal would be ridiculous. I avoid looking at him whenever possible so I won't develop inappropriate thoughts. "You want me to help? Fill this ass and make you come?"

He nods vigorously.

I chuckle. "Can you control yourself? Your moans?"

"Smother me with a pillow if you have to. I need it. You. Please."

I lift his lips to mine then sip from them, making sure he knows this is only naughty teasing, nothing serious. Then I say, "What if I don't? What if he hears how sweetly you beg and comes to help me take care of you?"

It surprises me when he trembles in my grasp. His dick is fully erect and stabbing me in the side. Sort of similar to how hard I am.

Except that's not quite the fantasy I have playing in my mind. I'd much rather Cortez use me and show Rogan how much we're really alike.

A spurt of precome trickles onto my belly.

Rogan runs his finger through the puddle, then sucks

on it. His strangled groan cuts through our hushed intimacy.

"What did I tell you about being quiet?" I pinch his ass.

He stiffens against me. Not for the right reasons. "Kaden, that wasn't me."

"Then who—?"

Another noise echoes down the hallway, this one more guttural and less easily confused with a sound born of pleasure.

We sit up at the same time, our blankets draping around our waists.

Before either of us can decide what to do, the groans morph into a wail. Then full-on, horror-movie-worthy screams. I never quite understood the term blood-curdling until now. It literally clumps in my veins as I listen to the audible expression of Cortez's fear and misery.

"Santiago!" Rogan comes to his senses first. He bolts from bed without pausing to put on a stitch of clothing. I chase after him.

Though I'm sure Cortez would never harm Rogan intentionally, he's obviously lost to reality. Rogan has no idea how strong Cortez really is. Or how lethal. I've seen him train. He could snap Rogan in half before he even knows what's coming.

"Wait, Rogan! Don't go in there!"

He doesn't listen. I swear to God I'm going to have him over my knee for this stunt later. He has no right putting himself in harm's way when I'm right here to take that chance for him.

In all fairness, he probably can't hear me over Cortez's curses, whimpers, grunts, and moans. His shrieks and crying. At least the screaming has died down. I'll never forget that sound as long as I live.

What the hell happened to him? What has he survived since he left me?

I'm starting to think I may have had it easy compared to him. *Son of a bitch!*

When I reach the guestroom and stumble across the threshold, Rogan is already reaching out. The instant his fingers land on Cortez's shoulder, he snaps to consciousness. He flies toward my well-meaning boyfriend. I fling myself in front of Rogan, taking the brunt of the impact.

Cortez hits me like a human battering ram. We roll across the floor and slam into something immovable. Before I can catch my breath, he's on his feet, pinning me to the wall that stopped our tumbling hard enough I'm sure my skull dents the brand-new sheetrock. It also has me seeing stars.

Far in the distance, Rogan shouts, "Santiago! Don't hurt him! It's Kaden. You're here, in his house. Where you used to live. Remember?"

Dazed and concentrating on hearing over the ringing in my ears, I don't react at first when Cortez plasters himself against me and groans. "Kaden?"

I can't answer after that because his mouth slams down over mine. On instinct, I react, sucking his tongue into my mouth the moment it probes for access. His hands fly over my body as if making sure I'm really here, and okay.

When his cock nudges my belly, I realize he's naked. I'm naked. Rogan's naked.

Fuck! Rogan!

I writhe in Cortez's unrelenting grasp, finally

dislodging his lips. I shout his name. "Stop! Get off me! I'm not yours anymore."

His hands open automatically. Instantly.

I slide down the wall and curl into a ball at his feet.

Rogan rushes over, skidding beside me on the floor. "Kaden, are you okay?"

I look up in time to see Cortez touching his mouth as if wondering what just happened. He blinks down at Rogan and me, huddled together, then reels backward. "Oh, fuck. Shit. Sorry. I'm sorry. I'll go. Sleep in the car. Something."

I glance at Rogan. He's staring at me.

Without exchanging a single word, we stand together. Shoulder to shoulder, we advance on Cortez.

"You're not going anywhere," I decree in my best in-command voice. Something Cortez has never heard before. Ironic, since I learned it from him.

Rogan nods along with me. "Except maybe out to the kitchen. I'll make us some hot chocolate."

Neither of us mention the cold sweat pouring off of Cortez—down his temples, his chest, his abs. It drips onto his legs. My god, his leg. Ragged purple scars stand out even against the blotches of fresh pink skin left by extensive burns.

He's been through hell.

And managed to come back out.

For me? The look in his eyes says it all. What are we going to do?

I panic, sucking in huge lungfuls of air so I don't pass out from shock or bliss or shame or embarrassment. Rogan and Cortez are both scrutinizing me. When I turn away from them and rest my palms on the dresser, my gaze lands on a framed drawing I instantly recognize. It's the one I stuffed in Cortez's duffle after I'd talked to his handler, and before our final romp goodbye.

He kept it.

Treasured it.

Brought it with him tonight.

I finally thought I'd reconstructed my life. It's being blown apart again as obviously as Cortez's has been. Rogan approaches, slipping his hand into mine. It's clammy and tense.

When he turns me around and leads me toward the door, I can't help but see Cortez. He's slumped on the bed, also staring at the drawing.

We're a mess.

Rogan speaks first. "Time out, guys. Let's take a breather. Five minutes. When everyone's composed themselves, I think it's about time we talked."

For the man who's the most submissive person in the room, he doesn't do a bad job of taking charge. Can Cortez and I be as brave or honorable as he is?

Doubtful.

I guess we're about to find out.

31

ROGAN

The splash of the shower running in Santiago's room soothes me as I watch bubbles begin to gather on the bottom of the cobalt blue glass kettle I bought for our new kitchen. It's masculine yet beautiful. Like Kaden, who is sitting at the table in a pair of boxer-briefs. He's staring at me as intently as I'm gazing at the water, waiting for it to erupt into a vigorous boil.

Sort of like us.

The pockets of worry and restlessness have been accumulating for a while now, growing larger and more frequent, especially since Santiago reappeared. I'm ready for them to rise to the surface and burst. Hopefully without any of us getting scalded.

Seems like a long shot.

"What exactly are we supposed to discuss?" Kaden asks. "Is there really anything good that can come of including Cortez when we hash things out?"

"Maybe." I try to keep it from sounding like an accusation when I say, "You're not happy."

"I *am*. If you'd seen me a year ago, you'd know how far

I've come. Just because I'm not whistling and skipping all damn day doesn't mean I'm struggling or depressed or some shit."

"Okay, you're not completely satisfied, then. I can tell." It's time to be honest, even with myself. "You mumble about Cortez in your sleep. I can even see the difference in your paintings. They're darker lately. Angsty. If something doesn't change, I'm going to lose you."

"You're not. I swear."

I shake my head. "Then I'll walk away. I won't let you live half alive."

"You'd rather I was destroyed entirely? Because that's what it would do if you leave me. I thought you got that. Thanks a fucking lot, Rogan." He shoves back from the table, preparing to storm out.

"Hey, wait." I touch his shoulder lightly, urging him to remain seated. When he does, I sit in his lap and absorb the heat of his arms, which instantly slide around my waist. "I'm worried, okay? That your old urges are starting to resurface. Or could eventually. Maybe you'll find someone else and cave when I'm not around. Or maybe…I don't know. I think this could be a chance for you to get what you need without going behind my back or making yourself do without."

"Wait, *what* could be?"

I peer up at him from beneath lowered lashes. "A threesome with Santiago."

"Jesus." This time he does stand. Quick enough that he nearly dumps me onto the floor.

We face each other. I take his hands in mine. "You told me you still love him, Kaden."

"So what? That doesn't mean I like him. Or respect him. Or trust him." He breaks away and kicks the garbage can halfway across the room. "Sometimes love isn't enough."

"That's exactly what I'm afraid of." I put my fingers on his elbow, turning him to face me again. "There's part of you that still needs him. And if we don't take advantage of this situation, maybe the fact that I'm crazy in love with you isn't going to be enough to keep you."

"And what about you? What would you get out of it? Wouldn't it be awkward?"

"Nah. I mean, Cortez is smoking hot. Watching the two of you together..." I hum. "I could get into that."

"Seriously?" He narrows his eyes, seeing right into me, as usual. "Is that all it is? What exactly have you two been doing all day at the office?"

"Not cheating on you, if that's what you're implying." This time it's me that tries to recoil. He doesn't let me go.

"Maybe not, but I'm pretty sure a hot dog didn't fall into your shorts while you were getting the milk out of the refrigerator."

I glance down. Damn it. "I can't help it if you two are sexy."

"So you're attracted to him, too?" Kaden wonders. "I mean, I don't blame you. He's...yeah."

I can't ask him to bare his deepest secrets without doing the same. "You're right. I've gotten to know him over the past few weeks and I'm definitely interested in taking things farther."

"Have you ever slept with multiple guys at once before?"

"No." I can't believe this is an actual discussion we're having. "I've seen porn where guys are gangbanged. And got off on it."

Kaden leans in and kisses my flushed cheek. "You're

adorable. I'm telling you right now, as someone who's been fucked by Cortez, that it would be nothing like those stroke movies you watched. It would be much more intense and personal. But…"

"What?" I stretch up for a real kiss this time. It comforts me to know his affection hasn't dimmed after everything that's gone on today.

"Will you remember who you belong to? You're mine. I won't let Cortez steal you away. He taught me everything I know. He could blow your mind without trying. Mine too, for that matter."

"I'll never forget that I'm yours."

"Good. And about me bottoming…"

"What about it?" I blink up at him.

"Will it make you think less of me to see me submit?"

"I should punch you in the gut for that." I scowl.

"What? It's a serious fucking question." He tries to hug me. I slap his hands away.

"Do *you* think less of *me* because I bend over for you?"

"Rogan, of course not." He grabs me then and draws me to him for another kiss. This one communicates exactly how much he cherishes and adores me.

A little breathless, I look into his eyes and say, "So don't be a dumbass. Of course it wouldn't change how I see you, how things are when you're alone with me."

I can see his throat working as he tries to speak around the knot that must be lodged there.

"All I'm asking is for you to think about it. Okay?" I lay my forehead on his shoulder. "Let's see what Santiago thinks."

His arms wrap around me, squeezing me tight. He rocks with me as if he's putting me to bed.

Kaden whispers into my hair, "Okay. For you."

"For *us*. We're not going to make it unless something changes. That scares me more than anything."

"For us, then."

"Why do you two look like you're in the middle of something steamy?" Santiago asks from the hallway as though he might turn around and leave if we tell him he's interrupting.

"Because Rogan's trying to talk me into double-teaming you." Kaden probably could have picked a more suave method of delivering that message. I had to give it to him, though, it's fast and effective. Gets the point across before either of us can chicken out.

"You're *what*?" Santiago whips his stare to me.

I shrug. "Is it the worst idea you've ever heard?"

"Because I'm a selfish fucker who'd love to sleep with you both, no. For you guys and your relationship, it's got to be right up there." He glowers. "This isn't a game. I'm not a pawn who'll be responsible for fucking up your chances of winning at life together. Maybe I should go back to bed."

None of us believe he'll be sleeping anymore tonight.

Those perpetual sooty smudges under his eyes make a lot more sense now.

I leave Kaden's side, pour steaming water into a mug, add a handful of marshmallows, and a squirt of whipped cream that I can think of much better uses for. Because sweet, sticky sex makes everything better, right?

When I look up, he's still standing there. So is Kaden.

"We won't bite," I can't resist joking.

Santiago shuffles closer. He and Kaden take seats opposite each other at the table. I carry two mugs over and set one in front of each guy at the same time, then make a second trip for my own drink.

"I could add some bourbon if you guys prefer." I pause before returning.

Kaden shakes his head. "You know I stay away from the harder stuff these days."

"No thanks. Not with Ronaldo on the loose," Santiago reminds me that this slumber party isn't only for the hell of it. On second thought, I grab the bottle out of the liquor cabinet and add a splash to my own mug to dull the repercussions of my poor choices in men.

Hopefully I'm not making another enormous mistake tonight.

As if he realizes he needs to distract me from the past, Santiago asks Kaden, "Out of curiosity, what were you saying to your boy's proposal?"

"That I need to sleep on it. I think he's crazy. But he might also be right." Kaden takes a long drink of his hot chocolate, probably also rethinking that bourbon. Then he clears his throat and wipes the froth from his upper lip. Both Santiago and I are riveted to the motion. "Maybe I think about being topped from time to time. Unfortunately, my stupid ass won't yield to anyone except you."

Santiago's nostrils flare and his eyes turn glassy. "I'm so sorry I let you down, Kaden. I never should have gotten involved with you knowing I was obligated to the government. But...I met you and I couldn't resist."

"I did come on to you pretty strong. And I'm pretty fucking awesome. So, you know, I forgive you."

Damn. I hadn't expected that. I rush back to the table and sit between them, taking one of each of their hands in mine. I link them together since they're too stubborn and marred to do it themselves.

"You do?" Santiago's fingers shake in mine.

"Yeah. But if you do one single thing to hurt Rogan, that'll be it. There's no second chances when it comes to him. Do you understand?"

"Absolutely." Santiago nods. "He really is one hell of a man."

"You haven't even seen how good of a cocksucker he is yet." Kaden's eyes roll back.

Is it fucked up that I'm smug over his crass compliment?

Nah, not when he's trying to entice his ex-lover to become my lover, too.

I think it's working. Santiago brushes his thumb over the inside of my wrist, then releases me somewhat reluctantly, judging by the trailing of his fingertips over my skin. He wraps his big hands around his mug as if to help keep them to himself. "You two should go back to bed. I'm okay now. Going to stay up and watch the monitors for a while. Call in a few favors from guys I've worked with before."

"At this time of night?" Kaden wonders.

"It's not exactly a nine-to-five job." He chuckles, though it's the sort without much humor.

"Thanks for taking such good care of Rogan. I really do appreciate it," Kaden says.

Santiago nods. "You're welcome."

"Goodnight." I have an urge to kiss his cheek when I say it. I don't.

As we drift toward the hallway, he calls softly, "You guys think hard. If you decide a ménage is really what's best for you as a couple, you know I'm in. I could never say no to you."

This time, when we return to our bed, there are no more disturbances. I spend an hour or two really considering the ramifications of a fuckfest with Santiago and Kaden. The more I visualize it, the more I can only see the positives. Like how incredible it would be to suck both their cocks at the same time, or to be fucked by Kaden while Santiago watches.

"I guess I know what your final answer is," Kaden murmurs sleepily at some point. "You're about to poke a hole in me with that thing."

"Uh, sorry." I attempt to shift, angling my hips away from him.

He doesn't let me go. Instead, Kaden takes my hand and uses it to cover his equally hard cock. He doesn't allow me to stroke him or grant him any relief. He makes it clear he's into it, too.

"You're right, Rogan." He kisses me softly. "If we don't get a handle on whatever this is, we're going to spiral out of control. For you, for Cortez, and mostly for myself...I'm going to do it. Bring on the wild monkey sex."

"Tomorrow just got a lot more interesting." I'm nervous and excited at once.

Even still, I'm more peaceful than I've been in a while. Because if Kaden and I can work through this, we can work through anything.

"Rest up. You're going to need to be at the top of your game tomorrow." Kaden kisses my forehead like he does every night before bed.

"I promise I'll live up to your bragging."

"No doubt in my mind." He holds me close as our breathing shallows out.

Eventually I slip into a dreamless, rejuvenating slumber.

So do the other two men in our house.

32

KADEN

The next morning I lock eyes with Rogan, then take his hand in mine. After another quick double-check, I'm sure. We're in complete agreement.

Foolish or not, we're leaping together.

He squeezes my fingers and nods. So I clear my throat and yell, "Cortez!"

His slightly uneven gait is still fast as fuck as he dashes into our bedroom, gun drawn, and scans the area.

"Whoa. Sorry, didn't mean to alarm you." I put my hands up as if he's going to arrest me. Does he own handcuffs? Hmm...a question for another time. "Could you put that away? It's not the weapon we're interested in checking out right now."

"What's this about? I didn't get the No-Pants Saturday memo. Don't the two of you own any clothes?" He engages the safety on his gun, then tucks it into the holster at his hip. He's wearing jeans sans a shirt. The gorgeous sculpted chest I used to know so well is pocked with scars.

He's still handsome as ever, and seems even stronger now that I know how much he can endure.

I hope for an hour or two we can soothe his pain.

Cortez flicks his greedy stare between Rogan and me. Our nude bodies and stiff cocks are on display. For him.

As if our dicks are the world's flashiest lures and he's a powerful marlin, we reel him in. He stalks closer to the bed step by step. When he's no more than two feet in front of us, I let him off the hook. "It's pretty obvious to us both that there are unresolved emotions lingering between you and me, plus a new attraction blossoming between you and Rogan. We decided it's best not to waste this chance to get it out of our systems. He's mine. And for today at least, I'm yours again. So use us wisely."

"Are you sure?" He doesn't pounce immediately. "There's no taking this back. What if I screw up what's between you?"

"I guess we'll figure it out if that happens." I bite my lip and look at Rogan. He's smiling softly, reassuring me.

Still, Cortez doesn't advance. "So this is, what? An isolated hook up, right? One last fuck—spiced up by Rogan—so you and I can both move on?"

"I guess." I shrug. My gut says a single taste might not be enough to satisfy my appetite. But what exactly did Rogan sign up for?

We probably should have been more explicit about that in our discussion. I haven't even thought beyond what it will feel like to be sandwiched between him and Cortez. After that, my ability to reason pretty much evaporated.

"So are you going to get it on with us or not?" I mash Cortez's buttons with everything I have. If he walks away now, it will devastate me. Again. "If you've got better things to do this morning, I'll find someone else. I'm not going to disappoint Rogan now that he's decided to experiment with being naughty."

Cortez shoots us a wry smile. "Same insubordinate Kaden, I see. I should be a better man and turn you two idiots away before you fuck yourselves up."

Rogan opens his mouth as if to argue. One stern look from Cortez has him shutting it with a click of his teeth. Unleashed, Cortez is even more glorious than I remembered. Though it might not seem like it if you didn't know him like I do, he's been keeping his bossy tendencies under wraps. Hopefully Rogan is ready for Cortez set on full blast.

"Don't worry, I can't. I'm going to help you remember your manners and how to show a man some respect instead." He leans in, snatches a fistful of my hair then yanks me to my feet, hauling me toward the area rug that softens the hardwood floor. "Let's go, Rogan. Get over here. Now."

He hesitates until I second the order. "Rogan, come."

I scramble to keep up with Cortez. Even his bum leg doesn't slow him down. Not when he's this determined. Fortunately, we aren't going far. By the time my knees hit the carpet, Rogan is there beside me. He lends me his strength, making it possible for me to stay where Cortez put me instead of bolting.

Cortez removes his holster and sets his gun carefully aside. Then he turns back to us. "Why am I still wearing these jeans?"

Rogan looks at me. "Should I?"

"No, I've got this." I'm not going to lie; I can't wait to touch Cortez again. It's my right, my *duty*, to undress him. So I tuck my fingers in his waistband then undo his fly carefully since he always goes commando and his cock is already rock solid, mashed up against the front of his pants.

Before I can do more, Cortez shoves them to his ankles, then kicks them into the corner. He stands tall before us, completely nude. His scars fade from my sight as I see the man beneath. The one I've been missing for years.

Beside me, Rogan hums in appreciation when Cortez's big, thick cock is unveiled. It's impressive, I'll give him that. I've seen enough of them in the past year to know he's far above average.

"Maybe next time." Cortez smiles warmly at Rogan and ruffles his hair before looking at me. "You're about to be sucking my cock for a while. If you'd like to give your boy something to occupy himself with while you're busy, now would be a good time."

Fuck yes. "Rogan, lie down. Get on your stomach between his feet. Put your mouth on me. Show him how good you are at bringing me pleasure."

I've hardly finished speaking when he crawls between my knees. They're spread as I sit on my haunches. His lithe body stretches out between Cortez's legs and behind him on the plush rug Rogan handpicked for our personal retreat. I'm torn between staring at his pert ass and Cortez's cock. It's hard to figure out which is a greater temptation.

Cortez reaches down and cups the back of my head. "You better watch those teeth. Just because he's doing a damn fine job blowing you doesn't mean I'll excuse you if you bite me. Understand?"

I nod.

"Then tell him to start," Cortez orders.

I look at Rogan, who's staring up at me from beneath his thick onyx lashes. "Go ahead."

When he takes just the tip in his mouth and swirls his tongue around it, I slam my eyes closed. The pressure of Cortez's hand on my head while Rogan begins to take me deeper is enough to make me sure this is going to be a day I'll never forget.

It's like an electric current is running between us. The sparks have always been there but now that both of these men, who light me up so much individually, are touching me at the same time, the circuit is complete. I twitch and spasm as if I stuck my finger in a socket instead of my dick in Rogan's very willing mouth.

Cortez returns my attention to him with a light slap on my cheek. "Open wide. Careful, remember?"

I nod then drop my jaw, waiting for the moment he thrusts inside me for the first time in years. He's nothing like Rogan, who's progressing down my length with steady, gentle suction.

No, Cortez sets his cock against my lips then drives in, feeding me his entire length at once. I choke, unable to even gasp around his fat shaft. My eyes water and I look up. Just when I'm about to panic, he holds my head steady and withdraws. A strand of saliva stretches from his dick to my lips as he permits me to breathe before repeating the motion.

I never thought I'd taste him again. The zest of his skin makes me moan.

It's like waiting all year for that first scoop of ice cream from a seasonal concession stand. Even better because I thought my favorite flavor had been discontinued.

If my eyes grow damp at the corners, he lets me pretend it's because he's harsh, exploiting me like I'm not used to anymore. It could be overwhelming if it wasn't for Rogan and the pleasure he gives me. It mellows Cortez's coarseness and comforts me at the same time.

I could do this forever.

Recovered from my abrupt reintroduction to Cortez's cock, instincts begin to take over. I relax, allowing him to tunnel deeper into my mouth, prodding and slipping into my throat.

When I suck Rogan, it's nothing like this. I'm not giving Cortez a blowjob, he's fucking my face.

And I love it.

I put my hands on the backs of his thighs, bracing myself while trying to pull him closer.

"Hands at your sides!" he shouts. "Or I'll take my dick away from you and give it to Rogan. I swear I will."

I drop them so fast they slap my hips. Was it because of the ruined flesh I'd felt beneath my fingers that he reacted so strongly? There's a lot of healing left to do. For us all.

I raise my gaze to his and am surprised to see it bursting with affection. The taut muscles of his abs and thighs tell me how much he's holding back. Maybe it's too much for him, having me touch him. Could this mean as much to him as it does to me?

Being together again, like this? The impossible is happening.

Rogan purrs as he laves me, suckling and bobbing like a champ. His ass tenses and releases as he humps the floor, rubbing himself on that ultra-soft rug.

"Does he need you?" Cortez asks me. I nod, bouncing my mouth on his cock even as I confirm his suspicions. "All right then. Put on a show for me. Let me see how dirty you are when I'm not around."

Cortez whips his cock from between my lips, making me sigh at the loss. He wraps his hand around my arm and lifts, practically making me levitate. The motion tugs my erection from Rogan's mouth. He whines in protest.

"Shh, I'm going to take care of you," I promise him as Cortez steadies me.

"Where do you want him?" Cortez asks.

"On his back on the bed."

Without straining, he scoops Rogan into his arms and delivers him on top of the rumpled covers for me. Whatever physical limitations he has, he's determined to prove they don't hinder him here or anywhere else.

Rogan practically swoons. I don't blame him one bit.

Nor do I let him cool down.

The instant Cortez removes his hands from my boyfriend, I'm on him. I crush my mouth to Rogan's and show him how glad I am to be sharing this experience with him. He amplifies my excitement and joy. The enthusiasm with which he returns my kiss makes me sure he's on the same page. I have to make it even better for him.

I glance at Cortez. "Will you do me a favor?"

"Does it involve driving him wild?" He jerks his chin at Rogan, who's pretty much a puddle of blissful goo at this point. I nod. "Sure. What do you need?"

"Hold his legs up for me. I'm going to prep him well. I have a feeling we're going to be rougher than he's used to when I fuck him." Because we all know that's where this is going.

Cortez gives me a wicked smile. "You're so good at being nasty, Kaden. I love that about you."

"Thanks," I bow my head accepting his praise, then kneel beside the bed. Rogan's ass is on the edge of the

JAYNE RYLON

mattress, his legs dangling off the side. I grab his calves and lift so that his feet are propped on my shoulders.

Cortez climbs onto the bed—with one foot on either side of Rogan's arms, facing me—then squats. The position dangles his balls right in front of Rogan's face.

Rogan shivers in my grip.

"You want to lick them, don't you?" I murmur as Cortez runs his hands along the tops of Rogan's thighs up to his knees. He realizes what I have planned.

Rogan bucks and cries, "Yes! Please."

"Should I put a pillow under his head?" Cortez hesitates with a hand hovering over one. He's waiting for my authorization to do what comes naturally to him, because he knows as well as I do that Rogan is mine.

"Yes. Do it."

Cortez twists, and Rogan leans forward. Cortez jams the extra-fluffy pillow beneath him. With it supporting his neck, Cortez's balls rest on Rogan's mouth, maybe even covering his nose. He doesn't complain about struggling to take a breath around the warm, creased skin of Cortez's sac.

Instead, he uses his lips and tongue to spoil Cortez.

"Ah, fuck," Cortez growls. "You better reward this boy. He's so fucking excellent at that."

"I told you." I grin up at him, then gesture to Rogan's ankles. "Hold them for me, please. High."

He does, bending Rogan in half. His ankles are now somewhere near Cortez's pecs. That gives me plenty of room to dive in and eat his ass.

I'm not gentle about it. The point here is to get him as wet and hot as possible.

I'm sure that by the time I have my cock embedded in him, I'm going to be too worked up to ensure it's a gentle possession. He needs to be ready. So I lick him, spit on him, and prod him with my tongue. When even that is insufficient, I use the lube from our bedside table to coat my fingers and begin to pry him open.

Cortez and Rogan are grunting and moaning in chorus. With Rogan's talented mouth weaving its magic and my fingers spreading Rogan apart, we're pushing the limits. I sneak one hand up and pump Rogan a few times. Not too much. He won't last if I start jerking him more regularly. And I don't want this to be over.

Not so soon.

Maybe not ever.

"Enough," Cortez growls. "This is torture. Time to get serious. Fuck him, Kaden. Bury yourself in that tight ass so I can fuck yours. You know you want that. You in him and me in you. All of us fucking together."

He's right, I do. I have for so long.

Even before I was ready to admit it to myself.

Rogan is writhing beneath us, definitely not opposed to that plan. So I stand up and walk forward until my dick is nudging Rogan's hole. That puts my face even with Cortez's. He stares straight into my eyes and says, "Kiss me, Kaden. Kiss me while you invade his body."

Oh shit. How will I stand this?

I do as he commands. Advancing my cock into Rogan with small jabs that help me penetrate his grasping ring of muscles. Meanwhile, I set my lips against Cortez's and surrender to him. It feels like coming home after a long trip.

I've missed him so much. The emptiness I've carried within me for so long begins to fill with passion and devotion.

He wraps one hand around the back of my neck,

trapping me there while the other still holds Rogan's leg up. Rogan is moaning and shoving his ass toward me, encouraging me to slide in deeper.

I never knew multitasking could be so rewarding.

When I'm lodged entirely in Rogan, Cortez pulls away. He stares at the place where I'm joined with Rogan, then runs the tip of his index finger along the seam between our bodies. "That's so hot, Kaden. Do a good job. Fuck him right and I'll do the same to you."

My cock jerks inside Rogan, making him cry out. Cortez climbs off the bed and circles around behind me. He appraises my motions as I fuck. Encourages me when I lean forward and kiss the shit out of my boyfriend, who takes it so well.

Rogan's dick bounces off of my abs as I pound into him. The stroking of my muscles over his erection could set him off. Lust hazes his eyes, making them darker than usual.

While I'm distracted, Cortez is doing some prep of his own. Soon the slick glide of his thick shaft between my cheeks brings back steamy memories. Holy shit. It's been an eternity since I've experienced the weight and heat of a cock there. I almost forgot how much the anticipation caused by that weight in my crack could turn me on.

My dick gets even harder in Rogan's ass.

"You always did love my cock. Didn't you, Kaden?" Cortez is there, running his hands all over me. My arms, sides, neck, face. He inserts his thumb in my mouth, and I suck it as I keep pumping my hips. I swear I could shoot my load any second. But I don't.

Because this is too good to stop. And honestly, I think I can't without his permission.

One day with him back in my bed and I'm right there,

where I used to be, refusing to surrender to rapture until he gives me the go-ahead. It's ingrained.

"Yes. Fuck me, please."

He tucks the head of his cock deeper and I hesitate. Is it going to hurt much? I don't care. I need it anyway. I look over my shoulder at him and confess, "I haven't done this since the day you left."

"Are you asking me to go easy on you?" He runs his hand over my flank.

"Shit no. I'm telling you to make it good. I've been waiting a hell of a long time to have your dick in my ass again." I know what will happen if I sass him. He doesn't disappoint.

Cortez pulls back his hand and smacks my ass.

I shove it at him, begging for more.

He obliges, landing spank after spank that lights up my rear even as it turns it red with the imprint of his fingers. Since I'm balls-deep in Rogan, it serves the added benefit of making me grind against him.

Holy shit. If I'd only known what I was missing, I'd have insisted we find another guy to hook up with. This is heaven.

I lean forward and bite Rogan's shoulder. He groans. His dick twitches between our abdomens. I can't wait to watch him shoot all over himself. My chest will slide across his in the resulting slickness.

Cortez lines himself up again and begins to stretch me around him. Just before his blunt head pops inside, he whispers in my ear, "I haven't done this in all that time either. Not since I last was in you. So forgive me if this is too fast or rough. I can't hold back. Not with you. Never with you."

Rogan stares at me, a warm smile on his face. He

heard every word of that declaration and he's not jealous or angry. He's happy. For me.

"I love you," I promise him. He nods, too overcome to respond.

From behind me, I think I hear Cortez whisper the same three words right before he distracts me with full penetration. I embrace the shock and discomfort of that single full thrust. It helps me regain some of my control.

Rogan senses the slight softening of my cock and reaches for me. He pets me and riles me up again as Cortez begins to move within me.

It feels so strange, and so right, to be fucked again.

I'm overwhelmed. My stride falters. Until Cortez notices and picks me back up, like he always used to do. He ensures I won't disappoint Rogan, or him. All I have to do is give myself over to pure fervor, and the rest will be fine.

Spectacular, actually.

He guides my hips back and forth, inserting me into Rogan in one direction, then impaling me on his cock when I travel in the other. I crave more and more of this ultimate decadence.

Pretty soon, I find the right rhythm. I fuck into Rogan while Cortez fucks into me, bringing the three of us as tightly together as possible. Then I wait for him to retreat, pull myself out of Rogan slowly—nearly to the brink of his tight ass—before we do it again. Over and over.

The unrelenting pace and mixture of sensations has my toes curling where they dig into the carpet, keeping me balanced. Rogan aids with that too. His hands bracket my ribs. He anchors me so that Cortez's thrusts don't mash our faces together. No one cares to be interrupted by an accidental shiner in the middle of kinky time.

I can tell our slightly uneven fucking is working for Rogan, too. He's moaning and rearing beneath me. I shove my hand between our bodies so that I can cup his erection and rub my palm along his length. Damn, he's never been this hard before.

Will he ever be again if it's just the two of us?

I shove the stray thought aside and vow to commit myself to enjoying this liaison for however long it lasts.

The end is near.

Cortez has some of the most impressive stamina of any man I've been with. He can fuck all night. But me...no way, especially not when faced with the only two men I've ever loved, who are both showering me with fondness and attention.

I soak it up. Every second of this makes up for a week of my past depression.

A minute caught between them erases an entire year of pain. I'm sure of it.

I fuck and am fucked simultaneously. Every part of me, every facet, is indulged and cared for. My next few strokes into Rogan are harder than the last. Cortez takes his cues from me and ramps up his thrusts as well.

"You're getting close, aren't you?" he growls against my neck before raking his teeth down the corded tendons there. His arms wrap around me and he flattens his palms on my chest so he can thumb my nipples.

"Yes," I hiss. There's no use in denying it. Although I'd love to stretch this moment out for eternity, nothing this brilliant can burn forever.

Cortez pinches my nipples. Hard. He brings me around a little before allowing his hands to wander lower to my abs.

"Take care of your boyfriend first." Of course, how

could I not? Having Cortez there to direct me, even in this, is freeing. I know he won't let me down. And that means he won't let Rogan down either. "Don't you dare come before he does."

I lean in and kiss Rogan. He responds to my mouth on his, but I can see that he's retreated inside his mind, lost to his own ecstasy. When I begin to pump his dick, he roars. He drums his fists on the mattress. His jaw falls open and he throws his head back.

"He's gorgeous, Kaden," Cortez murmurs, so as not to interrupt Rogan's moment.

It's true. He's the most arousing sight I've ever seen. Especially when he freezes, about to explode. Better than any pill for stiffening my cock.

Cortez's too, going by the feel of him wedged within me.

Damn.

"Show me how you take care of him. Make it good." He directs my motions but stops fucking into me. Instead he holds still and allows me the room to really get my groove on. My hips swing faster, skewering myself on Cortez on the backstroke then pounding into Rogan as I jerk forward.

Rogan's chocolate eyes fly open. He pierces me with his stare, then rasps, "Please."

"Come for me, Rogan. So Cortez knows how much you love having my dick inside you. Shoot good and hard for us. Now." I punctuate my commands with the drilling of my cock.

Like the good boy he is, Rogan does as he's told.

Pearly fluid begins to fly from his tip before I've even finished my last word. It tags him on the chin, then slashes across his pecs and abs. I keep fucking him with both my dick and hand until he's completely empty.

Then I slow and lavish him with tender commendations. Kisses and comfort.

That doesn't stop Cortez from hammering away at me, though. He keeps up his unrelenting fucking, his hands clasped tight around my hips. The motion keeps me moving within Rogan plenty enough to set me on the edge.

"Your turn," Cortez says to me. "Fill that ass. Flood it. For me."

Rogan smiles at that. The combination of Cortez's possession and his sweet understanding does me in and takes Cortez down with me.

The instant my body clamps around his thick cock, he loses it.

We climax together.

His seed sears me from the inside with its taboo heat, making me realize we didn't use protection. I've been cleared. If he hasn't been with anyone in years, we're safe. That doesn't guard me from the intimacy of the act, though. When I think it can't get any better, Rogan cranes his neck upward and kisses me. I devour him as Cortez infuses me with his ecstasy.

My orgasm is the single most powerful release of physical and emotional energy I've ever experienced in my life. Come pours out of me along with a sound that's a horrifying cross between a moan and a sob.

All the times I got high had nothing on this. I'm transported to a place where there's no pain and no sorrow. Only hope and unbreakable bonds. Even my fingers twitch in time to the pulses of my climax, which drain me dry.

I have nothing left to give. They own me. Soul, mind, body. Everything.

In that moment, I have an epiphany.

It's finally and instantly clear to me. The reason I've never felt wholly complete or satisfied is because I haven't been doing this relationship thing right. Not with Cortez and not even with Rogan.

I'm not a top. I'm not a bottom.

I was born to be their middleman.

33

KADEN

After my revelation, and the sense of freedom that accompanied it, I crashed. Hard.

Several hours later, I rub my eyes and stretch. If someone told me right now that I had napped for a hundred years, I would believe them. I feel like a completely different person than the anxious, tense, frightened man who rose from this same bed this morning.

I smile when Rogan's warmth beside me sinks in. I know it's him because the familiar click of his laptop keys accompanies his presence.

My eyes focus and I blink some more. No sign of Cortez.

It shouldn't come as such a shock, but I sag, disappointed to find him missing.

"I told him to stay." Rogan leans over to kiss me. The exchange is full of even more love and shared intimacy than ever before. "I don't think he believed me when I said you'd prefer that. Maybe it's because he couldn't see your face while he fucked you, like I could."

He's right, there was no pretending or concealing my emotions in that moment. Everything I felt was written there.

"You were his before I was yours, Kaden." Rogan winces. "You belong to him."

"I was his, but he was never mine." I grip his hand, refusing to let him slip through my fingers. It's critical that he understands my desire for Cortez doesn't diminish how much I love him. "*You're* mine. I'm never going to throw you away like he did to me."

The tight set of his jaw relaxes. He puts his computer on the nightstand, then worms down until he's lying full-length against me. "Thank you for sharing this morning with me. It was by far the best experience I've ever had in bed."

"Me too." Without a doubt.

The only problem is that I've developed another addiction. This time to sharing my pleasure with *both* men I love. I might have said it was a one-time thing. But I'm sure now that I'll never be satisfied with less.

"I'm going to go paint." I can't stay here. Rogan will read the truth in my stare as easily as he did when we were embroiled in the threesome with Cortez.

"I'm feeling pretty inspired myself." He grins and kisses my cheek. "I think I might work out."

"How do you have any energy left after this morning?" I wonder. Maybe it hadn't impacted him as much as me.

He shrugs. "I feel...invigorated. Like I could do anything right now. It was such a rush."

"It was." A summit I'm afraid I'll never reach again. Could that have been the pinnacle of my sex life? Is it all downhill from here?

That doesn't seem fair to Rogan, who's being amazing.

As always. He deserves someone who puts him first. Someone who cherishes him above everything and everyone else.

"I love you, Rogan." Will that be enough this time?

"I love you too." He gets up with me when I climb from bed. "Do you want me to make you something to eat? You skipped breakfast."

I don't know if I'll ever be hungry again. Like the overly sated feeling after Thanksgiving dinner, I was stuffed full. And I'm not only talking about Cortez's meaty cock. Full of love. Full of acceptance. Full of pleasure.

What more is there?

"Nah, I'm okay. I gotta do something." Art is the only way to express how I'm feeling right now. I intend to zone out, lose myself in the colors and the motion of my strokes on the canvas. We'll see what comes to light.

"Have fun." He stands there, patiently waiting for me to kiss him temporarily goodbye.

And I do.

Rogan is comforting and familiar. My home. I'm not sure when that happened.

How would he react if I proposed another adventure with Cortez? Or maybe something more permanent? Would he do it because he's an incredible partner and because he's used to following my lead? Is it something he could actually want, too?

Or would he come to resent my outlandish needs for double the love and attention of a normal man?

What about Cortez? I could sense it when he held me as I flew apart. He still loves me too. I can't stand to see either of them suffer. But I may have put us in a situation where it's inevitable that one of us...or all three of us...do.

"See you in a while." I can already tell it's going to take

hours of isolation, relying heavily on my creative outlet, before I can work out what my next step should be.

I'll tread carefully, because one wrong step could crush my soul and theirs along with it.

34

CORTEZ

Everything aches. My arms, my legs, my back, my heart.

Working out like crazy is helping me regain the strength I lost while condemned to months of bed rest. It's doing nothing to burn off the extra energy still pulsing through my veins hours after my threesome with Kaden and Rogan.

What am I going to do when Ronaldo is out of the picture? How will I walk away?

I've loved Kaden for years. I might care even more for him now that I've seen how resilient and adaptable he's become. And Rogan. Holy hell. I used to think Kaden was the most ideal submissive in the world. Now I know there's one—and only one—better.

Because Kaden evolved into something else, something equally as magnificent.

Would they consider a rematch? If they did, would it be worth taking them up on it knowing another session like that would make it that much harder for me to slink back into the night when this is over? Is there any chance they'd consider opening their arms to me for longer than a night or two? Something deeper than a fling?

I drop the weights then towel my face. The pressure behind my ribs is either a sign that I've overdone it or that I'm in danger of ripping my heart out of my chest soon. This time for good.

I'll never be satisfied with anyone else as long as I live.

No one could be as good as those two in bed. I hardly even got a taste of Rogan.

I hope he realizes I was in it for him too, not only because of my history with Kaden. I should have done a better job of reaching out to him. Maybe then he'd help me convince Kaden that the budding affection between us has the potential to become something incredible when paired with the already fierce love he and I share.

While I've known all along my feelings for him haven't changed, this morning was the first time I was absolutely certain it was the same for Kaden. The way he'd unraveled in my arms was about more than physical intimacy. The anger and resentment fell away, revealing the love he'd been keeping untarnished beneath the mountain of other shit.

It took emotion to ramp things up to that level of intensity.

I'm willing to fight for a chance to prove I can be a good partner to both Kaden and Rogan. Whatever it takes, I'll do it. Just like I've rehabilitated my body. My leg throbs, but it works. That's more than I could say a few months ago. With effort and attention it will continue to improve.

Applying the same principles to a relationship should be no problem, right? Right?

Before I can bang my head against the wall, my phone rings. I dive for it. "Yo."

Only a few people have my number. Since it's not Kaden or Rogan, it's one of my ex-comrades. The one providing backup. You know, for the Ronaldo situation. The actual reason I'm here in Kaden and Rogan's inner sanctum.

"You're going to have to leave them there." Though the caller had no idea what's been going on in this incredible revamped old building, those words stung. They're everything I'm trying to avoid.

"Why?"

"Ronaldo's been circling, but he knows you're with those guys. Apparently he's not quite as dumb as we thought. He's afraid of you."

"So your solution is that I waltz out of here and leave them to fend for themselves?" I glare at the phone. No fucking way.

"Just for a bit. We can hear everything that's going on in there. As soon as we have him recorded committing a crime, you can go back in." The agent clears his throat. "I understand your desire to return to them as soon as possible, after this morning's soundtrack."

Yeah, I'd forgotten about our surveillance when it came to our earlier playtime. Or maybe I simply didn't care about anything other than the two men sharing the experience with me and what they thought.

"I do *not* like this. Not one bit." I've taken far greater chances in my operations. But this situation is much, much more personal than any of the others.

"Cortez, this is a minimal-risk situation. We're wasting our time here. Get your ass outside. We're in the blue van halfway down the block. Let's finish this."

"Okay, fine. Give me five minutes to explain the plan and I'll be out."

"I'd rather you didn't." The man sighs. "I'm sort of putting my ass on the line here. This isn't an officially sanctioned use of agency resources. The fewer people who know what we're up to, the better. Tell them you're going for a lunch run. You guys must have worked up a hell of an appetite. Before they know it, you'll be back and this will be behind you."

How could I ask my former associate to jeopardize his career? In our world, you don't just get fired. Breaking the rules could get us both thrown in a dank military prison. There could be repercussions for Kaden and Rogan, too.

"You're right. I'm overreacting. I'm coming. Just let me say goodbye." I punch the screen to end the call, then gather my gear before heading toward the common area. Not two steps from the door, I run smack into Rogan.

How much did he hear?

Shit.

"Hey." I paste a cheery smile on my face. Somehow it's a lot easier to lie to strangers than the two men who know me best. After what we shared, their bullshit meters are pretty finely calibrated to my emotions.

"What's going on?" He plants his hands on his trim hips.

"Nothing. I'm gonna grab some lunch. You said you like Chinese, right?"

He narrows his eyes at me. "That didn't sound like a takeout order you were phoning in."

"You're going to have to trust me on this one, Rogan. Please."

"Was that your old bosses calling?" He refers to when I told him they could have used his negotiating skills.

"Uh, not exactly. Kind of." I shrug.

"Are they trying to get you back?" He bites his lip.

"Nothing like that."

"Then what?" he asks.

I rub my palm over my face. "They want to talk to me about being a trainer, okay? I have to run over there quick and hear them out. Then I'll politely decline. I'm coming right back. I swear."

"You won't be tempted to leave again?" His worry improves my chances of talking them into letting me stay after this last bit of business is taken care of. The weak part of me, the one that has never wanted something as badly as I would like them in my life, urges me to test the waters.

"Does that mean you'd be upset if I didn't hang around?" I take a small step closer to him, definitely coming on to him.

"You're unbelievable." He shocks the shit out of me when he puts his hands on my chest and shoves. "If you make the same fucking mistake you made before, there's no undoing that. Haven't you learned anything? It would kill Kaden if you left again right after he's let you back in. Don't do that to him. I love him too much to let you mess with him like that."

I hold his gaze. "I'm asking about you. Would *you* be relieved if I left so you could have him all to yourself again?"

Rogan tries to evade my piercing stare. I won't let him. I clasp his shoulders in my hands and force him to look at me. "You know I wouldn't. I—I'm starting to have feelings for you too. Come back, Santiago, and I'll beg Kaden to let us be together. The three of us. Fully this time. Not just you with him and him with me, but all of us. Together."

"I'd like that more than you know." I can't help but gather him in my arms. I didn't mean to scare him. Once he's there, it's impossible not to steal a single perfect kiss.

Our *first* kiss.

I frame his face and hold him still as I direct the action. That way if Kaden objects, it's entirely my fault. Our kiss is sweet and spicy, tender yet full of angst. It goes on forever. Finally, I nibble on his lower lip, then pull back just enough to make sure he understands what I'm about to say. "You've got to trust me, okay?"

Rogan nods, if a little slower than I'd like.

"Everything is going to be okay. I'm coming back and I will make this right for all three of us. I swear."

"What should I tell Kaden?" he wonders breathlessly.

"Probably best if you stick with the lunch story. I've seen you dancing around that boardroom, remember? Your poker face is better than I'd prefer for one of my boyfriends. If...if that's what we're going to be. Just this once, use it to your advantage."

Rogan curses, then walks away. "You owe me one."

"I'll make it up to you tonight." I hope he can hear the sinful intent in that promise.

I mean it exactly how it sounds.

"W hat do you mean he left?" Kaden practically shrieks at me as he waves a paintbrush in the air.

"He went to pick up some Chinese food."

Kaden's face falls. He throws a sheet over the painting he's been working on. The one he won't show me. Then he marches toward the hallway. "Bullshit."

How does he know?

"Uh..."

"Rogan, you might be able to fool some people. Not me. Where did he really go?" Figures I can't sneak anything past him. He knows me too damn well.

"To talk to his old bosses. To turn down a job as one of their trainers."

Kaden's paintbrush snaps in half. Disgusted, he drops the pieces to the floor, splattering more paint over the concrete. To be honest, you can't really tell among the layers of colorful drips surrounding his work area. "This is exactly why I didn't want to fuck him again."

"Seriously? No one twisted your dick. You wanted to fuck him. You can lie to yourself, but you won't lie to me." I glare at his back.

"No. I mean. Yes. I *needed* to do it. But I didn't *want* to. Because I knew this would happen."

"He said he's coming right back. He swore it."

"I don't believe him."

I approach Kaden carefully and wrap my arms around him from behind. "Did he lie last time? No. He was upfront with you. Why assume differently now?"

"Because his priorities haven't changed. Saving the world comes before his own happiness. And ours." He sounds like he might fall apart. Or start breaking more stuff. "They'll convince him to go. Hell, he's already gone. I didn't even get to say goodbye."

Holy fuck. Kaden is spiraling downward right in front of my eyes. If I ever needed confirmation that he's madly in love with Santiago, here it is. The moment Santiago comes home, I need to talk to them both and convince them he should stay.

For their sakes. And mine.

I can't bear to watch either of them tormented like this.

"Well, isn't this a quaint scene?" The hair on the back of my neck stands up in response to the familiar and very out of place voice. It doesn't belong here in this new world I'm building for myself.

"Ronaldo?" When I turn, it's to stare down the barrel of a gun. What the fuck? How did he get in? Santiago would never have left without double and triple checking that the locks were set. But when I look, the front door of the gallery is standing ajar. Why didn't we at least hear those cute bells Kaden had hanging on the front door?

"Hello again, my dear."

Kaden steps in front of me. Despite my attempts to shove him out of the line of fire, he won't budge. "There's money in the safe. Let me get you some so you can buy a one-way ticket out of here. Away from the fuck-ton of trouble you're going to be in if you hang around."

I don't even try to stop him. Money is nothing compared to Kaden's safety.

"No thanks." Ronaldo grins. "I'd much rather take you. You're worth a hell of a lot more to Rogan than whatever you have on hand. Besides, I might get a few decent fucks out of the deal. I always did like the way you looked on Cortez's arm."

He waves the gun toward the door. No one moves.

"If you don't start walking, I'm going to put a hole in your boyfriend. Shame, too, since Rogan's pretty damn good at taking it up the ass himself."

Kaden growls. I put my hand on his shoulder to keep him from lunging at Ronaldo, who's clearly escalated from douchebag to psycho.

"I know what you like better," I try. "Take me instead. Kaden has access to my accounts. He'll do whatever you ask and I'll keep you entertained in the meantime."

Kaden whips around to glare at me. "Like fucking hell you will."

"Sorry, Rogan. Those days are over. I was bored of you anyway. Need to shake it up a little." Ronaldo wiggles the gun at Kaden, making me terrified he's going to shoot him by accident, if not on purpose. "Let's go. Now. Before Cortez gets back."

"Too late, fuckface." Santiago comes barreling through the door along with a second man, who's dressed entirely in black. I only catch a glimpse of him. What I do see is

James Bond-worthy. If I wasn't terrified for Kaden and Santiago's safety, I might have appreciated him more.

It's over before it begins.

Ronaldo's gun is skidding across the floor. Santiago's backup lifts it between gloved fingers and drops it in a plastic bag. In the two seconds it takes him to wrap it up, Santiago has Ronaldo slammed to the ground with his arms behind his back.

His treatment is rougher than entirely necessary. He glances at me. Without him saying a word, I understand that's payback for my broken arm.

"Cortez, I called this in to the cops. Here's the gun. I've emailed you the recordings of this shitbag's attempted kidnapping. That should do it, right?" the man in black asks.

"Yeah, get out of here before they show up and you have to explain where you came from. Appreciate it."

"Any time. We'll miss you. You were one of the best. I'm glad this is working out for you. Remy would be too."

"Thanks. Someday you'll also be on the other side of it," Santiago says to his friend. I'm sure that no matter how hard we try, Kaden and I will never fully understand the second life he's lived away from here and the petty troubles we think of as major problems.

He's a true hero. And so is this man.

Well, the man who was just here. I blinked, and he's gone.

Ronaldo thrashes wildly. Santiago holds him with one hand.

"I've tracked down and destroyed international most-wanted criminals. If you think I'm going to let a miserable little shit like you threaten, intimidate, or hurt my boyfriends in *any* way, you're even more insane than I thought." He warps into full-on protector mode, snarling at Ronaldo. "You're going away for a while. When that time is up, if you ever dare come near them again, you will die a painful death before you vanish. I promise you that."

Ronaldo stills. A puddle grows beneath him as he pisses himself.

I glance over at Kaden, who is staring. Not at Ronaldo, but at Santiago.

I nudge him in the ribs with my elbow. "That was hot, huh? How he called us his boyfriends? Plural. Sssssssss."

Santiago wings an incredulous glance over his shoulder. "Guys, not now."

Yet it's perfect timing. He's here. We're safe and free to share this life—one we've all struggled for in some way—with each other. Kaden gapes at me. Then we both crack up, unfazed by Ronaldo or his presence here today.

Nothing is going to split us apart. I think, finally, we're sure of that.

I hold my hand out to Kaden. He takes it, linking his fingers with mine.

"The *three* of you?" Ronaldo's bug-eyed stare flies between us, or as much of us as he can see with his face smashed against the concrete. I smile and flash a thumbs up.

Santiago shuts me down. "Don't antagonize him."

Fine, I'll behave. Or maybe not, if it means he'll punish me later while Kaden lets me suck his cock.

Santiago fists the back of Ronaldo's shirt and lifts the guy from the ground. The wail of sirens are approaching, so he shoves his captive toward the door and doesn't catch him when he trips and falls.

"Hey." Kaden steps over and puts his hand on Cortez's shoulder. "That's not necessary. Don't get yourself in trouble. We're better than him."

Cortez hauls Ronaldo up and snarls right in his face. "*They* are better than that. I'm not. Don't forget it, either. I have no qualms about ripping your dick off with my bare hands and stuffing it down your throat so you can't ever screw over another innocent man again."

The full-on glare of Cortez's angry eyes must be enough to get his point across. Ronaldo whimpers and flinches.

"In fact, I think it's best if you move to another city once you're out of the system. Somewhere far away from here." Cortez takes a step forward and Ronaldo scurries backward. I don't blame him.

He dusts himself off, minus that giant wet spot on the front of his pants, then attempts one final show of bravado. "I hear there are lots of rich gay guys down in Key West. I've always wanted to live somewhere warm, by the beach."

That last bit is a barb for me. I know he's thinking of the house I used to love so much. The one he stole from me. Little does he know that I've moved on. Into the place I was always meant to be.

Kaden takes my hand and squeezes it.

"I'd rather live somewhere that's warm inside, from the love of the people who make it a home." Santiago shrugs as if it's an offhanded statement. But when he glances over at Kaden and me, I know he means it for us. He's planning on sticking around and figuring things out.

I know it. From the enormous smile on Kaden's face, he knows it too.

If I hadn't already started to fall for Santiago, that would have done the trick. Anyone who can put that look of sheer euphoria on my boyfriend's face is a keeper.

Santiago fists Ronaldo's collar and leads him outside to the police.

36

KADEN

I thought the amount of paperwork we had to fill out after Ronaldo broke Rogan's arm was ridiculous. The barrage of reports, signatures, photographs, interviews, and various other red tape required when someone tries to kidnap you borders on obscene.

Rogan and I are finished long before Cortez, though. The authorities have a lot of additional questions for him, most of which he's not permitted to answer.

While we wait for the authorities to quit badgering him for saving our lives, I wander into my studio. I can't stop myself from reaching for a paintbrush. Not when the image I want to bring to life is now so clear in my mind. I don't care who is in our house, who might see.

This is my truth and I'm no longer ashamed of it.

I won't deny it, especially not to myself.

The only people whose opinions matter to me are Rogan's and Cortez's. Both of them are banned from my studio until my masterpiece is complete.

It's the most beautiful thing I've ever created. There isn't anything I'd alter.

I put down my brushes and palette then stand back and admire what I've done. It's perfect. For the first time in my life, I wouldn't change a single detail.

Smiling, I leave it to dry and rejoin the circus still ongoing in our kitchen. At least the crowd has thinned out. It seems like officials are packing their things and scattering.

I sit at the table for nearly another hour before it's just me and Rogan.

We're both impatiently waiting for Cortez.

Holding hands, we don't say anything as if we both understand it's not right to talk about our future until the other person it concerns rejoins us. *If* he does.

When the backdoor opens and he strides inside, we perk up. He seems to do the same when he spots us. Until he comes nearer and shuffles from foot to foot. "It's done."

"Thank you," Rogan says softly.

"I guess that's it then." Cortez says, "Give me a few minutes to collect my stuff and I'll get out of your hair."

I don't expect him to move in or declare his undying love after having been gone so long and only knowing Rogan for a few weeks. But something else. *Anything* else would have been nice.

My worst fears are coming true. The things we shared today didn't mean as much to him as they did to me. Or Rogan.

Rogan calls him on it. "Are you joking? You're not even going to have dinner with us so we can talk this out?"

"If I don't leave soon, I'm not sure I'm going to be able to go at all," Cortez admits, flicking his gaze between us.

Rogan looks at me. "Is that a problem? I think he should stay."

"Like for dinner, or the night, or more..." I know which option I would vote for.

"A *lot* more." Rogan squeezes my hand. "And I don't only mean sex. You two already know you work together as a couple, and I feel like Santiago and I could, too. I didn't really get the chance to be with him fully this morning, but I'd like to see where that could take us. You know, if it wasn't chain fucking—or chain loving, rather—from him to you to me. What if it was about the three of us, in every combination?"

My heart trips in my chest. "Would you really be into that? Not only for me, but because you want it too?"

Rogan nods. Then he turns to Cortez. I see the heat in their gazes as they exchange a poignant stare. "Do you?"

"I honestly can't believe you're asking. Either of you. Both of you." He rubs his chest, and not over one of his scars this time. Over the healthy part of him that hopefully we've touched and encouraged to regenerate, healing old wounds.

"So that's a yes, then?" I prod, unable to wait another second for his answer.

"Not just a regular yes, but a *hell* yes. Get over here. Both of you."

We hurry to his side. He whoops and squashes us to his mammoth chest. One arm around me and the other around Rogan. Rogan and I exchange a private smile and a quick kiss, which soon becomes a not-so-quick kiss.

"That's right. I think this calls for a celebration, boys." Cortez puts one hand on each of our heads and directs our making out. Once we've had our fill, he takes his. First he kisses the shit out of me.

Then he eyes Rogan.

It occurs to me that we've already had a threesome, but they've never even tasted each other's lips.

"I want to watch your first kiss," I tease Rogan. "Don't tell me you haven't thought about what it would be like if he wrapped his hands around your neck and hauled you up against his body, which is so much thicker and more muscular than mine."

Rogan whimpers.

Cortez chuckles at Rogan's distress, then admits, "I sort of stole a taste before I left earlier. May I kiss him again, Kaden? Properly this time."

I've never heard him ask for permission like that before. He's asking me not as his sub or even a peer. He's asking me, as Rogan's top. It shocks and thrills me.

"Yes, but not here. If we don't take this show into the bedroom, someone's going to end up with bruised knees from fucking on the floor."

"Nice thinking ahead." Cortez grins. Then he reaches for me and tosses me over his shoulder. I'm certain that if he were up to full strength, he'd put Rogan over the other. For now, he claps one hand over my ass and leaves that up to me.

"Rogan, stay with us."

"I plan on it." He sticks close on Cortez's heels as we march to our room. I'm so grateful that Rogan had insisted on the largest damn mattress known to man. I have a feeling we're going to need all the space we can get. Today, and every day from now on.

Cortez tosses me onto the bed then gestures to my clothes. "You're wearing too much."

The three of us practically rip off our shirts and jeans, flinging them every which way. I put my hand on my cock and stroke slowly as Rogan and Cortez come together for the very first time. Hey, I say it doesn't count unless I get to watch.

Cortez makes the initial move, drawing Rogan to him. He inhales sharply when their bare chests press together. With his mouth open, Rogan makes an easy target for Cortez's lips and tongue. He raids Rogan's mouth.

I cup my balls and roll them in my palm as I think about how fucking great it feels when he kisses me like that. Taking what he wants. Rogan goes slack in his hold.

It's no longer right to act like we're indulging in some sort of experimentation. This means something to them. I can see it in their eyes and the tenderness with which they touch each other.

This time is different. It's not just Cortez fucking me and me fucking Rogan anymore. This is going to last because they're into each other, too. We're equals in this relationship, no matter what roles we play in the bedroom.

When they have to come up for breath, Cortez is in full bossy mode. "You're such a good kisser. I'm ready to have that mouth working my cock. What do you say, Kaden? Should he suck us both at once?"

"Fuck yes." I hop off the bed and stand next to it, at a right angle to Cortez's torso.

Rogan sinks to the ground between us. He puts one hand on my thigh and the other on Cortez's good one, bracing himself as he glances back and forth between our cocks, which are at the perfect level for him to devour.

"You want to taste Cortez?" I ask, my arm wrapping around Cortez's waist and his doing the same to me. Rogan nods. "Do it. Make it good too. So he knows I was telling the truth about how fucking fantastic that mouth of yours is."

I monitor his response as we venture into uncharted territory. I shouldn't have worried. He wraps his fingers around the base of my shaft, staying connected, then swallows Cortez in one long slurp. Impressive.

Even I couldn't manage that without gagging.

"Shit!" Cortez shouts, then turns his attention on me. He rests the fingers of his free hand around my throat. With him holding me there, and Rogan clasping my dick, I'm already unbearably aroused. It only gets worse when he leans in and kisses me.

We make out while Rogan bobs between his legs for a while before switching his lips to my shaft and his pumping fist to Cortez's hard-on. He knows exactly how much we can take before he needs to torture the other.

He may be the one kneeling, but he's got more control than he realizes.

We're slaves to his attention.

He elevates our pleasure to the next level when he tucks our cocks together. They rub against each other, making us both moan. Even louder when Rogan takes us both into his mouth at once. He can't swallow as much of us together as he did individually, but he sure gives it one hell of a try.

Just the thought of being wrapped together with Cortez's cock in Rogan's mouth is enough to have precome leaking from me.

"Enough," Cortez growls. Thank God. "It's time to reward Rogan for what a good job he did," he tells me.

"I will. I'm going to fuck him." I help Rogan stand then guide him to the bed. "And I think you should let him keep blowing you while I do. He loves having a dick in his mouth. He'll enjoy my cock in his ass twice as much if you'll feed him yours."

"If you insist." Cortez shoots me a wicked smile.

"I do."

Rogan moans. "Hurry."

Cortez doesn't let me go that easily, though. He bites my jaw then growls, "And when you're done with him, I'm going to fill you up, too. We may be playing nice right now, tag-teaming your boy, but that ass is mine. Don't forget it."

He smacks it, hard, so I can't.

The sting of his palm lingers as I put Rogan where I want him. I stand while he lies on the bed on his back. A lot like yesterday. Except this time Cortez leaps onto the mattress, with only a slight wince, then sits on his heels by Rogan's shoulder. He draws my boyfriend's head into his lap and strokes his hair and cheeks affectionately.

The gentle exchange riles me up even more and before I know it, I'm slathered in lube and drilling into Rogan. When he opens his mouth to groan, Cortez is there, slotting his cock between Rogan's lips.

Cortez and I push each other higher and higher. We begin thrusting into Rogan in sync, filling him from both ends. It's like we're drawn to each other. Pretty soon we're both leaning in so we can make out above Rogan as we use him to bring ourselves pleasure. He doesn't seem to mind. His cock is rock hard and leaking where it bounces against his belly.

I can't wait until it's my turn to be as blissed out as he is right now. He's soaking in every touch. He's also working over Cortez's cock. The man is nearly superhuman, but he's still got his limits.

"Time for your ass to join in the party," he says to me. Then he reaches over to our nightstand and tosses me a condom.

I realize what he wants. I cover myself so I can put my

cock in Rogan's warm, wet mouth despite having just been plowing his ass. I'm glad Cortez is looking out for us both. It's been so long since I could have blind faith in a partner to have my best interests at heart. It's a feeling I've missed and craved.

And here it is again.

Here *he* is.

"Hurry up. Put it on."

I do as I'm told then crawl over Rogan. He's flipped around so his head hangs off the edge of the bed. He doesn't waste any time before he's sucking me down. So I return the favor.

Rogan is beneath me. We're linked in a never-ending circle—my mouth to his cock and his on mine. We suck, sixty-nining. It's one of our favorite ways to get each other off. Except I've never been ridden while doing it before.

There's a first time for everything. I sincerely hope it isn't the last.

I swallow Rogan to the root just before Cortez inches closer. While I'm holding all of Rogan's cock in my mouth, Cortez begins to prod at my hole. He stretches me, causing some zings of erotic pain before he breaches my ass. Sinking a few inches deeper with each stroke, he begins to fuck me.

When I'm sure I'm going to lose control and fill the condom I'm wearing, which is not at all what I want, Cortez abruptly pulls out of me, leaving me empty and open. I lift off Rogan's dick with a wet noise and look over my shoulder.

"What's wrong?" I ask.

"Nothing. Except..." He pauses.

"What?"

"I want to fuck Rogan, too." He groans. "Can I?"

Rogan is nudging my shoulder, encouraging me to flip to my back. So I give him what he's asking for.

"Absolutely. Please do," I say.

We roll and Cortez switches sides of the bed. In seconds, he's exploring Rogan's ass for the first time. He curses and praises Rogan as he plunges inside. A lot larger than me, fatter and longer, I'm sure it's a lot for Rogan to get used to.

He doesn't flinch.

Instead he blows me twice as well, showing me with every flick of his tongue, rub of his fingers on my balls, and the increasing suction he applies to my tip that he's a very content man.

Cortez keeps going, rotating us so that he spreads the fucking out evenly. I told you he has incredible stamina. Soon I'm barely hanging on, even when it's Rogan he's plowing.

Rogan is shuddering and moaning out of control. Only then does Cortez lead us closer to the greatest pleasure imaginable. He spanks me and orders me to stretch out beside Rogan.

I strip off my condom then capture Rogan's hand and bring it to my cock. I do the same for him. We jerk each other off as Cortez looms above us. His hand flies over his own shaft in a blur. He stares at us as he tips over the edge.

The sounds he makes when come shoots from his cock is nearly enough to have me joining him. He showers Rogan and me with spurt after spurt of his seed, making sure we split it evenly. Rogan runs his thumb through a line that cuts across his nipple then brings it to his mouth, savoring Cortez's taste. I roll to my side and kiss him so I can share in the flavor.

Cortez is taking huge heaving breaths as he continues

to rub his cock and tease his own nipple. He keeps himself engaged because he's not quite done yet.

"Rogan seemed to like that a lot. Why don't you give him some more?"

"Damn straight I will." I roll to my knees, planting one on either side of Rogan's hips before jacking myself off. Cortez tips me into orgasm when he slips his thick middle finger into my ass and uses it to massage my prostate while I spill my load all over Rogan's face. He opens his mouth to catch as much as he can and licks more from his lips when I'm finished.

Spent, Cortez and I crash to the bed on either side of Rogan. We cradle him between us. Now that we're more clear-headed, we can focus on him and his pleasure.

I kiss him sweetly as I trace light circles around his nipple. In my peripheral vision I see Cortez pinching his other one before trailing his rough fingers over Rogan's smooth, hairless torso. We can't torture him much more. His cock is already bulging and rouged from staying hard this long.

It's time to grant him release so he can float along with us.

Cortez looks to me and I relay my game plan. "I'm going to jerk him off. You use your magic fingers on him. He loves being stretched wide when he comes. We're going to get him off together."

Rogan groans and shivers between us.

Exactly, love. Exactly.

I kiss his forehead as I wrap my hand around his shaft and begin to stroke, making sure to caress every bit of him from the root to his tip. Meanwhile, Cortez detours to test the weight of Rogan's balls and brush the pad of his thumb over the sac that holds them.

I bet that feels fucking great.

Not as amazing as when Cortez uses the come splattered across Rogan's abdomen to coat his fingers. He walks them down Rogan's pelvis to the apex of his thighs before tucking them under his balls. I can tell he's pushed them inside Rogan's gaping hole when our boy bows up and calls our names.

Rogan thrusts into my fist. I increase the pressure of my grip and match the pace Cortez is setting with his hand, which drills into Rogan, massaging him from the inside.

In tandem, we bring him pleasure.

He's gorgeous, straining to meet our touches, giving himself over to the rapture we induce. His eyes fly open and he stares directly at us when he surrenders.

His orgasm surpasses ours, drenching him.

Only when he's finished coming does Cortez knock my hand out of the way then lower his mouth over Rogan's cock. He cleans Rogan off, despite the sensitivity of his still-engorged penis. He's diabolical like that.

Rogan seems to love it as much as I do.

Almost as much as I love these guys.

Cortez shoves me to my back on the bed again then takes his time cleaning both of us, and himself. He cares for all three of us before climbing into bed. This time he's not leaving.

I'm nestled between Cortez and Rogan, snuggled tight to Cortez's chest while Rogan curls up behind me. I could stay here for the rest of my life.

The only way I can do that is if I convince Cortez and Rogan that this is how it should be.

The three of us against the world.

And I think I might know a way to do that.

"I have something I want to show you. Wait here." Before they can pin me down, I sprint into my studio and touch my finger to the canvas I finished earlier. Not *too* wet. I carefully lift it off the easel and carry it into our bedroom.

Ours—as in Cortez's, Rogan's, and mine.

We're a unit now. I'm certain of it.

When I have their full attention, I turn the canvas around. I truly believe this painting will be regarded as my magnum opus. If not by the world, then certainly by the two people whose opinions I give a shit about.

It's a depiction of us, embracing. More importantly to me, it represents our relationship. Cortez is on the left, one hand wrapped around the back of my neck and the other resting on my waist. I'm pulling him toward me. Our lips are about to touch. Behind me stands Rogan, kissing that spot between my shoulder blades he loves so much. His head is slightly bowed and his eyes are closed. He's wearing a serene expression of surrender.

I'm trapped in the middle and loving every second of it. For once not torn between the two halves of myself but embracing them both instead.

It's titled, "Meant To Be."

"That's incredible." Rogan sinks to his knees to admire it up close. Cortez stands behind him with his hands on Rogan's shoulders.

"It's the most amazing thing I've ever seen," Cortez agrees, his voice husky.

"I want to hang it in the other room. Beside the painting of Rogan and me. Then I'll add the drawing of Cortez and me on the far side. Above the three of them, I'm saving a spot for another painting, one that's not as clear in my mind yet, but will be. One of the two of you."

I'm not sure where that plan came from, but it must have been brewing in the back of my mind. "All four of those relationships are precious to me. I want to love you guys in every way possible. Honor the bonds between us in every variation."

"Same here," Cortez says.

"Me three," Rogan adds. Then he looks up at Cortez and asks, "I only have one more question. Did you actually bring Chinese food when you came back? If you really loved us, you would have."

My stomach rumbles in response.

He shakes his head. "Sorry, no. And for the record, I never really left. But I still remember the number for delivery."

Maybe we'll get lucky and—for the third time—find the same fortune Rogan and I each cracked open, the one that inspired my painting's title. It seems impossible, but I can tell you from personal experience that sometimes people beat the odds.

Look at the three of us. So different—brains, brawn, and creativity—each with our own priorities and goals. Despite everything we've faced, and the countless things that could have destroyed us, we're finally where we were always meant to be.

It's not a physical place, but a state of mind.

Open to a lifetime together.

37

KADEN

ONE YEAR LATER

The buzz of three tattoo guns running simultaneously sounds like a swarm of bees. Kind of feels like it, too, as one of my artist friends attacks my thigh. Oh well, I've learned that sometimes it takes a lot of pain to end up with the best things in life.

"How you doing over there, Cortez?" I grin when he grimaces.

"You must be crazy to have so much ink. This is not fun."

"To each their own. I happen to like pain more than you do." I wink at him. "I'll show you later."

Rogan chuckles from where he's laid out, getting a coordinating design to mine and Cortez's tattoos. His hand is stretched out, wrapped around Cortez's ankle either for moral support or because the connection bolsters his own sense of security. It's funny to think that he has more experience in the chair than Cortez, but identifying marks were strictly prohibited before our lover retired from super-spydom.

As much as I've enjoyed the past year we've spent together on a selfish level, shattering my personal record for the number of orgasms I've had in a twelve month period, it's been even more amazing to nurture the sprout of their attraction so it could grow into affection. Finally, it blossomed into a vibrant expression of undying love that makes all of our lives more beautiful.

There are no more doubts.

The three of us fit together like pieces of a puzzle that form a perfect picture. Take away any one and there's clearly something missing. Not only in bed, or in our broader personal life, but in business as well.

These days Cortez is the Chief Security Officer of Clearwater Industries. He didn't fuck his way to the top, either. He earned the title by implementing improvements that have already reduced incidents within the home office and at the properties managed by Rogan's real estate powerhouse by more than fifty percent company wide.

In the meantime, Rogan has expanded his empire and recently won his industry professional group's Developer of the Year Award for the third time in a row.

My guys are simply amazing.

They're even rubbing off on me. Ever since Rogan drew an insane amount of publicity to my studio, I've been booked solid on commissions. He convinced me to substantially raise my prices to whittle the queue to a manageable level and maximize profits from my artwork.

It seems that move made collectors take notice and increased demand yet again. It's unbelievable. In addition, he followed through on his promise to help me write a business plan for a traveling exhibition. Cortez arranged the security needed for my insurance company to approve the remote showings. We attended the kickoff of the international tour a few weeks back. Now that Rogan is a super model as well as a mogul, he's a household name. He's been bombarded with new and exciting opportunities for his company.

Every dream I've ever had, and some things I never dared to imagine possible before I met Cortez and Rogan, have come true.

Rogan clears his throat. I look over at him. He says softly, "I like that look on your face."

"Oh yeah?"

"It's the one I hoped I would see someday. You're finally at peace."

"I am. Or I will be, once this is finished."

Cortez and I are getting tattoos on the outside of our left thighs while Rogan is getting one on his right. That way they'll make sense when we're in our favorite position —Rogan lying on his back while I make love to him missionary style and Cortez fucks me from behind.

Romantic, isn't it? I think so, too.

What could be a greater testament to our love than being joined like that, bringing each other indescribable pleasure?

Nothing.

So what are we permanently inscribing on our flesh to commemorate our first anniversary as a committed polygamous triad?

A variation on our favorite Chinese fortune, of course.

Three words, one each. Surrounded by elaborate linework that, to me, symbolizes exactly how entwined our lives have become. Inseparable.

Meant

To

Be

Because we always were. I'm sure of it now, and so are my partners.

We plan to make it official with a simple ceremony on the beach of Rogan's island, attended by the three of us and the widow of Cortez's handler, who has agreed to officiate our spur-of-the-moment commitment ceremony when we elope next week.

Cortez stunned and thrilled us when he dropped to one knee and proposed to Rogan and me, putting titanium engagement bands on us this morning. I can't wait to slide his matching one on his finger. It will be the best day of our lives.

Today's not too shabby either.

Regardless of when Cortez and Rogan make an honest guy out of me, they've already turned me into the sort of man I want to be.

A middleman for life.

WANT MORE STEAMY MENAGE ROMANCES?

If you've enjoyed Middleman, check out another of Jayne's menage romance series Powertools and the related series Hot Rods. Powertools kicks off with Kate's Crew. Read it by clicking here.

Nothing's sexier than men with power tools.

Sultry summer heat has nothing on the five-man crew renovating the house next door. No one could blame Kate for leaning out the window for a better view of the manscape. The nasty fall that follows isn't part of her fantasy—but the man who saves her from splattering the sidewalk is definitely the star.

When Mike personally attends to her injuries, she realizes her white knight in a hard hat has a tender side, giving her no choice but to surrender to the lust that's been arcing between them since day one. In the aftermath of the best sex of her life, she whispers her most secret desire: to be ravaged by his crew.

She never expected Mike would dare her to take what she wants—or that the freedom to make her most decadent desires come true could be the foundation for something lasting...

Warning: This book may cause you to spontaneously combust as five hot guys bring a woman's wildest fantasies to life during one blazing summer affair.

Excerpt From Kate's Crew:

Kate wiped her palms on her paint-splattered cutoffs before adjusting her grip on the rebuilt window casement. A flash of tan skin drew her attention to glistening muscles. They rippled over five sexy frames as the crew renovating the townhouse next door hammered nail after nail into their first-story roof, just a few feet below her perch.

From inside the bedroom where she worked, she inched to the edge of the ladder rung then craned her neck through the opening in front of her for a glimpse of the intricate tattoo spanning Mike's broad shoulders. Instead, she caught him reaching up to their stash of supplies for another pack of shingles. When her gaze latched onto the drop of sweat that slid along his neck, she forgot to breathe. She watched in fascination as it journeyed over his defined pecs and six-pack abs. After it was absorbed in the ultra-low-riding jeans snugged to his trim hips by a bulging tool belt, she heaved a sigh of relief.

Kate swiped at a blob of paint that had plopped onto her wrist unnoticed while she'd ogled Mike. Her tongue moistened her lips as she imagined licking a similar trail down his body. The edge of the fresh trim gouged her thigh as she strained for a better view. The gasp she made busted her. His head lifted, catching her spying. Great, now she'd never convince him to take it easy with his persistent innuendo or date invites. And, no matter how much she wanted to, she couldn't indulge either of their desires.

Mike threw her a dazzling victory grin. The anticipation sparkling in his cocky stare blasted a shockwave through her, screwing with her balance. The ladder wobbled then tipped. She probably could have righted herself if she hadn't been standing on tiptoes to maximize her view of the scenery. In slow motion, she watched his expression morph from flirtatious to horrified.

Kate flung out her arms in an attempt to catch the frame before she tumbled through it but the momentum swung her around. Her temple grazed the custom-made pewter latch she'd installed the day before. She hung, suspended in midair, as Mike rose from his crouch. The other guys began to turn toward her, but he was already sprinting for the edge.

Terror froze her insides when he launched himself across the ten-foot gap between their houses. Then she spun away, losing sight of him. She braced for imminent impact.

Shit, this is going to hurt.

Everything happened at once. Air whooshed from her lungs when she slammed, on her side, onto the roof. She rolled, flexing her ankles in an attempt to find purchase that would halt her skid toward the brink. But her knee wrenched at an awkward angle while she continued to rake over the slate. Her hand caught the ridge of an attic vent, slowing her descent, but gravity overcame the tenuous hold. Her frantic fingers recoiled from the sharp metal edge.

The gutters rushed closer, her last hope. After that, she'd have to pray the evergreen shrubs would cushion her, preventing any broken bones. The heels of her work boots hit the aluminum edging but kept going. Her legs dangled in thin air.

Then a strong hand banded around her wrist. Her arm nearly jerked from the socket as she lurched to a stop. Kate shoved on the edging shingles with her free hand, fighting to stay on the roof.

"Son of a bitch!" Mike hauled her the rest of the way up.

To keep reading Kate's Crew, click here.

WANT TO KNOW MORE ABOUT THE COUPLE FROM KADEN'S MAGAZINE ARTICLE?

When Kaden tells Rogan about the couple he read about in his magazine, he's talking about Lucas and Ellie from Jayne's Men in Blue series. Their book is called Wounded Hearts. You can check it out here.

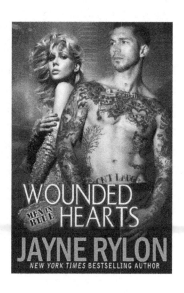

Attraction, fear, danger—an unlikely recipe for healing scars.

Men in Blue, Book 5

In the year since Ellie escaped The Scientist's ghastly dungeon, she still can't stop looking over her shoulder. Or stop feeling guilty over the man who sacrificed so much to save her.

He lost everything. His career, his aspirations—even part of his body. It's no wonder he wants nothing to do with her. Too bad he's the only man she can think about.

Lucas has vowed to stay away from Ellie, but not for the reason she thinks. The woman he craves doesn't need to waste her life taking care of a man with a missing leg, not when she needs to focus on her own healing.

Despite the best matchmaking attempts of the Men in Blue—and their wives—the emotional and physical gap between them seems uncrossable. Until Ellie is threatened again, and the only choice is to work together until she's safe.

But to stay in the land of the living, they'll both have to fight through their pain—and relive a few nightmares—to guarantee their demons won't destroy her future.

Warning: Contains an alpha male with a broken body, but whose best bits are in fine working order. And a woman who survived hell, and is determined to fit enough of their jagged edges together to make a whole. Vivid PTSD flashbacks of sexual violence could be disturbing for some readers.

NAUGHTY NEWS

Want to win cool stuff? Get sneak peeks of upcoming books? How about being the first to know what's in the pipeline or where Jayne will be making appearances near you? If any of that stuff sounds good then sign up for Jayne's newsletter, the Naughty News. She never shares you information, pinky swear!

www.jaynerylon.com/newsletter

WHAT WAS YOUR FAVORITE PART?

Did you enjoy this book? If so, please leave a review and tell your friends about it. Word of mouth and online reviews are immensely helpful and greatly appreciated.

JAYNE'S SHOP

Check out Jayne's online shop for autographed print books, direct download ebooks, reading-themed apparel up to size 5XL, mugs, tote bags, notebooks, Mr. Rylon's wood (you'll have to see it for yourself!) and more.
www.jaynerylon.com/shop

LISTEN UP!

The majority of Jayne's books are also available in audio format on Audible, Amazon and iTunes.

ABOUT THE AUTHOR

Jayne Rylon is a New York Times and USA Today bestselling author. She received the 2011 Romantic Times Reviewers' Choice Award for Best Indie Erotic Romance. Her stories used to begin as daydreams in seemingly endless business meetings, but now she is a full time author, who employs the skills she learned from her straight-laced corporate existence in the business of writing. She lives in Ohio with two cats and her husband, the infamous Mr. Rylon. When she can escape her purple office, she loves to travel the world, avoid speeding tickets in her beloved Sky, and–of course–read.

Jayne Loves To Hear From Readers

www.jaynerylon.com
contact@jaynerylon.com

ALSO BY JAYNE RYLON

MEN IN BLUE

Hot Cops Save Women In Danger

Night is Darkest

Razor's Edge

Mistress's Master

Spread Your Wings

Wounded Hearts

Bound For You

DIVEMASTERS

Sexy SCUBA Instructors By Day, Doms On A Mega-Yacht By Night

Going Down

Going Deep

Going Hard

POWERTOOLS

Five Guys Who Get It On With Each Other & One Girl.
Enough Said?

Kate's Crew

Morgan's Surprise

Kayla's Gift

Devon's Pair

Nailed to the Wall

Hammer it Home

HOT RODS

Powertools Spin Off. Keep up with the Crew plus...

Seven Guys & One Girl. Enough Said?

King Cobra

Mustang Sally

Super Nova

Rebel on the Run

Swinger Style

Barracuda's Heart

Touch of Amber

Long Time Coming

STANDALONE

Menage

Middleman

4-Ever Theirs

Nice & Naughty

Contemporary

Where There's Smoke

Report For Booty

COMPASS BROTHERS

Modern Western Family Drama Plus Lots Of Steamy Sex

Northern Exposure

Southern Comfort

Eastern Ambitions

Western Ties

COMPASS GIRLS

Daughters Of The Compass Brothers Drive Their Dads Crazy And Fall In Love

Winter's Thaw

Hope Springs

Summer Fling

Falling Softly

PLAY DOCTOR

Naughty Sexual Psychology Experiments Anyone?

Dream Machine

Healing Touch

RED LIGHT

A Hooker Who Loves Her Job

Complete Red Light Series Boxset

FREE - Through My Window - FREE

Star

Can't Buy Love

Free For All

PICK YOUR PLEASURES

Choose Your Own Adventure Romances!

Pick Your Pleasure

Pick Your Pleasure 2

RACING FOR LOVE

MMF Menages With Race-Car Driver Heroes

Complete Series Boxset

Driven

Shifting Gears

PARANORMALS

Vampires, Witches, And A Man Trapped In A Painting

Paranormal Double Pack Boxset

Picture Perfect

Reborn